The Girl in the Gallery

The Second London
Murder Mystery

Alice Castle

From the same series:
Death in Dulwich

CROOKED
CAT

Discover us online:
www.crookedcatbooks.com

Join us on facebook:
www.facebook.com/crookedcat

Tweet a photo of yourself holding
this book to **@crookedcatbooks**
and something nice will happen.

In memory of
Domonic Noble

Acknowledgements

To Ella, Connie and William, with love.

Thank you to my mother, Anita, and my brothers, Clive and Marcus, for all their help and support, and to Connie, Seth, Clive, Penny, Matthew, Natasha, Marie-Louise, Lucy, Clare, Oliver, Emma and Bill.

This mystery was inspired by the wonderful Dulwich Picture Gallery, celebrating 200 years of art for the public this year. I found *Soane's Favourite Subject: Dulwich Picture Gallery* by Francesco Nevola very useful, as was *Dulwich Picture Gallery: Complete Illustrated Catalogue* by Richard Beresford. Thank you to all the friends who have heard so much about the progress of this novel and all those who've been so generous in their enthusiasm for my first in this series, Death in Dulwich, giving me the impetus to continue. Thanks, too, to Laurence, Steph and Christine at Crooked Cat for making it all possible.

About the Author

Alice Castle was a national newspaper journalist for The Daily Express, The Times and The Daily Telegraph before becoming a novelist. Her first book, *Hot Chocolate*, was a European best-seller which sold out in two weeks.

Alice's first book in the London Murder Mystery series, *Death in Dulwich*, topped Amazon's satire detective fiction chart. The third instalment in the London Murder Mystery series, *The Calamity in Catford,* will be published by Crooked Cat next year.

Find Alice's website at www.AliceCastleAuthor.com. Alice is also a top mummy blogger, writing DD's Diary at www.dulwichdivorcee.com, and is on Facebook at www.facebook.com/alicecastleauthor/ and Twitter at www.twitter.com/DDsDiary

She lives in south London and is married with two children, two step-children and two cats.

The Girl in the Gallery

Alice Castle

**The Second London
Murder Mystery**

Chapter One

Beth Haldane gazed helplessly in front of her, trying to decide between the Gainsborough and the Romney. The flames might be flickering up the walls, the silk damask covering the chairs starting to singe, but still she dithered, her serious grey eyes flicking from one large canvas to the other. *Which work of art would you save in a fire?* It was her favourite museum game, but it was just so hard to play, here at Wyatt's Picture Gallery.

Should she rescue that perfect, frilly vision of the English countryside, with its bewigged and powdered owners preening centre stage? Or would she plump instead for the dimpled cheek and laughing eyes of a delicious daughter of the nobility, immortalised in the brief interlude between smallpox and childbirth?

She wanted them both, basically.

It was a lovely idea – to run out of the burning building with, say, a Reynolds up your jumper, and be hailed as a heroine instead of slammed into prison as an art thief. The fact that she would be more than tempted to gallop straight back to her tiny house a few minutes away in Pickwick Road, and stick her salvage straight onto her sitting room wall, was beside the point. She would never do it, even if she could get away with it. A life of crime was not for her. She knew that much for sure, no matter how many pictures were dying to be liberated from this elegant building and relocated to her own beloved but slightly down-at-heel home.

She trotted across the parquet of the central gallery, worn smooth by 200 years' worth of art lovers' feet, hardly believing her luck that the place was still deserted. The girl on the ticket desk had only just arrived when Beth had popped in on a whim. She didn't have to be at work at Wyatt's Endowment School's archive office – or the research institute, as she had to get used to calling it, after her stratospheric recent promotion – until 11am today, but she did have to pick up some cannelloni for supper from the Italian deli in the Village. Cannelloni had made her think irresistibly of Canaletto and, before she knew it, she was prancing up to the impressive yellow brick building, its rows of blind windowless arches like quizzical eyebrows raised at her small sturdy figure, her pony tail swishing as she passed the still-closed café and the beautiful old mulberry tree to the side of entrance.

She always felt so lucky to have great works, including the Canaletto, the Gainsborough and all their friends, right on her doorstep in Dulwich. The place had pretentions to village status, but really – whisper it softly – it was just another south London suburb. By rights, a collection this good should have warranted a train trip into the centre of the city, with all the hassle and planning that entailed. But, through a quirk of history and the founders' affection for this leafy pocket, the Gallery had opened to the public here in 1817 – and she was certainly dedicated to making the most of it.

The Friends' desk, where Beth usually showed her £30-a-year, come-as-often-as-you-like pass, was staffed by volunteers. It had been deserted at this early hour, but she'd been waved through by the flustered assistant at the other end of the counter who usually dealt with the normal ticket sales. She'd been switching on her computer with one hand and flipping the light switches with the other, and couldn't have been less interested in checking the fine print of Beth's pass. So, Beth was savouring every moment of being the first visitor of the day.

The sun flooded in through the central roof lanterns, the brainwave of 19th century architect Sir John Soane. They ensured that, although there was not a single conventional window in the place, every painting was bathed in an equal share of light from above. The uninterrupted sweep of the walls was studded with gem after gem – Tiepolo, Rembrandt,

Poussin. A few motes of dust danced in the central pools of brightness, and the air had that heaviness that betokened that it was going to be a hot day in Dulwich.

Beth's gaze slid from Rembrandt's little girl, leaning out from her canvas to beguile every viewer that passed with her frank, bright-eyed gaze, to one of her all-time favourite pictures, Gainsborough's full-length portrait of a lady, *Mrs Elizabeth Moody*. The lovely Mrs M held her rather pensive toddler nestled into her silken waist, while her long fingers curved possessively around the wrist of her eldest boy, as he stood close to the sheeny swish of his mother's taffeta skirts.

Beth shivered, despite the gathering warmth of the day. Sometimes knowing too much could spoil even the most innocent moments. She'd only been a small girl herself, little older than the boy standing at his mother's side, when she'd learned the secret of Gainsborough's lady in blue. Mrs Moody, with her faraway gaze, had died aged twenty-six – which seemed like early childhood now to Beth, from the vantage point of her mid-thirties. The little boys, dressed so much like girls to modern eyes, had been painted into the pre-existing portrait after her death; a sentimental gesture toward the dead that had rebounded horribly on the living.

The picture, which seemed such an innocent record of an everyday stroll with mother and sons, was as much a work of imagination as Beth's own save-the-painting game. It turned out that poor Elizabeth Moody had died when her youngest boy was a newborn baby, not the self-possessed child Gainsborough had captured, and the little family had never once taken a walk together in the woods like this one. In fact, despite the grief which had initially prompted Elizabeth's widower to alter the picture and paint his growing boys with the mother they missed, Mr Moody had rapidly remarried. Elizabeth's boys hated their new stepmother, and ended up estranged from their father, too. Thomas, the painted toddler, had bequeathed the valuable Gainsborough to the public Picture Gallery on his death, expressly so that his stepmother and her own children would never inherit it.

Had this fantasy of devoted motherhood helped to wreck

5

their real life? Beth wondered. It was amazing to think of the grief, jealousy, and anger which hid behind these wistful painted smiles.

The rich russet walls seemed to close in and, despite the light wells, the place started to feel claustrophobic. Maybe it was a dose of reality, or maybe it was because Beth was approaching the part of the gallery she always dreaded. She wanted to see the latest exhibition while the going was good, and today was the perfect moment while the place was deserted, but her route took her right past a strange stone nook built into the museum's heart. It always gave her chills. It was a mausoleum, housing the dead bodies of the place's founders. She knew it was silly, but she had a superstitious horror of the spot. It was such a bizarre idea – a cemetery hidden in plain sight, right in the middle of an art gallery. While tourists, the cognoscenti, and amateur enthusiasts like herself idled away moments looking at these walls, the original collectors who had hand-picked everything here, lay rotting in their midst.

All right, she had to admit, Sir John Soane had packaged the bodies of the art dealer, Francis Petty, his business partner Noel Devereux, and his wife, Margot, with his usual flair. First, there was a circular stone antechamber, with a flagged floor radiating out from the central roundel. Quite a few patios in Dulwich sported this design, and Beth knew that the B&Q in Norwood High Street even sold the slabs in kit form. They made a nice terrace feature in a suburban back garden, but here the effect was sombre. Six tall, fat marble columns edged the circle, supporting a high ceiling with a glass lantern, its panes in murky orange and cold yellow-green, drowning the place in cheerless shadow. Even here, an unwitting visitor could drift in and still not realise what they were seeing, though they might wonder at the gloomy décor. But at the end, the circular room opened into a smaller, darker, oblong annexe, again with a high, high ceiling. And here were the three marble sarcophagi which the entire gallery was built around.

Francis Petty was in what looked like a long, low, marble

filing cabinet, right opposite the entrance to the mausoleum. As a last resting place, it was very plain. There seemed to be a vacant filing cabinet just above him – perhaps for a woman who had gone off the whole idea when she saw what lay in store for her mortal remains. Two white marble busts topped off the cabinets. Flanking Petty on either side were tombs containing the bodies of his friends, the Devereux. These were more recognisable as enormous coffins. Again, drab dark-orange and yellowish-green panes up above filtered the light, so it had a cold, flat, and mournful quality.

It was quite possible to walk past this set of two creepy rooms without knowing their purpose – and Beth heartily wished she had never been curious enough to find out about it – but it was open to view if you were so minded. Although she quite liked the joke that the art dealers had made a spectacle of themselves, her 21st century mind recoiled from the reality of death. And, after recent events which were still horribly vivid, she was all the keener to canter past the whole business.

And that's what she started doing. But as she sped on to the last gallery, containing the current exhibition, she stopped for a second opposite one of her favourite canvases – the spectacular red, white, and blue bouquet of Jan van Huysum's still life; one of the jewels of the collection. She'd heard that 18th century flower painters were paid extra for insects, and it was one of her little habits to try and spot the wriggling wildlife every time she came. This time, it wasn't a beastie in the bunch of flowers that caught her eye, though. It was something on the very edge of her peripheral vision. Something that jarred, didn't make sense. Shouldn't even *be* there. Something that, she realised with dread, was in the mausoleum antechamber. Something that meant, however much she did not want to, she had to turn back and look.

Beth's heart started to thud. It was a flash of scarlet.

Someone had once told her that Constable had added a dash of red to all his canvases – it was 'the salt in the soup'. Beth felt quite vehemently that her life did not need even the tiniest jot more seasoning. In fact, she could no longer even think of the shade crimson lake without shuddering from head to toe, after making a ghastly discovery on the first day of her job at Wyatt's.

No, this time, if anything bad was happening, she was not going to stumble across it on her own. Resolutely shutting her eyes, she sidled back past the niche and then ran straight for the ticket desk. She'd get that girl on the desk to come with her, if she had to drag her all the way.

***

Tricia, the gallery assistant, was surreptitiously washing down a fistful of paracetamol with a bottle of water purloined from the gift shop when Beth arrived, panting and shouting.

Feeling just as harassed now as she had been when Beth had first breezed past her, Tricia had been looking forward to a clear twenty-minute breather to get her hangover under control. She needed it, before the daily stampede of Dulwich mummies, OAPs, and art students began traipsing in and ruining her day. Looking Beth up and down crossly – seeing a short but determined little person, with surprisingly intelligent eyes peering past a long fringe – Tricia summed her up as probably another one of those women with nothing better to do than make a massive fuss about the pamphlets having run out in the main gallery. Which Trish knew all about already, as she'd promised faithfully to replenish them. Last week.

'Ok, ok, I've got a load of them here. Somewhere…' she said, pushing a mess of bleached hair out of the way and rooting around half-heartedly under her desk, where her stash of biscuits was hidden. If anyone had told her that her first job out of uni would be this dull, she'd have… At this point, her imagination failed. For what was there for her, but the treadmill of exams, college, and dull jobs, until, maybe, marriage to a Dulwich banker beckoned? Shame she'd just dumped her boyfriend. But the woman leaning annoyingly over her counter wasn't calming down at all, despite Trish's efforts to appease. If anything, she was getting a lot more agitated.

'You don't understand. I've seen something… It's all wrong…'

'Oh, you mean on the kids' trail? Yes, we've got a few spoof captions up. For April Fool's Day, you know?' Ok, so the first of April had been some time ago. But, God, she couldn't get round to everything, could she?

'It's not that. Look, I'm sorry, but you've got to come with me. Now!' There was no mistaking the note of command in Beth's voice. Trish was willing to bet this woman was a terror with her kids. A workshy intern was no match for her. Clearly, if she had to come round and drag Trish with her, she would.

Trish sighed and admitted defeat. Brushing a few crumbs off her lap and screwing the cap onto her water bottle with an aggressive twist, she levered herself off her chair and sidled out from behind the desk. This wasn't as easy as it had been when she'd landed the job, four months ago. Close proximity to the gallery's outstanding café, not to mention the plethora of coffee shops in the village, was not doing much for her embonpoint, though Rubens – well represented in the collection – would have heartily approved of her pale and bountiful flesh.

'Ok then. What's up?' said Tricia crossly, wincing slightly as her own harsh voice jarred the Jägerbomb-jangled contents of her skull. Beth didn't waste any more words but, taking the girl's wrist in as firm a grip as the late Mrs Moody's, led her through the main gallery. As they approached the mausoleum, Tricia dug in her heels.

'Oh no you don't! That's just part of the gallery, that bit. Don't ask me why they thought it was a good idea, but yes, those marble chunks are, like, coffins and the owners of the gallery are in them, dead. It's all legit.'

Beth stopped and looked Tricia in the eye. 'I know all about that. But there's something else in there today. Something that shouldn't be there.'

Tricia, a head taller than Beth, looked down at the serious oval face before her and measured the look in the clear grey

9

eyes. This woman wasn't messing about. Suddenly, Tricia felt afraid, and not just because the zip on her skirt was starting to give.

***

Just the day before, Beth had sneaked in an early coffee with her friend at Katie's absolute favourite café, Jane's, in the heart of the village. It was a measure of Beth's ebullient mood that she was happy to meet at this insanely popular spot. If there was anything even remotely confidential on her mind, she would no sooner go to Jane's than she would have stood at the corner of Calton Avenue and Dulwich Village with a loudhailer, announcing her business to the passing hordes. Ears were not just on stalks at every table at Jane's, they were arrayed in giant bouquets and attuned to catching every nuance of a promising-sounding conversation. Not helped by the fact that the proprietors of Jane's had crammed in as many tables as possible to maximise custom.

As they took their seats, the table wobbling precariously as usual – Beth couldn't actually remember sitting at a table that didn't wobble in this place – Katie was all smiles. Her perennially supportive husband, Michael, had finally agreed that they could revamp the upstairs of their already gorgeous home on Court Lane.

'But what on earth needs doing? Your place is perfect. Oh no, actually, it's not,' said Beth.

'It's not?' Katie wrinkled her brow. She and Beth were among the few that could pull off this feat in Dulwich, since Botox had become a hobby of the mummying classes.

'Nope, it's not. I distinctly remember seeing a hair out of place on Scabbers. And wasn't there a speck of dust in your spare room the month before last?'

Katie laughed in relief. Beth knew how cordially she loathed Scabbers, her son Charlie's beloved hamster, who had the temerity to chuck straw out of his cage onto her pristine floors. And her spare room was a hermetically-sealed area where no dirt ever gained admittance. 'Anyway, you

10

can't talk about cleaning, Miss OCD,' she said pointedly to Beth.

There was some truth in what Katie said. Beth had been known to alphabetise her spice rack in times of stress, and Marie Kondo's *Life-Changing Magic of Tidying* was a permanent fixture on her bedside table.

'Well, cleaning, I concede. But my whole house could definitely do with a lick of paint. And it's not going to get it, unless we win the lottery.'

'Why not?' said Katie, with the airiness of someone with the whole of Farrow & Ball, and a team of decorators, at her disposal whenever she snapped her fingers.

'Well, time, money, stuff like that.' Beth shrugged her shoulders briefly, and set about shipwrecking the last of her cappuccino's foam with a vigorous stir. While Katie theoretically understood her friend's struggles as a single parent, the day-to-day reality was so far removed from her own silky-smooth existence that Beth sometimes felt she was like Cinders, picking dried peas out of the fire, in front of her alter ego, already clad in her ice blue frou-frou ball gown, complete with crystal coach at the door. Kind, tender Katie was all sympathy; she'd just never known struggle. At least she was a million miles from the ugly sisters, thought Beth fondly.

Over on the next-door table, a mere hand span away, Belinda Mackenzie held court. The Queen Bee of Dulwich mothers was in full flow as usual, this time about her youngest daughter's flute teacher, who was not coming up to scratch. Her acolytes sat in reasonably contented silence, glad just to be in the chosen band that accompanied Belinda everywhere. Belinda owned the best babysitters, she threw the best playdates, and her kids' birthday parties lasted days and put the *son et lumieres* of Versailles in the shade.

While space in the café was at a premium, and the ladies at her table jostled thighs and shoulders, Belinda's handbag took its rightful place on a chair of its own, its fixtures and fittings gleaming like bright copper kettles. Beth sighed with envy. She loved handbags. She kicked her own ratty old

11

number surreptitiously as it skulked under the table, shamed by its neighbour's magnificence.

'So, what are you having done in the house?' Beth asked Katie, and let her mind wander a little as her friend outlined plans to paper the upper reaches of her house's hallway in a striking Osborne and Little print, and change the paintwork from the current custard cream to a more Dulwich-friendly biscotti shade.

'I just feel that, now Charlie's getting older, we don't have to have everything so *child friendly*, if you know what I mean,' said Katie earnestly. Beth, though nodding, felt a little sorry for Charlie, who was still very definitely only nine and probably not yet ready to put away childish things. Though, having said that, Katie had gone a bit nuts when he was born – after an exhausting and pricey struggle with IVF – and for a long while she could only really see in triumphant primary colours. When Beth had been invited round for her first bonding cup of coffee at Katie's after they met at the St Barnabas playgroup in the Village, she had slightly wished she'd been wearing dark glasses, though it must have been November. Maybe it *was* time they junked the alphabet-themed tiles in the master bathroom.

It made Beth think. Perhaps she could have a little revamp of her own at some point. Nothing super-fancy, a couple of cans of B&Q's finest magnolia, and the most reliable worker she knew – herself. She could definitely afford that. She was so used to counting the pennies that sometimes she forgot things weren't as tight, money-wise, as they had once been. That was all thanks to the job at Wyatt's. Despite the stickiest of sticky starts – so sticky that, if she'd been face-down in a vat of molasses wearing a jumpsuit full of honey, it could hardly have been worse – her job had developed into a source of real joy.

Initially, her role had been to sort out the archives of the venerable school, which had been relentlessly collecting play programmes and other chaff, as well as the odd genuinely important document, for three hundred-odd years and counting. Rapidly, with all the hoo-has that had occurred, her role had morphed into something she was eminently better suited for – curating and developing a permanent exhibition exploring the way that Thomas Wyatt, the school's founder, had become involved in the slave trade.

Although the exhibition was going to be a life's work – there were so many elements that Beth intended to draw into it, that sometimes her head was spinning – the initial phases were shaping up nicely, and she was almost ready to unveil her progress to the headmaster and school board. This week was going to be dedicated to finishing touches. Next week would be the big reveal – of the outline of her plan, at least.

For Beth, finally getting to use her history degree was a dream come true. She had pootled along since her son Ben was born, doing whatever freelance journalism work came up, as long as it fitted in with all the pick-ups and drop-offs that today's maximum-security parenthood required. Ben, nearly ten, had still never walked anywhere on his own – though he did have his own scooter, as of a couple of weeks ago. According to him, he was the last child in Dulwich to get one. Now, he was just a distant dot on the horizon that she was theoretically accompanying.

They talked about separation anxiety, but these days it often seemed to be the wrong way round, with the parents clinging on while the child did its best to break free. She tried hard not to go down this cul-de-sac herself. She worried about him, of course she did, but she knew he couldn't be clamped by her side forever, even if he wanted that.

She remembered there had been a massive furore a few months ago, when it was discovered that a five-year-old was cycling to school *on his own*. It was no exaggeration to say that the Village's pitchforks were sharpened. Five did seem very young, but it was up to the parents, she supposed. The miasma of disapproval had taken its toll and the family had suddenly upped sticks to Blackheath, where standards were rumoured to be lower – making a tidy profit on their desirable Dulwich property, of course.

Beth couldn't disagree with the current predilection for locking down childhood – her absolute worst nightmares centred around something bad happening to her boy – but it was tough maintaining the required standard of vigilance when you were a lone parent. At least couples could act as a security guard tag team, even if in practice one parent often got the lion's share of the crap job of hanging around judo class or tennis lessons for hours waiting for them to end. Beth also found it impossible to imagine racking up the hours that any employer now expected of their full-time workforce. When she had last held a big office job, people had often gone home jacketless, just so their chairs wouldn't look empty *all night long*. Even in her child-free days, Beth hadn't been that dedicated.

Yes, Wyatt had been a lifesaver. And even her deeply inauspicious start there had worked out for the best. She was loving delving into the murky background of Thomas Wyatt, even though what she found was often disturbing.

But Wyatt's had somehow managed to come out of the whole slavery debacle without too much tarnish clinging to its beautiful wrought iron gates. By admitting so openly that the school had been founded on a tainted fortune, Wyatt's had pulled off a reverse public relations coup as miraculous as Hugh Grant's rehabilitation after that grubby Sunset Boulevard hooker incident. The excoriating – and sincere – apologies Dr Grover had made so fluently and heart-searchingly had bumped the school up a bushel of places in the rankings, and the fees had increased by more than the rate of inflation.

He'd looked flamboyant yet penitent on *News at Ten*, and grave yet slightly twinkling on *Newsnight*. Thomas Wyatt himself couldn't have pulled off the feat with any more chutzpah. It didn't hurt that Oxford was still wrestling, much less successfully, with its own Rhodes problem, now that everyone's collective amnesia about the man's white supremacist views had worn off. Even Princeton and Yale turned out to have very unsavoury founders lurking behind their ivy-clad facades. In fact, it was now almost fashionable to have an off-colour benefactor in the closet, like an ageing relative spouting politically incorrect views at Christmas lunch.

Once Beth had found the first horrifying ledger detailing Wyatt's slave ownership, she'd then uncovered a whole cache of documents. Thomas Wyatt, or his clerks, had been meticulous. At the time, there had been no stigma attached to slave owning – rather the reverse – and Wyatt had shown great pride in watching his fortune accumulate. It was a delight which showed in every exuberant curlicue etched onto the series of vellum-bound ledgers by his managers' quill pens as they recorded the sums piling into his coffers. His ownership of men, women, and children was as diligently registered as every plantation he'd bought.

It meant Beth could now lay bare all the fascinating – and revolting – facts, which made for compelling reading. The Board was considering opening a permanent museum in the school grounds and even, possibly, charging admittance – though there was lively debate about whether, in all conscience, Wyatt's could be seen to be profiting from slavery again, even if the proceeds went to increasing the number of bursary places it offered.

The tinkling of Katie's spoon against her now nearly empty coffee cup brought Beth back to the present. She had missed quite a lot of Katie's explanation of the new colour scheme, but she felt sure she'd see enough swatches between now and the finished upgrade to comment intelligently if necessary. There was other urgent business to discuss, though, as Katie had a new neighbour, with a boy who had just started in Ben and Charlie's class. Already there were rumours swirling the playground. The family were Swiss, they owned a ski resort, they were Spanish and into bullfighting, they were French and ate nothing but offal...

'She's an Italian doctor, he's Belgian, and their son, Matteo, is just lovely. There's a daughter as well, Chiara, fourteen-ish I think, got straight into the College School. Perfect English, the whole lot of them,' said Katie.

'How come?'

'They were in Kuwait before; the kids went to one of

15

those international schools. They have a sort of transatlantic accent.'

'Like 1990s radio DJs?' said Beth.

'Exactly,' laughed Katie. 'I think *he's* something in the City.'

Beth nodded. The husband would, indeed, need a job in one of the big London banking houses to afford Court Lane prices – houses were changing hands for upwards of £3million these days.

On the neighbouring table, Belinda was still in the middle of an anecdote in which her latest au pair was coming off a sorry second. Belinda had nothing to rush back for: her children safely being minded by the best teachers in south London; her house being groomed to within an inch of its life by the much-maligned au pair and a cleaner; her lawn being manicured by the gardener; and her dogs were towing their long-suffering walker around Dulwich Park. Later, her personal trainer would stop by to make sure she expended equivalent calories to dog walking/cleaning/gardening in the latest carefully selected fitness fad, before her husband staggered home at 8.30pm to hear how relentless her day had been.

Katie, meanwhile, was off to give an exercise class. And Beth – well, she had ten thousand things to do, and didn't really want to think about any of them. Katie had wound her airy red georgette scarf around her neck, and they had both stood up to go.

***

It was the red of that scarf which Beth was remembering, she realised. Her pulse slowed a little from its frenetic pace as she repeated to herself that it was probably nothing, absolutely nothing. She'd dragged this reluctant gallery assistant with her for no reason, and they were bound to find nothing more sinister than a lost scarlet scarf, forgotten by some ditsy Dulwich mum, abandoned in the mausoleum niche. She was about to feel *so* silly. That's what she was hoping, anyway.

As they approached the mausoleum, their footsteps instinctively slowed until they were mimicking the pace which Ben adopted every night, when he was being forced up the stairs to bed. Beth wasn't *quite* dragging her feet, but the unwilling assistant at her side really might have been. It didn't help that, as soon as they stepped into the small, circular room, the temperature dropped by about ten degrees – this portion of the gallery was constructed entirely from solid marble, and the coldly coloured glass high above them shut out the bright Dulwich day as effectively as the fanciest designer sunglasses. Beth shivered.

But the mystery was solved. Right in front of them, and hardly over the threshold of the room, was the splash of red that Beth had seen out of the corner of her eye – a scrunched-up, empty-looking backpack in the brightest of vermilions. It lay in a bit of a tangle, long straps left lying anyhow, not far from the simple wooden bench which had been placed incongruously in the centre of the space. Beth supposed that you could plonk yourself down on this basic structure – no better, really, than the sort of garden bench you might pick up in Ikea – and sit and contemplate the dead founders of the museum. Why anyone would want to do that, though, was entirely beyond her.

Beth turned to the gallery girl and they both tittered a bit nervously out of sheer relief. 'Well *that's* all it was!' said Beth, with forced jollity. Her delight at avoiding a grisly discovery was rapidly giving way to embarrassment. 'Just some lost property. I'm so sorry to have made you...' she started.

But the girl's expression, all smiles the moment before, had become strangely fixed, while the corners of her mouth trembled and dropped. Her gaze was on something over Beth's shoulder, something that was causing her stare to become more and more saucer-sized by the second. Her mouth opened in horror, but no sound came out, and she stuffed a hand, complete with grubby, chipped black nail varnish, into it.

17

She started to back away, out of the mausoleum. She reached the archway that they had just come through, and sagged against it, still making no sound, still gazing over Beth's shoulder.

Beth didn't want to turn round, but knew she had to. She did it slowly. Behind her, set at an angle away from the bench, and following the curve of the circular wall, was the long, low box of smooth dull maroon marble, about six feet long – the stone coffin housing Margot Devereux's bones. And then there was no mystery at all about what was terrifying the intern.

Lying on top of the coffin was the body of a girl. She was dressed in a white slip dress, sequins shimmering slightly in the half light, her skin as pale and lucent as the material. One tiny spaghetti strap had fallen off her shoulder, which would have lent a casual air to her look, except that both arms had been crossed over her chest, and her hands lay still as death, fingers fanned. Her eyes were closed. Her hair was dark and wavy, blonder at the tips. It rippled down the marble and onto the cold floor. Her feet were bare, electric blue painted toenails garish against the pallid flesh.

Beth stared in horror. It was Millais' Ophelia come to life, but so much more bleak. Millais had garlanded his corpse with greenery; this girl lay starkly abandoned, in this cheerless mausoleum, with only the long dead for company. It was horrifying. Rooted to the spot, Beth gazed helplessly. Then the girl's chest moved. Not so much Millais, whose model had died of pneumonia after posing for months in baths of cold water, as Sleeping Beauty.

Chapter Two

Eighteen Hours Earlier

Sophia Jones-Creedy sucked in her cheeks and looked deep into the lens of her smartphone, flicking on the saucy smile that had won her thousands of Instagram followers. Way more than her nearest rival, Louisa, thought Sophia smugly. Not surprising. Wet little Louisa was in her class. Her Instafeed was all outdoorsy rubbish, with great chunky captions under every shot: 'this weekend my family and I walked 15k up a mountain for charity, blah blah blah.' Meh. Who frigging cared? Maybe it was because Louisa was still only thirteen. A child. Sophia's own fourteenth birthday had been months ago.

Louisa's trouble was that she had no idea what people really wanted, Sophia reflected as she pointed, pouted, and papped in her cluttered bedroom in the largest house on Court Lane. She then ran the pictures through a couple of apps to make minor adjustments – it wasn't cheating to plump up her lips a bit or airbrush that spot coming up on her chin, it was just editing. Everyone did it. Or everyone with any sense. She had a duty to make sure that she was looking her absolute best. When she was completely happy, she uploaded the picture.

A minute later, the likes started rolling in. Her party pics always got the most hits. Well, let's face it, she thought, in this little number, she looked hot. She smoothed the pale, sequinned dress down her slim body, the silk sliding cool against her skin. It was Armani. Her mum had bought it for her as an apology for being away in the States that time, literally for ever, lawyering away on some huge case or other.

Mum had made a really big deal about the dress, so Sophia had Googled it to see if she could make some money out of it on eBay later, once she'd worn it. It was some old-school design classic, and yes, really pricey, but she would have preferred something a bit racier from Asos. And, to be honest, she'd have preferred her mum being around for all that time, instead of any dress. Like that was going to happen, though. Her mum had always made it clear – her career was a big deal. And she wanted Sophia to have a big deal career, too. That meant slaving away for ever, exam after exam after exam, and then getting a really super-dull job. Sophia didn't see the point. Not when people her actual age were making lorry-loads of money just becoming influencers and writing blogs and... ok, she wasn't a hundred per cent on how all this translated to hard cash. But she knew it did. Look at Zoella. All she did was put on make-up at home and say 'craycray' a lot, like she didn't even have time to pronounce things properly. Sophia could totally do that.

Meanwhile, Mum was away again. It had been a boooring week. She'd been stuck at home with the au-frigging-pair, her kid brother, and a dad who worked such long hours at the hospital that sometimes she almost didn't recognise him when they coincided at the breakfast table. Just because he was some big-shot surgeon. Well, he might be saving all those mangled people, sewing on legs or whatever – and she felt for his patients, she really did – but poor little Matthew would have loved a game of football in the garden. She didn't care any more, she was used to it. And anyway, she was too busy now to worry about her parents and all the mistakes they were making. She had to keep her public happy.

Suddenly her blank, pale face lit up, her mouth flicking up at the corners in that characteristic way that had launched ten thousand posts. She'd just had a brainwave. If she'd got that many likes for just a straight shot in the dress, how about if she pulled the straps down, accidentally on purpose, and leant forward – with her special smile, too, of course. That would really get them going.

***

'Oh my God, she's alive. Call an ambulance!' Beth shouted, dashing forward and kneeling at the girl's side. There was silence behind her. Beth turned round, where the gallery assistant was still standing, stock still, knuckles in her mouth. 'Ring the police!' she yelled again, then turned back to the girl.

Beth grabbed her hand, knew she should be feeling for a pulse, but the cool skin defeated her and she couldn't remember which bits of the wrist to press. She gave up and shook the girl gently instead. Maybe she'd just wake up, say it was all a joke? To her horror, the slight form slithered all of a piece from side to side on its marble slab, and she stopped. The last thing she wanted was to knock the poor girl off her plinth and do more damage. She leaned over her, touching her face, which was still faintly warm, thank goodness.

'Can you hear me?' Beth said urgently. 'Are you ok? Can you wake up?' At the same time, she was fishing in her bag for her phone, which as ever was hiding under a heap of jumbled junk and hoping for a quiet life. With one hand, she chucked the contents of the bag out onto the floor and picked out the phone, prodding the three 9s with shaking fingers. The other hand she kept around the girl's face, patting her cheeks, feeling her forehead – though that was ridiculous. Was she thinking she might have a slight fever, like Ben with an ear infection? Was she going to dose her up with Calpol and send her on her way?

Beth turned, exasperated, to bark at the gallery assistant. 'Is there anybody else here? Anyone who can help?' Beth was just being treated to a trembling shrug when her call connected. 'Which service? Um, ambulance? Please, as quickly as you can. Yes, it's Wyatt's Picture Gallery, Wyatt's Road, Dulwich, you know, the first proper picture gallery in the UK…' She was rambling, and she mentally slapped herself round the chops. There was no way the emergency operator needed a history lesson.

'Look, there's a girl here, she's unconscious, I can't get

her to come round… I don't know what it is… yes, she could have taken something, I have no idea what… how old is she? Um, well, I'd guess she's in her teens… do we want the police? Um, well, yes… though, hang on, no, I'll ring the police myself. If you could send an ambulance as quickly as possible… I don't like the way she won't come round. Something's *wrong.*'

Replaying the conversation in her head later, Beth thought how ridiculous she had sounded. Of course, something was wrong. You didn't just happen across moribund teenagers every day of the week, especially in a place like Dulwich. And the way the body – no, the *girl,* she was alive – had been posed? That was just plain weird. Someone had a sick sense of humour. Or a degree in art history. Maybe both.

The idea of explaining all this to the police made Beth's heart sink. She needed someone who knew the place a bit, who could understand that there was more to this than just some stupid teenage game that had gone wrong. Before she knew it, Beth was scrolling back in her call history with an unsteady hand, until she found the number she was looking for. She pressed dial.

The phone rang out, and a deep voice clicked on. Beth started to speak, then realised it was just an answering machine. Should she leave a message, or just ring 999 again? She was pondering it when she realised she was pretty sure the girl's skin was feeling cooler. They had to keep her warm. It might be sunny in Dulwich, but it was cold as the grave in here. Beth whipped off her cardigan and draped it round the girl. 'Do you have any blankets? Anything to keep her warm?' she asked the assistant. 'Did you bring a jacket in this morning? Anything at all?'

The girl's cluelessness was beginning to exasperate Beth. 'Ok then, go to the gift shop, get any scarves, tea towels, there must be loads left over from the Vanessa Bell exhibition, whatever you can find. And a cushion, if there is one.'

Beth was almost sorry she'd sent the girl off, listening to

her slightly flat feet slapping across the parquet flooring as she ran the length of the gallery to the gift shop. Alone in the niche, with the scarcely-breathing girl lying so still, Beth realised what an enormously successful bit of mortuary design she was kneeling in. The cold marble beneath the girl must be leaching all the warmth from her body, while the sepulchral stillness of her three long-dead companions seemed to beckon her to join them.

Well, not on my watch, thought Beth. She clasped the cold, splayed fingers in her own warm ones, and chafed them as best she could, breathing on them to try and chase away the deadly chill. She kept up a constant stream of babbling chat, though she was useless at small talk at the best of times, and this was hardly that. Should she be trying to walk up and down with the girl, as you sometimes saw in hospital dramas? She wasn't sure she should attempt it. For a start, the girl might have broken bones – and Beth wasn't sure if she could support her, anyway. Though the girl was thin to the point of emaciation, Beth could see she was tall – certainly taller than her.

While she was lying so still, Beth had a perfect chance to have a good look at her. She was beautiful, and much younger than Beth had first thought; little more than a child. Her skin was translucent, the Anglo Saxon, skimmed milk type, dead white with a blue tinge, veins traced over her eyelids and at her temples, the colouring Beth associated with naturally blonde or sandy hair. The eyelashes, extravagantly fanned out on the girl's cheeks, as Ben's had been as a sleeping baby, had been inexpertly encrusted with thick mascara, while the eyeliner edging the lids was smeared. When she woke up, she'd have panda eyes. When? *If.*

The girl screamed youth, dressed up to ape something more sophisticated, in her party dress. Beth could see that the delicate straps of the dress were silk, as was the lining which was, eerily, the same ice-blue as Mrs Moody's extravagant frock. The girl's chest was barely moving now. It was heartbreakingly sad, to see her lying here. Beth felt the desperation of sheer panic. She was going to die. What

23

should she *do?*

The phone broke into her worries. Automatically, she clamped it to her ear. 'Hello?'

Immediately, a deep voice filled her ear. 'Harry York here.' Her immediate feeling was one of relief. At last, here was someone who could help her, take a bit of this burden off her shoulders. The gallery assistant was worse than useless, and there seemed – incredibly – to be not another soul in the place. Weren't there supposed to be curators, guards; a boss, even? It seemed a bit bizarre that she and a work experience girl should still have the run of the place. And, apart from anything else, she had to get in to work sometime today.

'Inspector York, thank God it's you.'

There was silence for a beat. She could forgive DI York of the Metropolitan Police for being surprised to hear from her. When they had last met, a few months ago, there had been, well, a heated exchange. From Beth's point of view, Harry York had been much too willing to accept that some mysteries could never be solved. As she had been one of the prime suspects in a bloody murder, she hadn't been nearly as sanguine as he about the case languishing on the Met's books, and had nearly got herself killed while trying to wrap things up neatly and clear her name. York had given her what he described as a firm talking-to – and what she remembered as a massive, shouty dressing-down.

But this was no time to worry about social gaffes, and the wisdom of revisiting painful scenes. Beth needed someone useful at her side and, annoying and insufferable though he certainly was, she'd never had cause to doubt York's essential good qualities. He might be too much of a pragmatist, in her view, but he was the best police officer she knew. Ok, the only police officer she really knew. But, after the last investigation, he was wise in the ways of Dulwich, and that counted for a lot.

'Beth, er, Miss Haldane. Your voice sounds odd. What's going on there? How can I help?'

'I've found a body…'

Immediately, York groaned.

24

'But listen, it's not like that! This time, she's alive. Well, at the moment,' said Beth, her gaze going again to the girl lying on the slab. She was very, very pale. And still as death.

'Right. I'm on my way.'

***

Harry York had a polystyrene cup containing alleged coffee in each hand as he strode down the corridor of the police station in Camberwell. He had to hand it to Beth, she managed to stumble across some top crime scenes. This one, complete with a teenager in clubbing gear draped over a coffin, was spectacular by any account.

The girl had been shipped off to the A & E at King's College Hospital, with the paramedics shaking their heads gravely even before they tried to drive her two miles across London. This journey made squeezing a camel through the eye of a needle seem a doddle, as they contended with crazed Uber drivers; kamikaze Deliveroo cyclists; joggers darting across the road whenever the mood took them, as though their quest for fitness raised them above the mere highway code; not to mention the lumbering red buses; and, of course, a whole bunch of mothers crashing around in Chelsea tractors they could hardly control.

It hadn't been much easier getting Beth and the dippy intern over to the police station. First, they'd had to winkle the rest of the gallery staff out of a hush-hush meeting in the new wing of the place, then Beth had had to square her absence with the school, *then* they'd had to drive to Camberwell. It had all been a lot easier when Dulwich Hospital had its own casualty department and there'd been a police station in Lordship Lane. The cuts. York was beginning to feel like his own stepfather, who sat in a chair all day complaining about the world. But really. This case was going to be hell to deal with, without the victim perishing as a result of the government's austerity programme.

***

York pushed open the door of the interview room with his foot, and deposited the two cups on the table. Beth, who'd been sitting nervously in the featureless room, with its institutional yellow-painted walls and unlovely lino floor, was just glad there wasn't a two-way mirror anywhere. She knew from hopeless addiction to cop shows that if there was, a team would be sitting in an adjoining room dissecting her every move, discussing whether her fidgeting made her guilty, or just desperate for the loo… but she wasn't a suspect. She wasn't even 'helping the police with their enquiries', or whatever the euphemism was. She had just stumbled into something. Again.

She smiled her thanks for the coffee, saw the contents of the cup and sniffed a little suspiciously. She took a sip and smiled again, bravely this time. York pushed his own cup away.

'So. Here we are again.' York fixed Beth with a cross blue stare, and she felt obscurely guilty. Then she thought better of it – it really wasn't her fault that she'd run across the girl today. And, in a way, thank God she had. The longer the child had been left there – and chilling wasn't the right word, but it had popped into her head and wouldn't go away – *chilling* in the mausoleum, the worse her chances would have been. At least Beth had raised the alarm and got her off for some treatment.

She sat up a little straighter and decisively flicked her fringe out of the way. It swung back as inexorably as a fire door, but Beth had made her point. She wasn't going to apologise, again, for being in the wrong place. Maybe she'd actually been in the *right* place this time.

'We've got your fingerprints on file from last time. Just run me through your reasons for being in the gallery?'

Beth thought for a moment. She was already feeling defensive, thinking she should come up with valid reasons for being in the place… but stuff that. She had as much right as anyone with a Friends' pass to pop by.

'Well, mostly, my only reason for being there is that I love the Picture Gallery,' said Beth, shrugging. 'Simple as that, really. I'd gone to pick up some stuff from the Village before work, but it was such a lovely day... I found myself walking to the Gallery gardens, then I thought I'd just take a quick peek while the place was really quiet... there was no-one there at all, apart from the girl on the desk. Tricia Stroud, I think she said her name was...'

York grimaced slightly. Of course, Beth thought. He'd just come from trying to make some sense of Tricia's scrambled account of events.

'I was just going to look in on a few friends and then get on with the day...' Beth went on.

'Sorry, friends? I thought you said there was no-one there?' York broke in.

She blushed. 'Oh. Well, some of the pictures. I've been visiting them since I was a little girl. I think of some of them as... friends. Sorry, that sounds so lame. Well, you get called a Friend of the Gallery, and that kind of makes you friends with the pictures...' she tailed off.

York turned a smile into a cough. Beth could just imagine how twee he thought she was being, and so completely *Dulwich,* too. While she might consider herself one of the saner residents of the borough, she did have the time, during the working day, to commune with artworks when she felt like it.

'I bet you wish you had that sort of job,' she smiled ruefully.

He met her eye and laughed. 'More free time would definitely be good. But art galleries? To be honest, probably not. They remind me of school trips – or visits with my boring aunt that were supposed to be 'improving', but only helped my daydreaming. I can't image *wanting* to see a picture.'

'They lift my spirits,' said Beth, simply.

'Not this time,' said York with some irony.

'Well, it wasn't the pictures' fault,' said Beth protectively. 'It's whoever played that evil joke.'

27

'A joke? Is that what you think it was?'

'Well, maybe. It's just that she was arranged… artistically, for want of a better word. Her hands were posed. The way she was lying. The *place* she'd been put.'

'You don't think she just lay down there herself?'

'I can't think how she would get in. You'd know all that better than me, how easy it is to get into the gallery, whether she was on camera and so on. But she was so still, so out of it… when I saw her anyway. I don't think she can have walked far, can she? Her feet were bare.'

York sat back in his chair, ignoring its creaks. It seemed to be one of those ancient plastic seats that protested too much – they might sound as though they were falling apart but they had years of loud, uncomfortable service in them yet to come.

'How did she get in there, that's the question? And what on earth was she doing last night?' York mused.

'Isn't there another question we should be asking?' said Beth.

'What's that?' York said.

'Well, isn't it obvious?' Beth said. 'Who *is* she?'

'You didn't recognise her?'

'No, not at all. I was with her for a while before the ambulance crew came, and I'm sure I've never seen her before. Such a beautiful girl, though… I hope she'll be ok?'

York ignored the note of enquiry. 'You don't recognise her *at all*?'

'No, should I?' asked Beth. 'It looks like she'd been to a party… there must be some parents out there going nuts that she's not home. Has anyone reported her missing?'

York gave her an old-fashioned look. As usual, he seemed to have no intention of sharing any knowledge with Beth. Useful though she may turn out to be in this investigation, she could see that she wouldn't be allowed to forget for one instant that her role was to provide him with nuggets of information. Not the other way around.

'Do you know much about the party scene here? For teenagers?' York asked her.

Beth shrugged again. 'Well, Ben's only little still, and I'm much too old. So, no, not really. I mean, I know that parties go on... some of the mums with older children talk about them. But thank goodness, I don't have to worry about that stuff yet.'

'That stuff? What's 'that stuff'?' said York, leaning forward a little, to a symphony of protest from his chair.

'Well, I suppose, underage drinking. Being out late. Even drugs...'

'Is there much of a drug scene in Dulwich?' asked York, incredulous. Despite herself, Beth felt a little stung. While no-one wanted junkies lolling outside Romeo Jones, the Village's chichi café-cum-deli, that wasn't to say that Dulwich was such an unsophisticated backwater that they couldn't get drugs if they wanted them.

'I wouldn't say the place is awash, but if you think about it, we are in London. It's only a few minutes into the centre on the train, then there's plenty of drugs if you know where to find them. And alcohol, well, that's even easier to get.'

'Is it easy? That girl definitely looked under-age to me.'

'She did look young, didn't she? But if you think about it, these kids have money. They have parents who almost certainly drink the odd glass of wine, at least, so they can pinch booze from home. And I'm sure they can buy it. We always used to when I was that age.'

'Really?' said York, head on one side, as if considering this new view of Beth as a determined teen rule-breaker.

Beth nodded. She wasn't sure if she wanted to admit it to a policeman, but she'd always been the one who had to go into the off-licence to get the Saturday night supplies of cheap cider, while her friends milled around outside, giggling guiltily. She'd been pretty, in a tiny show-pony way, yes, but more importantly, she had always looked sensible. Shopkeepers gave her the benefit of the doubt. Until everyone else had grown so much taller than her, that is. Then she'd been pushed to the back of the queue – which suited her just fine. She wasn't sure what happened nowadays, when people were hotter on ID, but there were bound to be ways. You could probably get fake cards online somewhere. There had always been techniques for weaving a merry slalom around the rules, and teenagers had the time, energy, and motivation to make sure they exploited every loophole they could find as they flirted, innocently, with what so often turned out to be not such innocent pleasures.

***

The rumours at the College School started to circulate at about midday.

Miss Troughton wasn't surprised that the class was having trouble concentrating today. Year 9 was when they started tackling the tricky stuff. No more days of the week, *je m'appelle,* and *quelle heure est-il?* The nursery slopes of French were being left behind, and they were ready to tackle the slalom race that was sentence construction.

Mind you, Miss Troughton knew these were fine minds that she had before her. Standards may have slipped elsewhere in her twenty years of teaching, but the College School remained a fixed point; a centre of excellence, if one wanted to use the detestable jargon people tossed around with gay abandon these days. And that reminded her sourly that she couldn't say gay any more, or not in that context. Tsk.

Anyway, her point was the entrance exam to the school was fearsome, the academic standards rigorous, and there was an unspoken understanding that any girl who didn't make the grade one year, would mysteriously vanish from the school roll the next. Quite right, too, in Miss Troughton's view. There were plenty of able girls queuing up to get a chance at this sort of education.

If this lot concentrated for a few minutes, they'd easily get the hang of what she was trying to impart. But this morning, they didn't seem capable of focusing at all. 9C was not Miss Troughton's favourite form – there were some 'big characters', as teachers euphemistically described bossy troublemakers – but the worst of them wasn't even here today. That dreadful Jones-Creedy girl. Ridiculous narcissist.

Spent her entire day in the loos, if she wasn't kicked out, flicking her hair around and playing with her phone. It was a damned shame. She'd been a nice girl, then something had gone awry. Miss Troughton had no idea what, it wasn't her business to pry. The girl had parents, didn't she? They should be keeping her on the straight and narrow. Still, no time to worry about that now. At least it was making her job a little easier this morning, without Little Miss Jones-Creedy making a quip every two minutes that half the class would giggle at, bunch of sycophants. Absurd.

But despite the girl's absence, every time she turned round from the board, everyone seemed to have their heads hanging down, drooping where they sat, like tulips deprived of water. She knew what this meant. They had their phones under their desks, just out of sight, and were squinting at them in the hope that she wouldn't notice.

Well. Nothing made her crosser than the arrogance of youth. If they thought for one second they were pulling the wool over these experienced eyes... They weren't even supposed to have the dratted phones on them in the classroom in the first place, on pain of suspension. In her view, the development of mobile phones was having a sadly deleterious effect on the children, or the *students* as she was now forced to call them. She could demand everyone's phones and make them troop off to see the headmistress. But that was draconian, even for her – and, ultimately, pointless. She knew to her cost that parents complained furiously if their little dears were separated from their mobiles. Phones had now become replacement umbilical cords, with anxious mummies and daddies fondly imagining their kids were safe as long as they were getting a good signal.

In her view, there was no point in having this rule against the presence of phones if it was virtually unenforceable. As it was, she was having to connive with flagrant rule-breaking every day, and was unable to do anything about it. But, thank God, she wasn't running the school. Just this blasted class, and that was bad enough.

Now, she turned to face the class again and asked,

31

somewhat wearily, 'How would you start a sentence with *voulez-vous?*' She had taught this lesson many times before, and was braced either for sniggers, for those few who'd bothered to decode the words to that dratted raunchy Lady Marmalade song, or for a burst or two of ABBA, thanks to the popularity of the musical *Mamma Mia* in the West End. What she hadn't expected was a volley of suppressed beeps from phones all round the room, followed by a collective shocked silence that was as deafening as the chorus of swooping ABBA *ah-has* that she was braced for.

She looked around the pale, set faces, and watched, aghast, as little Lily Courtauld burst into tears. It would be her, of course, the class wimp, who was the first to faint at the childbirth film, had to be excused from all rumbustious school trips, and was allergic to anything you could shake a gluten-free breadstick at. But something was definitely up, and Miss Troughton had had enough of this nonsense.

'Girls? Will someone please tell me *what the hell is going on*?'

***

Beth unlocked the new archives HQ, now housed on the ground floor of the geography block. While hardly palatial, it was a million miles from the glorified shack she'd started work in not so long ago. Wyatt's had rearranged its priorities, she was glad to say, and the archives had gone from being something dusty, pointless, and neglected, to something important, worthy – and shameful. She wasn't sure if she totally approved of the way the English tended to wallow in their guilt. But since it had bought her a rather nice mahogany desk, lifted from some forgotten staffroom somewhere, not to mention a fleet of lovely matching mahogany bookshelves for her beloved records, she was willing to let it go. Best of all, she had an ergonomic office chair that was both comfy and did that swivelling thing, and she wasn't above taking herself for a spin when things got stale.

Today, after the horror of the Gallery, followed by a rather grim time down at the police station making a full report, a spin would have been altogether too much excitement, and she really needed the strong cup of tea on the desk in front of her. Not to mention the packet of digestive biscuits she'd liberated from the staff room, which she was absent-mindedly nibbling. She'd square it with the wonderful school secretary, Janice, later. Janice would understand. These biscuits were strictly medicinal.

Part of Beth wanted to blot out the morning entirely, turn on her computer, and lose herself in work. She had lots to do, deadlines looming, reports to write, plenty to organise... but her thoughts kept turning irresistibly to that slight, cold form lying on the marble slab. That poor girl. Poor *child*, really. She'd looked so forlorn, so abandoned. A shocking, pitiful sight.

Now Beth did turn on her laptop – but only to Google Wyatt's Picture Gallery. The usual site came up, with opening hours, highlights of the permanent collection, details on the latest exhibition. No links to any news items with mentions of girls left for dead.

Next, she tried 'missing girl'. A depressing litany of familiar names jumped out at her, Shannon, Suzie, Millie... nothing recent. Nothing involving Dulwich.

Beth sat back, stumped. Surely the girl had been missing long enough – far too long – for someone not to have noticed? She knew how parents were in Dulwich. If a kid was late leaving Scouts, there were helicopters sweeping the area. This just didn't make sense.

Much though she didn't want to feel involved, Beth knew that she couldn't escape her ties. She'd been the one who had found the girl. All right, Tricia had actually seen her first, but the gallery assistant might as well have been made of marble herself for all the use she'd been. It was Beth who'd contacted York, got an investigation going. In a way, it made the whole matter her baby – and the girl most of all, as she was at the centre of it all. And it did really look as though the poor girl needed a mother. Beth drank the last of her tea, brushed the crumbs from her lap decisively, and settled down at her keyboard. She had a lot to do.

***

Harry York pushed a hand through coarse, dark blond hair that could have done with a cut. There wasn't time; there wasn't time for anything. He felt like a dog chasing its own tail most days. This case, in particular, made him feel as though he was drowning. It was the worst kind of thing to get wrapped up in. A closed community, full of secrets, shunning outsiders, refusing to talk to strangers. And that was just the teenagers. The adult residents of Dulwich were going to be worse still when this hit the papers. And hit the papers it would. He'd just put the phone down on the hospital. They weren't holding out much hope.

'Trouble is, we think she's taken a shedload of different types of stuff. Usually, we can drag people back – if we know what on earth they've got inside them. Sometimes not. It depends which bits of them the toxins fry,' the A&E Consultant at the hospital had explained wearily over the phone. 'If they destroy the liver, you've basically had it. If you've just knackered your kidneys, then, on a good day, we might be able to do something. But we have to *know*. In this case, I take it, there was nothing at the scene? Nothing at all to indicate what she might have swallowed?'

The doctor sounded just as exhausted as York felt. King's College Hospital was huge, and busy round the clock, as the TV show *24 Hours in A&E*, filmed there for three years, had amply demonstrated. This girl was just one of many problems which had landed on the consultant's shoulders since his shift had started, what probably seemed like a lifetime ago. Yet, despite the fatigue, York could hear compassion in the doctor's voice, a wish to do the best for the girl, however bleak her prospects might appear.

'There were no injection marks? It was definitely pills?' York asked.

'She was clean for punctures, but it could have been

34

powder, pills, liquid, a spiked drink, something she smoked or sniffed, you name it. That's why we need some sort of indication…'

'Can't help you there at the moment. There was nothing at all at the scene. Just the girl herself, no shoes, no phone, nothing. We've got people combing the grounds. If there's anything there, we'll find it.'

'I really hope you do. Without any clues, well…'

York put the phone down. Already, he hated this case. There was nothing worse than seeing kids getting hurt. And he had a bad feeling that this poor girl in intensive care was just going to be the start of something very nasty. Someone, somewhere, was pulling strings, and he didn't like it at all.

***

Miss Troughton didn't usually run. In fact, she hadn't really walked anywhere fast since her knee had started troubling her, oh, five years ago. But today she sprinted all the way to the headmistress's office, bypassing the astonished secretary Leanne, who usually guarded the door like Cerberus with a particularly juicy bone.

'Angela, I have to speak to you,' said Miss Troughton, clinging onto the door frame to get her breath back. Her blouse had come adrift from her skirt and her face was most unbecomingly flushed. Her mighty bosom heaved with the effort of compensating for more physical effort in the space of five minutes than was usually required during a full year.

Angela Douglas, her spine perfectly straight as she sat in a chair that was, not by accident, rather like a throne, betrayed her surprise by an involuntary tightening of the nostrils. She briefly touched the double strand of lustrous, heavy pearls at her throat – the one sartorial frippery she allowed herself – then dropped her hand to her lap, sheathed in an expensively non-committal Eileen Fisher black dress. Those who didn't know her would think she had remained entirely impassive. Bernie Troughton, who'd known her since their student days at St Andrews, realised she was

35

shocked to the core.

'It gets worse. Look at this!'

With a shaking hand, Miss Troughton held out an iPhone in a battered case that screamed 'FAB' in pink neon letters. Miss Douglas recoiled a little from this garish artefact, then leaned closer, curious despite herself. The two women stared, perplexed, at the darkened screen. Miss Troughton *tsked* crossly, poked the 'home' button, and the screen came to life. Out of the darkness emerged the pale limbs of the girl in the Gallery, looking so ethereal and insubstantial that she seemed to be floating above her maroon marble slab. It wasn't a particularly good shot. Whoever had taken it had had scant regard for centering the image, and the whole thing looked rather blurry. Whatever its compositional defects, however, it certainly packed a punch. The two teachers looked at each other in dismay.

'Good grief,' said Angela Douglas, consternation cutting two deep horizontal lines into the smooth cream of her well made-up forehead.

'Exactly,' said Miss Troughton, nodding vigorously, her chins shaking emphatically with every movement.

'Are you sure it's her?' said Miss Douglas, weakly.

Miss Troughton looked at her quickly. She'd never known her friend to be indecisive or to shy away from battle. And now was not the time to be developing new character traits, particularly unhelpful ones.

'Of course, it's her! I'd know that little… minx… anywhere. The question is, what is she doing there? Why isn't she at school? Why is someone sending this picture to the rest of her class? What is *going on*?'

'That's four questions,' said Miss Douglas crisply. While Miss Troughton could have hit her, she was also relieved. That was more like the Miss Douglas the school needed in a crisis. And this was most definitely shaping up to be a crisis. *Most* definitely.

'So, she's not at school, we've established that much. She's probably just at home, recovering from… whatever that stunt is. I don't suppose you know when the photo was taken?'

'Last night. There's a date on it.'

'Right, well, maybe she's having a late morning… won't be the first time, will it? Such disciplined parents, and then they take their eye off the ball with the children. We've seen it so many times before, haven't we?'

Miss Troughton nodded sadly. It was a tragedy. High-achieving parents, with little time to be present in their children's lives, always seemed to feel the need to compensate their offspring with *objects*. It never worked. The children scented blood in the water. Weakness. Guilt. The parents, then faced with bad behaviour, failed to set boundaries – they didn't want to spoil what scant time they had with the children by laying down the law. Little did they know, thought Miss Troughton, that there was nothing these kids liked better than a few rules and someone willing to put in the effort to enforce them. Before you knew it, a very unhelpful pattern had emerged, with the children getting the upper hand and the parents constantly on the back foot – too many limbs, by anyone's reckoning. And the result was almost always an unpleasant mess. Parenting was so much easier when you didn't actually *have* children, she reflected.

'Do you think it is a stunt, then? Whatever that photo is about? Because her class is very upset. They're all crying.'

Miss Douglas pressed the home button again and the picture materialised in all its ghastly pallor. She zoomed in on the girl's impassive face.

'It's very chilling. She looks…'

Miss Troughton looked up anxiously. 'You don't think she's…'

'Absurd! Whatever else that girl may be, she is not an idiot. And whatever "issues" she may be incubating,' Miss Troughton smiled faintly at her friend's scathing inverted commas, 'she does not have a death wish. No, I would say this is an elaborate prank, designed to throw us all off course and make us worry about the little… madam. Now. First things first. We need to put a call in to the parents, establish the child's whereabouts. Everything else devolves from that,

37

wouldn't you agree?'

Miss Troughton, deeply relieved that the normal order had been restored and she was being bossed about, nodded fervently. 'So, you want me to ring?'

'*Voulez-vous*?' said her friend, with a small smile.

Miss Troughton didn't quite walk backwards out of the headmistress's room, but she did close the door softly and return to the staff room at her usual ambling velocity. As always, there was nothing like a quick chat with Angela to set her mind at rest.

Alone in her room again, Miss Douglas slipped her hands down to the heavy arms of her chair. Her face, if Miss Troughton could have seen it, wore a ferocious expression, and the two lines were back, cruelly bisecting her snowy forehead.

Chapter Three

Harry York strode quickly down the pale green corridors, head low, deliberately pushing all hospital-type thoughts out of his head. Though he was used to big institutions – hell, he worked in one – he absolutely hated hospitals. Whether it was the smell, the thought of the suffering being endured, or whether (and he realised this was not great) it was all the actual sick people hanging around, they were his least favourite places. King's wasn't the worst, by any means, but like all London hospitals, it had to keep growing to keep pace with the population it served.

He'd spent a botched weekend with a girlfriend in Paris a year or so ago and, while the romance hadn't lasted, her history lesson about the strategic rebuild of the city in the nineteenth century had stuck. Paris had emerged chic, but London had never had a makeover. Like a patched suit, it was stuck making do and mending, and the result was not pretty. Buildings at King's had been tacked on haphazardly as need demanded, and the result was a maze of corridors, like this one, leading with no logic to unexpected dead-ends and banks of apparently unused lifts.

Today, this was serving York well, as his mystery girl had been filed away, far from prying eyes, in a room with a door. These were far and few between in London hospitals, where the rule was now mixed wards with only a flimsy curtain between patients. Finally, York found the right place, thanks to the PC slumped on a hard, plastic chair outside. He'd been sitting, peacefully zoned out, vaguely listening to the burble of his police radio, for a couple of hours now, but snapped to attention as he registered York's purposeful form bearing down on him.

'All right, sir? All quiet here.'

'No-one hanging around?'

'Not seen a soul. Apart from nurses.'

'No visitors?'

'Not one, sir.'

Of course not, thought York, as he opened the door gingerly. After all, who knew the girl was even here? As far as he was aware, no-one had yet been reported missing. He didn't mind admitting that it surprised him. In a place like Dulwich, he was pretty sure that parents were all over their children. Ok, he didn't actually know many Dulwich parents to speak to – Beth Haldane was one of the few he'd met in the flesh, and she seemed fine, concerned about her kid of course, but this side of insanely over protective. But during his previous Dulwich case, he had had his ear bent by some very odd parents who'd thought that, just because he was investigating a death at their sons' school, he needed to explain his every move to their mums and dads. Well, he'd put them straight, of course. But he'd definitely got a certain impression about the way these parents liked to throw their weight around. Although he wanted this poor girl to receive all the support from her family that she could get – she'd need it, according to the doctor – he wasn't looking forward to having to deal with parents who were going to be over-privileged and pretty sure of their exalted status, as well as anxious and probably vengeful. He sighed, and pushed the door open.

Stepping inside the room, he was aware of the heavy silence, punctuated only by regular electronic beeps. He had no idea what all the various tubes and monitors attached to the figure in the bed were doing. He registered only that the monotonous sounds were proof of continued life, and therefore comforting. Steeling himself, he stepped forward.

The girl was tiny, her outline barely disturbing the standard, NHS-issue, cotton blanket, a faded blue from multiple boil washes. The blanket had been smoothed across the girl's slight chest, and lay as peaceful and tidy as the covers a little girl would tuck over her doll. It was clear that she hadn't moved at all since she had been hooked up to the machines. The little face was waxen pale, blank as a fresh page of his notebook. She had no lines. It was tempting to think that was because she'd had no experience, yet, but York knew that probably wasn't so.

She might be an English rose, if there had been any animation in her face, any flush of life. There wasn't. York had seen the photos from the Gallery and noticed that the crude make-up had been washed away, maybe while they'd been pumping her stomach or doing whatever it was they'd had to do to keep her alive thus far. He had previously thought she must be fourteen or fifteen, in her sophisticated party frock, though it was always difficult to guess a teenager's age. Now, stripped back to the essentials, she could easily pass for a ten-year-old.

It didn't seem right that she should lie here, alone, so close to death. Where were the people who loved her? And who had done this to her? York, against his own will, felt a vow rising. He didn't want to do this, he didn't even need to, but nevertheless – he swore he would find the people who'd put her here. Because, if he was sure of anything, it was this. The girl lying here was just a pawn. There was something else going on. And he wanted – needed – to know what it was.

He turned to face the window, and looked out. The view from this floor was uninspiring, to put it mildly. The backs of various buildings, a couple of high, wire-sided wheeled trolleys filled with used blankets identical to the one here, abandoned on their way to the laundry. An exit, surrounded by a throng of die-hard smokers – in all ways. One was wheeling a drip attached to his arm and, York could see from here, doubling over into a hacking cough; there were a couple of white-coated doctors, who should surely know better; a nurse in maroon scrubs; a patient in a thin, NHS-issue dressing gown; and an admin worker. They shared the uneasy camaraderie of addicts. As he watched, one of the medics ground out his stub and went back into the building.

Beyond the black railings, the traffic of Camberwell

rushed by, on its way to the Elephant and Castle or down to Dulwich, its roar not quite reaching York through the dusty double glazing, but so well known to him that it felt like part of his being.

As he watched, he heard a double beep back in the room. It was a misstep, a breaking of ranks from the machines surrounding the girl. Something was off. He swung back, but there was no discernible change – she lay still, the blanket perfectly shrouding the tiny hillocks of her breasts. Only an added flashing light from the bank of monitors signalled distress from somewhere within that small body. He rushed to the door.

'Get someone. Something's happening,' he said urgently to the PC, who shot out of his seat and bolted down the corridor, hefty shoes squeaking frantically on the lino.

***

Bernie Troughton sidled from one rubber-soled brogue to the other, outside Miss Douglas's door. She didn't usually hover – she didn't have the build for it – but today it was clear she was anxious. Very anxious. Watched by the cool dark eyes of Leanne, the headmistress's secretary, Miss Troughton's restless swaying reminded Leanne irresistibly of the time one of the oak trees had come down on Peckham Rye in a storm. People had seen it moving from side to side, and not paid it much mind. But once it had really got going, there'd been no stopping the momentum.

Leanne fiddled idly with one of her giant, gold hoop earrings. She needed to pop to the shops in her lunch break, but she didn't want to miss the moment when the Old Trout (as poor Miss Troughton was fondly known to everyone except the headmistress) finally toppled and hit the deck. They'd feel the reverberations in Brixton, for sure.

Before Miss Troughton finally made up her mind to knock, the door suddenly swung back, and Angela Douglas appeared. 'Oh, you're here, good, good, come in. Leanne?'

Leanne uncoiled herself from her seat and loped over

with two covered platters. This emergency lunch meeting was her chance to escape, and she was going to seize it. 'I'm off now, yeh?'

Miss Douglas waved a distracted hand. 'Yes, yes, *fine*.'

Leanne mentally expanded her shopping trip to cover making hair and nail appointments down Norwood High Street, as well as dropping her party shoes in at the menders. Clearly, no-one was going to be watching the clock today. She grabbed her jacket and was off before the headmistress's door had shut.

Miss Troughton and Miss Douglas faced each other in the large, quiet room. It wasn't as grand as the headmaster's room at Wyatt's, much to Miss Douglas's chagrin. Though her job was every bit as important to the reputation of the paired Endowment Schools, her own establishment was a Johnny – or should that be *Jill?* – come-lately affair, founded some two hundred and fifty years after the original school, when someone had belatedly realised that girls might just be worth educating, too. Wyatt's itself was a baroque redbrick palace to knowledge, complete with a cupola atop the Grand Hall, stained glass left, right, and centre, and acres of manicured greensward sprawling louchely beside the snarling traffic of the South Circular. Meanwhile, her own beloved College was a standard-issue, nineteenth-century school building, tucked unpretentiously into a residential street, and with a rash of higgledy-piggledy outbuildings clustered around it like the dreariest suburban shanty town, struggling to contain the school's constant expansion.

The headmistress's room was of a piece with the main school building, in that it was solid, workmanlike, and without architectural frills. Angela Douglas had chosen to emphasise this lack of fussiness in her own style of dress, but there were days when she yearned to be looking out onto something even approaching the billiard-table perfection of Wyatt's lawns. Instead, her view was a sea of bog-standard black tarmac, plain iron railings, and a couple of measly tubs of late tulips standing to attention by the sign saying The College School, like the afterthoughts they very much were.

Sometimes there was a comfort in grandeur, and today she felt as though she could do with all she could get. Even the high-backed chair behind her desk was restrained. It was a little throne-like, yes, but in an austere, medieval way, definitely more Edward the Confessor than Elizabeth I. She sighed a tiny sigh. Having exceptionally good taste could be an utter pain. Today, she would have liked an enormous ruff, and a massive fuck-off gown studded with seed pearls. Even a couple of handsome courtiers wearing golden hoops in their ears and rakish smiles on their faces would have cheered her up.

She looked over at Miss Troughton crossly. She loved her friend dearly, but the stress of the day had left the woman red-faced and rumpled, her choices of man-made, easy-care fibres being revealed as seriously flawed on many grounds.

'Let's sit,' she said to Miss Troughton, indicating the round table at the end of the room, more suitable for brainstorming sessions than the seat from which she handed down polite but unmistakable reprimands and diktats to recalcitrant girls – and their parents.

Miss Troughton whipped the covers off the plates and dived straight into the serried ranks of sandwiches, beautifully cut into equilateral triangles and arrayed points uppermost. Once she had an egg mayonnaise in one hand and a ham-and-pickle in the other, with bites missing from the apex of each, she took a breath and relaxed. Miss Douglas averted her gaze a little from her friend's feast – she had always been quite the trencherwoman – and shook out her linen napkin. She took a smoked salmon triangle and nibbled the edge, then put it to one side. The tang of lemon juice was a little astringent for her taste.

'The question is, how are we going to approach this mess?' she asked, the horizontal lines on her forehead now deeply scored.

Miss Troughton, moving on now to cheddar versus tuna, munched silently. Her shoulders rose up a couple of inches, but she remained focussed on chewing. Miss Douglas threw down her napkin crossly and stood up, striding to the window. Much to her annoyance, she caught the eye of the postman, who'd been strolling up to the school entrance with his little red trolley. He grinned cheerily, and she withdrew from sight, hoping she hadn't given him quite as fearsome a grimace as he deserved.

So much of this job was about appearances. Don't frighten the postman. Don't alarm the parents. Always show the best possible side of the school in public. Never let on that there were any problems rumbling beneath the surface. Never lie, but don't ever quite let any cats out of the bag either. And there lay the essence of her dilemma today.

Sophia Jones-Creedy might have been the envy of her peers for her tiny build and highly photogenic features, but her latest escapade was still going to represent a huge and very ugly moggy indeed being let out of the College School bag. Not that Miss Douglas didn't have compassion for the girl, and her family. Of course, she did. If ill had befallen her – and it very much looked as though it had – her heart went out to them all. But she had to think about her other charges, too, and the effect all this would have on the school.

The College was bigger than one silly schoolgirl. Always had been and, if she had anything to do with it, always would be. But reputation was everything. And the exam results! This summer's GCSEs and A levels were looming. The last thing she needed was the entire exam cohort going off the boil because some wayward child had got herself... What, exactly? That was what they needed to know.

'Any response from the parents?'

Miss Troughton chewed vigorously, swallowed and spoke. 'Father's in surgery until they don't know when. Mother's flying back from Dubai, she doesn't land until this evening. I've spoken to the au pair, but she knows nothing. Didn't see Sophia this morning, but that's nothing new. Can't tell whether her bed's been slept in; room's such a mess. Doesn't want to search the place for her phone – terrified of the girl. Well, she has a temper on her, as we know. Didn't see her last night, but that's nothing unusual either, and frankly it sounds like the less this au pair sees of the girl, the

45

better pleased she is.'

'What a situation. A fourteen-year-old girl, and her family has absolutely no idea where she is or what's she's up to. How can this happen? And with one of *our* families, too?'

'Angela. You know it happens. It's not good but it's the modern way. Remember last year?'

The women exchanged stricken glances. An eleven-year-old had been teased by her classmates because she smelled. They'd discovered, eventually, that the reason was her mother, newly divorced, had taken a month-long work assignment in Paris, leaving her daughter to cope alone with a stack of ready meals, a fork, a microwave, and a nightly FaceTime chat. The calls sufficed to reassure the mother that everything was ticking along. They did not, however, replace parental injunctions to shower, clean teeth, brush hair, and wash clothes. Getting to school on time and coping with her huge homework load had taken all the girl's organisational skills. There had been nothing left for the domestic front.

The mother returned to find her charming three-bedroomed terrace reduced to a byre, while her little girl was half-feral and wholly stinky. She had been overwhelmed by guilt. But she insisted she had had no choice. Facing swingeing cuts to her income when her husband ran off with the statutory younger woman, she had needed to take the work in order to pay the school fees.

That had been another moral nightmare, thought Miss Douglas. She had wrestled over whether to contact social services, or whether even the police should be involved – child abandonment could be a matter for the courts, with the threat of criminal charges, if it could be shown to have caused unnecessary suffering or injury to health. In the end, despite her conviction that a month's worth of solitude and processed food had probably stunted the girl's growth, if not worse, Miss Douglas decided to be merciful.

The problem had been solved with a bursary, though the child was still ostracised – there a streak of cruelty running through most schoolgirls, as vivid and unmistakable as the lettering in Brighton rock. They could smell an outsider – this time, quite literally – and they shunned her accordingly. Running with the pack was so important; no-one could afford to court the unpopularity that would be caused by showing this poor child a bit of friendship.

Miss Douglas sighed, though she told herself firmly her job was not to change the essential nature of humankind. It was just to turn out girls with excellent results that fitted them for life in a sharp-elbowed world. This time, though, it looked as though things were much more serious. There was no avoiding the obvious course of action.

Miss Troughton, still munching, looked questioningly at the headmistress. Miss Douglas inclined her head.

'It's got to be the police. I can't see another way. Though what the publicity will do to us, I shudder to think.'

Miss Troughton chewed frantically again. 'Wyatt's have managed, though. When you think about it. A murder, and that whole slavery business. And their stats are up!'

Miss Douglas looked sourly down at her salmon sandwich. 'Don't remind me. If they had Jack the Ripper as an Old Boy, their waiting list couldn't be any longer. They just can't seem to put a foot wrong. But, as usual, *it's different for girls.*'

It was the mantra they had both been fighting for a lifetime. Why was it the case that Wyatt's, and its personification, Dr Grover, had been able to shimmy around their recent scandal like the most shameless of pole dancers? Double standards. A man behaving badly got public sympathy, or not-so-sneaking admiration. A woman behaving badly had always been, and always would be, a harlot. And a teenage girl acting up was days on end of headlines for the red top papers, a gaggle of journalists posted outside her gates, plummeting applications, even some removals from the register, not to mention so-called think pieces on modern morals popping up on Radio 4 and a thousand blog posts from sanctimonious parents pointing out the school's failings.

'I'll ring them now. There doesn't seem any alternative,' said Miss Douglas, sitting up a little straighter, and brushing imaginary crumbs from her superbly tailored dress. Its strict lines and her set face made her look, thought Miss Troughton admiringly, like a slightly more mature Joan of Arc ready for her hot – very hot – date with the stake.

'It's the right thing to do,' said Miss Troughton sadly. The sandwiches were finished, but she would stay and offer whatever support she could. She snaked out a pudgy hand and laid it on her friend's slender arm. 'Might as well get on with it.'

***

That was *it*, thought Beth. She'd had enough of crouching at her desk, peering into her laptop as though it were a crystal ball. She could still find no trace of any official report of a missing teenager on the internet, but at least her hours spent on Facebook had borne some fruit.

And what bitter fruit they were. Though she kept telling herself that she had no reason to worry about Ben yet, it was the *yet* that loomed large. She felt a little like someone who had innocently gone searching for heffalumps in the woods, and got caught in her own trap.

Parents of kids Ben's age were protective, there was no doubt of that. There was a perception that danger lurked on every street corner, and that children were safer closeted at home with their parents. But this stifling world where no child played outside at any time – let alone after dark, unless they were under full parental supervision – led to both sides escaping the claustrophobic lock-down with their phones, laptops, iPads, or whatever they had that possessed the golden charm of connectivity.

No parent, however dedicated, could play Uno all night long, or Minecraft, or the Sims, or whatever else their child loved to do. She already knew that after a bout of playing Scrabble or Cluedo or Pandemic with Ben, she loved to curl up gratefully with her phone for some peaceful, mindless surfing, and *he did the same.* All their kids were learning, by example, that what you did for a bit of peace and quiet was disappear off to your own world online. You might be physically sharing the same space, in the same sitting room, but all members of the family could be in entirely different zones – and not all of them good ones.

Beth had started off her investigation into teenage life with little expectation of finding anything. Did she even know any teenagers? She was used to seeing gaggles of lovely girls, uniformly gorgeous, long-limbed, usually laughing, drifting through Dulwich Village at home time, making for the expensive cafes like giraffes moving towards a watering hole. But did she ever speak to any? Sometimes she glimpsed them in their natural habitat, when dropping off or picking up Ben for play dates with his friends, though these big sisters of small boys never deigned to acknowledge his presence. And she, as a much older woman and mummy to boot, was of no interest either, beyond a polite 'hello'.

Then she realised. Though hardly a party animal, Beth did occasionally venture out for dinner or to the theatre, and when she did, Zoe Bentick was Ben's favourite babysitter. The fact that she lived two doors up on Pickwick Road was a massive help – no Uber fares to tag onto the night's tariff, and Beth could see her home by sticking her head out of her front door. Zoe was a dream babysitter, one of those swotty girls who'd been liberated from terminal uncoolness by J. K. Rowling's wondrous invention, Hermione Grainger, patron saint of over-achieving girlhood everywhere.

Zoe was also a definite teenager, being in year, what was it, 9 or 10 at the College School? That made her fourteen or fifteen. Possibly young to babysit someone of Ben's age, but then Zoe was special. She was responsible, incredibly clever, and best yet, big sister to no fewer than three brothers of her own, so she was great with small boys. The Benticks were bursting out of their tiny Pickwick Road house, even though it was one of the few which had not only had a loft extension, but also had the side return covered over to enlarge the kitchen. There was a home studio plonked in the tiny garden, too. The long-suffering and prolific Bentick parents needed it, so that they had one reasonably quiet spot to quaff their Merlot in the evenings – and presumably gather their strength for more procreation, uninterrupted by the ones they had made earlier.

So, Beth had started out by crawling Zoe's Facebook page for clues. It felt like stalking, and it probably was, but she'd justified it because she needed information – and the girl she'd found in the Gallery needed help.

Before Beth knew it, she had been deep in a teenage world that she'd previously known nothing about. Zoe herself was not very active on Facebook – she was one of the few girls her age whose nose was permanently inserted in a book. In fact, the last time she'd come round, when Beth had been summoned to Katie's for a lovely but dauntingly grown-up dinner party, the teenager had been reading *Wuthering Heights*. They'd chatted about it before and after Beth's dinner outing, and Beth didn't mind admitting that she'd enjoyed their talk a lot more than the Brexit squabbles and hand-wringing over American politics that were still dominating Dulwich supper table talk.

But, though Zoe was not a leading light of social media, she had friends who had tagged her in various group shots at school. Before Beth knew it, she was following a trail that was a lot better signposted than crumbs scattered on a woodland path. By clicking on this or that group shot, she could harvest a bunch of names. Then she searched for them on Facebook, and their profiles came up. Depending on their privacy settings, she could see some, or all, of what they posted.

And many of these girls seemed to post every time they drew breath, let alone did something interesting. Considering most of their daily life ought to consist of school and homework, it was amazing how prolific they were. Every hairstyle was documented, every expression practised in the Facebook mirror, every outfit photographed, every party dissected as though the Rosetta Stone was being parsed. There were snaps of them drinking. All right, you couldn't tell if it was alcohol in the plastic cups they clutched, but the effect on them made it pretty clear that a lot of underage boozing was going on. There were pictures of them smoking, too. And, in some cases, falling over in the street. Always laughing. Because it was all just such fun, wasn't it? If they were in Zoe's class or year at school, the fact that they were well under the legal age for any of this behaviour was apparently irrelevant.

Beth had been amazed that posting these tipsy, toking pics wasn't getting them into big trouble with their parents, with the school – with everybody. They were breaking laws here. All right, the British had a very peculiar attitude towards alcohol, which cut through all ages and all social barriers. Given half a chance, and free access to booze, Brits, from dukes to dustmen, would simply drink until they fell over, and there was nothing much anyone could do to stop that deep-dyed predilection. Beth was beginning to feel sanctimonious, but knew she enjoyed a drink as much as the next person, yes, to the point of word-slurring giggliness in social situations, to take the edge off a little.

Teenagers, dealing with all kinds of awkwardness and blessed with fresh young livers that brushed off the abuse, were notorious for experimenting whenever they got the chance. She'd sometimes nipped behind the bike shed at school to take a puff on an illicit cigarette – who hadn't? But she hoped even her teenage self would have had more sense than to slap pictures of it all online.

And this was just booze and cigs. Where they were, drugs were sure to follow. Were all those actually cigarettes? And what exactly had everyone taken before thinking it was a great idea to take every photo at a 45-degree angle?

Beth had shaken her head slightly as she pulled up another shot of one of Zoe's friends, looking as though she'd passed out on the shoulder of some Wyatt's boy on a bench which had to be in Dulwich Park. Yes, she recognised the rhododendron bushes in the background. They were near the boating pond. Lots of joshing comments under the shot made it clear that this was particularly hilarious. Poor girl, thought Beth. A time would come, and soon, when she would so regret not just that evening, but the fact that it was plastered all over the internet as well.

51

And Beth had had access to all this simply by leaping from one profile to the next, without becoming anyone's friend and without her growing interest being signalled at all to those whose pictures she pored over.

If it was this easy for her, Beth realised, how much simpler might it be for someone who really knew what they were doing, who could delve further, and who had the time and inclination to befriend these girls – all of whom, horribly, seemed desperate for approval and appreciation? To a paedophile, it must be like supermarket sweep. These girls posed in bikinis on summer holidays, wearing tiny shorts in the park, lolling about in their back gardens in cropped tops and minis, at festivals in tiny dresses. They were young, they were beautiful. They were stupid. They were so vulnerable. It made Beth want to cry.

Among the mêlée of faces crying out for recognition, there were a few who stood out as that bit more outrageous, more determined, more attention-seeking. Either they were prettier, more photogenic, more prolific in their posts, or just seemed more desperate to get likes. One, in particular, seemed to the be superstar of the bunch. Her dresses were lower, or higher, or just plain sassier. She had a cheeky look, though she was not necessarily prettier than any of the rest. But she was ubiquitous, and shameless. She had a trademark smile, that crooked her mouth up a mile on the right-hand side, making her look a little bit knowing. Whenever she produced that smile, she got a deluge of likes. It seemed to be her 'Blue Steel'. Beth smiled wryly. She'd loved the film *Zoolander,* a parody of the fashion world, where a male model spends his days perfecting a repertoire of looks that are actually identical. Ironic that nowadays it was being used as a template to achieving Instagram glory by Dulwich teens.

Thanks to that certain smile, this girl's popularity seemed to be growing inexorably, post by post. She had far more Facebook followers than there were pupils at the College School, or at all the schools in Dulwich put together, plus those of Camberwell, Sydenham, and even Lewisham for that matter. Beth clicked on the serried ranks of fans to find out how that could be, and realised many of them were people who looked well over school age, who should surely have better things to do.

And behind the bland profile pics of teenage lads, who knew who could be lurking? The lonely thirty-stone truck driver from Minnesota pretending to be thirteen was an urban myth everyone had heard. Everyone Beth's age, anyway. Anybody who was safely in Minnesota was ok with her – while they stayed that far away. The real danger was the man round the corner pretending to be the girl next door. And why so many grown-up women would want to watch the posturing of a teenager was a complete mystery to her.

Maybe these kids were still innocently presuming everyone was exactly who they seemed. She knew that they had some sort of cyber-threat training in secondary school. The trouble was that this generation – like all generations before it – assumed they knew everything. Having grown up with these marvellous devices in their hands, they would listen with barely concealed irritation to some dumb old guy trying to scare them.

Beth sighed and turned again to the girl's posts, clicking through the now familiar stream of poses wearing little dresses, tiny playsuits, cutesy hats... The girl was striking, you had to give her that. It wasn't until Beth had got to a shot of her wearing white, in a dimly lit room, that she realised what had been troubling her about this particular girl for some time. With growing horror, she realised she bore a striking resemblance to someone she had seen before.

Someone she had last encountered lying on a cold marble slab in the Picture Gallery.

Was it the same girl? Beth pressed her nose almost to her laptop screen. She was pretty sure, but not certain. Still, there was no doubt in her mind about what she had to do next. For once, her phone was easily to hand. She grabbed it, and dialled.

Chapter Four

Harry York sat with his head in his hands. It had been a dicey half hour, to say the least. The first misstep from the machines had turned out to be just the opening salvo in a cacophony of horrible noises, from increasingly urgent beeps from the heart monitor to the buzzing of the panic button he started pressing, when the interval between his PC running for help and the help itself arriving looked as though it would never end. Then his ears were full, suddenly, with the sound he'd dreaded most of all; the remorseless low squeal of the pulse monitor as the girl finally flatlined. After that came the thunder of the crash team charging up the corridor with a cart filled with yet more equipment, as if the poor child wasn't attached to enough machines already. He had been glad to be pushed out of the room as the professionals fought over which bit to poke, prod, and shock next.

He wasn't expecting anything after that. The public, fed on a diet of miraculous hospital dramas, saw resurrection as everyone's God-given right as soon as the defibrillator paddles came out. But York knew that fewer than three per cent of attempts to restart the heart were successful. It had been part of his training, not least to ensure that police on the streets weren't too downcast when their own best efforts almost always failed.

Yet, against the odds, this girl had rallied. Who knew what germ of a survival instinct still fluttered within? York wondered if any of her ribs had been cracked during the CPR, or whether she was one of the few who had effortlessly floated back to life. Somehow, given her traumatic day so far, he doubted that anything had gone smoothly. And this might not be her last brush with the grim reaper. No-one yet knew if there was anything still going on in that pretty head of hers, even if her cells had decided they wanted to live on.

The white-coated doctor, sweaty after his efforts, had been in a rush to get somewhere else. He had also looked young enough to still be working for his Scouts first aid badge, despite the rigours of his training and the punishing NHS hours he was putting in at A&E. 'Got her back. Close one. Has she been conscious at all?'

Naturally, he wasn't the doctor who'd treated the girl earlier, or the one York had spoken to on the phone, and he wouldn't be the one caring for her later, either. The NHS's mysterious shift system seemed designed to ensure that you never had the same doctor twice during the course of your treatment.

'Nothing so far. I was told earlier that these next few hours were crucial – that if she is going to regain consciousness then the sooner the better. They weren't sure about any brain damage…'

'Well, this little episode won't have helped, that's for sure,' said the doctor, his straight fair hair flopping over a face which was unlined but grey with exhaustion, apart from two hectic patches of red on his cheeks.

'Will it have set the timings back? Will she just wake up later now?'

The doctor shrugged widely, then unhooked her chart from the foot of the bed. 'Drugs, we don't know what… She's been under, what? 12 hours now?'

'As far as we know. She was found unconscious, no idea when or how she got into that state.'

'Mmmm.' The doctor's lips were pursed, like a housewife presented with a bruised apple by an unscrupulous greengrocer. 'I suppose you're waiting for her to open her eyes and tell you who gave her what?'

York smiled ruefully. 'That would be excellent. If she could provide names and addresses, then better still.'

The doctor put his head to one side. 'Yeah. You could be waiting a long while.'

'Is that your medical opinion?'

'For what it's worth.' He turned back to the bed, where his patient lay, still and apparently serene under another smoothed blanket, the bank of machines at her side now purring benignly, perfectly placid again, whatever was going on inside her body. He rested his hand gently for a second on her inert arm. 'Her situation wasn't great before this cardiac incident, from what I've seen on her chart. But inevitably something like this is a setback, a deterioration of her condition.'

'Are you saying she won't regain consciousness, Doctor?'

The young man gave York a long, level look. He was used to breaking bad news to relatives. In this case, it wasn't family ties going down the tubes, it was an entire criminal case. It was clear it mattered to this policeman. A lot. 'I'm not saying anything for sure. You can never say never with the brain. There are people who've woken up after years... but there are a lot more who simply never do. It's unpredictable. What I can say is that she is stronger than she looks. She's still here, and that's against the odds. Keep hoping. We don't see a lot like this, thank Christ, but even one is too many. Good luck.'

York's – and the girl's – ten minutes were up. There were plenty more people suffering downstairs and only one boy in a white coat to sort them out. He collected up an armful of folders, nodded to York and dashed away, harassment marring his pleasant face.

And now it was time for York to leave the girl, too. He took his head out of his hands, got up from the chair, and took a last look at her. He was curiously reluctant to go, despite the loathing for hospitals that told him fresh air and a change of scene were urgent requirements. Though no-one had yet mentioned the word coma, he knew the longer the girl dallied before waking, the worse things were. And wasn't it family that was supposed to bring people round? The whispering of a mother, the playing of favourite tracks by a sister, the silent hand-holding of a dad or brother. These were the things that ripped people from the velvet of the deep unconscious and forced them up into the jostling world again. This girl was getting none of the stimulation she needed. The only attention she'd really had, in hours, was the terrifying mugging of the CPR.

But York was not family. He might feel for her, in her lonely splendour. She was more than ever now like Sleeping Beauty, waiting for her prince to awaken her. But if he had any hope of finding out what had happened to her, he had to abandon the silent vigil. She'd have to make do with the pimply PC stationed outside. He could ill afford it, but the lad would stay put outside, with an ear straining for any more nonsense from those monitors and a promise he'd get help more quickly next time. At least he knew where to go now.

York, meanwhile, had another princess to protect – in his mind, anyway. He dreaded to think what Beth would do or say if she got an inkling of the way he saw her. But, though she'd never admit to being in distress, she'd certainly been in mild peril this morning and her phone call just now had given him pause for thought. It was time he picked her brain about all this. Knowing her, she'd be a gold mine of information. Would she divulge anything to him, though? He'd just have to use his wiles, he decided with a grin, slipping his phone back in his pocket and giving the PC a brisk pat on the back as he sauntered away. The PC sat up a little straighter, and listened intently to the beeps from the room. All was well – for now.

*****

Miss Troughton sighed as the bell shrieked and the girls – 7D this time; quite a nice bunch but not a single linguist amongst them, alas – repacked their bags, which seemed to require immense amounts of giggling and argy-bargy. 'Ah, we'll move on to the next lesson *in silence*, please. *Taisez-vous,'* she said, raising her voice to that teacher pitch which always cut through the babble.

Thank goodness, this lot were fresh enough to the daunting world of Secondary School to quieten down immediately, and they trooped out of the door giving a pleasing, though probably erroneous, impression of docility. Miss Troughton wiped the last of the names of vegetables – which she had a horrible feeling that some of them wouldn't recognise in English, let alone a second language – off the white board, and then stuck her head out of the classroom door, wondering if she had time to sprint to the staff loo and back before the next lot.

Outside, she spotted a gaggle of girls – Year 9s, if she wasn't mistaken – in an intense cluster outside the girls' toilet. Uh-oh. She stepped closer, then could tell even by their back views that this was the group she thought of – political correctness could go hang itself – as the Skinny Minnies. While the school had no-one at present who was in any sort of medical danger from anorexia (and yes, she knew there were plenty of caveats in that sentence), this bunch were on her list as a group to watch. She tiptoed further down the corridor, thanking the Lord for her soft soles. Angie Douglas might well turn her nose up at such comforts, and she was never going to argue that these lumpen shoes represented the most stylish choice out there for a woman of her build, but there was a lot to be said for rubber. She felt like the hippo in *Fantasia* creeping up on a load of half-starved gazelles.

'But what are we going to do? Sophia always tells us what the calorie count is. I don't know if I'm allowed this snack,' said Alexa McKinnon, her cheekbones so sharp they looked as though they might pierce her skin, her uniform jumper hanging off her in swathes. She had a carrot baton clutched in her scrawny hand.

Miss Troughton noticed the whole band (what was the collective noun for anorexics? A diet, maybe, or a rattle, she thought with a silent snort) was huddling in sweaters, despite the warm day. It was partly, she knew, a technique to disguise their weight loss. It was also necessary, as extremely skinny girls felt the cold acutely, no matter how hot the weather. Indeed, if they continued to full-blown anorexia, they would start to grow long, downy hairs on their arms and legs as their bodies tried to conserve warmth. Their periods would stop. Their hair and teeth might fall out. It was ugly facts like this that Miss Troughton was constantly urging Miss Douglas to disseminate. No teenage girl wants to look like a gummy, wizened yeti. But making such announcements would acknowledge that there was a problem, the girls would tell their parents, the parents would tell their friends…

Poor Angela. She couldn't be the Head of a school with a major anorexia problem. She had so much to balance. Reputation, publicity, *health*… these silly children made Miss Troughton so angry. Why wouldn't they just eat a slice of cake, for the love of God? Her own stomach was rumbling just at the thought of what these kids were *not* consuming. Even that carrot baton looked rather tasty. Oh, they were ridiculous. She took a big step forward, forgetting that stealth was her watchword. The girls looked up from their confab, startled. Their eyes, already rendered huge in their slender, starved faces, opened even wider. 'What's all this, girls? Shouldn't you be in a class?' thundered the Trout.

Lizzy George, her long dark hair framing her oval face like a medieval Madonna – though no Van Eyck would have painted the Mother of God so urgently in need of a pie – spoke up. 'Do you know what's happened to Sophia? We need to talk to her… we were just wondering…'

'Now, what would you need her for so urgently, hmmm?' said Miss Troughton, scanning the pinched features of the little gathering. There was a slight shuffling as no-one met her eyes. 'Desperately wanted to discuss your French homework, did you?' This was Miss Troughton's attempt at a joke, but the girls were too startled, too directionless without their leader, possibly even just too hungry, to realise.

'Yes, about the homework…' Lizzy nodded a head that looked much too large for her scrawny neck. Alexa McKinnon had hidden away the carrot stick. She had not, Miss Troughton surmised, eaten it.

She looked once again round the half-starved circle. 'Listen to me, girls, you do not need Sophia Jones-Creedy here, bossing you around and telling you what to do. Now go to your next class – and for goodness' sake, have a snack!'

At the mention of their leader, and maybe the word 'snack', the girls' faces suddenly looked shuttered again, and they gathered their bags and moved off.

Miss Troughton sighed, '*Bloody* girls,' and made her way back to her classroom, where Year 10, hovering on the brink of GCSEs and therefore with fear making them a little more manageable, were murmuring while getting their books out of their overstuffed bags.

***

Beth stood outside the Picture Gallery, hitching her bag from one shoulder to the next and looking at her watch. York was already five minutes late. It wasn't like him. Though Ben had been picked up from school by Katie, and was thrilled to be spending a rare midweek supper with Charlie despite his friend's hectic tutoring and piano practice schedule, Beth was on edge.

A tiny bit of this was because Ben wasn't the only guest tonight – Charlie had already had a playdate fixed up with the new boy in the class, Matteo. Beth had been surprised when Katie had said this, given that the tutoring routine was usually sacrosanct.

Beth was also a bit wary. If Ben had a fault, it was that he could be possessive. He was used to having his mother all to himself, with no father to claim any of her attention. Beth knew he felt the same sense of entitlement to all his favourite people's focus – and that included Charlie.

Three was never a good number on a playdate, but she could hardly complain, having foisted her son on Katie at a moment's notice. She prayed this Matteo kid was nice and, though she didn't like to admit it, she hoped that if anyone got left out of things – as inevitably happened with these eternal triangle relationships – it would not be her boy.

And she was still feeling jittery, being back here. It wasn't hard to guess the reason. There was still a bit of police tape attached to the Gallery entrance, and the other visitors were peering about them a lot more than usual. Either it was

Beth's imagination, or the place had a different, much less benign aura after the events of the morning.

Though she felt distinctly wimpy admitting it, Beth wasn't mad keen to go back inside the Gallery at all. Maybe she was being oversensitive, but every time she shut her eyes, that pale body floated across her consciousness, the feel of the girl's cold, unresponsive hand, the blue veins under the white skin, the incongruously festive shimmer of her sequinned dress... This morning, the girl had reminded Beth of Millais' *Ophelia*, but now the vision in her mind's eye had changed and the girl was more like the *Lady of Shalott*, pale and bound for death, drifting downriver to Camelot with her dress and hair streaming free. They were not happy visions.

Beth shivered and, despite the warmth of the day, wrapped her arms around herself. She was just wondering if she should go and sit in the café, safely in the concrete and glass extension abutting the Gallery itself, which was bound to be a lot less conducive to creepy visions, when she saw York striding towards her. Relief flooded through her. It took him seconds to cover the distance, and one searching glance seemed to tell him all he needed to know.

'Bit spooked? Don't worry, it won't be as bad as you think. Let's get it over with.' He pushed open the heavy door to the Gallery with its ornate panelled and studded door, and held it with his shoulder, allowing in a couple of elderly ladies before ushering Beth through. She automatically started hunting through her uncooperative bag for her Friends' pass, but York waved his warrant card at the ladies on the desk, leaving them muttering to each other in his wake. Tricia had, of course, seized the opportunity to go home and had probably spent the rest of the day spreading rumours far and wide from her sofa.

'Look, we've not got much to go on, so I thought it would be helpful if we just went through exactly what happened this morning,' said York, trying to keep his voice down discreetly. But his size, sense of purpose, and obvious lack of interest in the pictures had already drawn both disapproving and curious glances from the art lovers meandering though the rooms.

'You mean she hasn't woken up?' Beth was shocked, eyes wide and anxious.

York looked at her. 'I wish I could tell you that she's sitting up in bed, shovelling down a Full English, with roses in her cheeks. But…' He shrugged unhappily.

'The longer that goes on, the longer she stays unconscious…' Beth didn't finish the sentence, but her stricken face said it all.

'The worse the prognosis is. That's why we've got to try and find out what happened from this end,' York said, purposeful again. 'Now. When you came in this morning. Where exactly did you start?'

Beth was back on safer ground now; with the paintings she'd loved since childhood. These canvases had seen it all in their time. They'd witnessed savage spats between lovers, family rows, bad behaviour of all possible types from the streams of visitors who stopped and bickered in front of them over the centuries. They'd seen her squabbling with her own brother often enough, when their mother had dragged them round on rainy childhood Saturdays. An attempted murder was, well – not nothing new, but something the pictures, at least, could take in their stride. They hung as peacefully as ever, reminders of the interests and obsessions of past centuries, not the lusts, wild angers, and rages driving whoever had dumped the girl here.

But dumped was not the right word to use, Beth corrected herself. The girl had been nothing if not carefully positioned, posed even, and by someone who had a curious sense of place or theatre.

'Why here? That's the question you need to answer,' said Beth, turning to York. But he was distracted, poring over his phone.

'Damn. I'll just have to return this call,' he said to Beth over his shoulder. He was already striding back toward the exit.

Beth, standing in the centre of the main gallery, realised this was what she had been dreading. Though there were knots of visitors here and there, admiring a picture or craning to read the little potted biographies beside each frame, she felt alone. It was the same as this morning – but so different. Then, she'd been perfectly content to have the place to herself, had even relished her little game of picking the day's favourite to save from conflagration.

Now, things had changed. Sir John Soane's lavishly-hung walls suddenly seemed oppressively cluttered and the background colour the pictures were displayed on, easily identified by Beth and any other Dulwich resident as Farrow & Ball's delicious Eating Room Red, now looked like nothing so much as congealed blood. She couldn't help shuddering. She was close to the mausoleum now. Did she have the courage to retrace her steps?

Chapter Five

Beth was dithering as York walked into the gallery again. He paused as she made up her mind, and set off bravely to make the left turn that would take her to the forbidding stone annexe. He caught up with her in three strides, taking her by the arm.

'Do you want to do this?' No need to spell it out.

Beth swallowed, and nodded.

'Ok then,' he smiled. They moved forward together.

It was proof, for Beth, that things are never quite as awful as you imagine. The mausoleum, masterpiece of Georgian elegance and restraint, was always going to be forbidding. It was a frankly bleak place, designed to make the onlooker contemplate the eternal, and its involvement in this morning's escapade did nothing to diminish its atmospheric power. But aside from the thin plastic yellow and black police tape, which York stepped over and Beth slipped under, there was nothing here to give any indication that the three bodies already lying here in state had had a recent visitor who'd been a little less moribund.

'Tell me exactly what happened,' York said, as they stood in the small round anteroom which led to the mausoleum proper.

Beth looked up at him. Was it her imagination, or did he seem a little more purposeful, after that phone call? Something seemed to have shifted. There was a new sense of urgency and resolve about him. She responded to it. This puzzle must have a solution. Together, they could find it.

'Well, it's not a part of the gallery that I love. It's always given me the heebie-jeebies,' she said, peeping up at him for understanding, quickly enough to see him suppress a smile at her choice of words.

He wiped it from his face, saying, 'Go on.'

'So, I wasn't planning to go in at all, but as I passed by, I saw something. After what happened, *at the school,*' she said, with an emphasis that told him she was referring to their blood-drenched first meeting, 'I knew I wanted someone with me if I found um… anything again. So, I went back and got that intern, Tricia. Well, you saw what she's like,' said Beth, with a shrug. York grimaced. 'I finally got her back here, for some moral support, and for a moment it was as though I'd imagined the whole thing. We stepped into that little round anteroom,' said Beth, pointing, 'And the relief was incredible. There was nothing sinister at all. I was just starting to feel really silly, and then – well, Tricia caught sight of something over my shoulder.' She glanced at him for understanding. He nodded back.

'It was like one of those scary films. I was just saying to Tricia, "Oh, it was nothing," and feeling a bit of an idiot, frankly, when her face completely changed. She was standing *there.*' Beth pointed to a spot right opposite the maroon marble sarcophagus that was now, again, the last resting place of Margaret Devereux alone. 'And she saw… Well, she just froze. People talk about the colour draining out of your face. It really does happen. Then she was just… catatonic.'

'The girl? Or Tricia?' York asked.

'*Both,*' said Beth sadly. 'That's when I called you.'

They were silent for a moment. Meanwhile, the cold orange light from the lantern above them was beginning to fade, and longer and longer shadows starting to stretch along the sides of the three sarcophagi.

'Who was on the phone just now?' Beth blurted, to break the stillness. Standing here, among the dead and with her discovery so fresh in her mind, was seriously creeping her out. 'Was it to do with the case?'

She knew it was none of her business, and she wasn't expecting an answer. But York took her arm again and led her back out into the main gallery. It wasn't until she took a huge heaving gasp that she realised she'd almost stopped breathing while they'd been in the mausoleum. His determined footsteps, as usual, had people jerking their heads round from their peaceful contemplation of the art.

'Let's get out of here,' he said, and towed her after him, making her take two steps to his every one. But Beth wasn't complaining. The Picture Gallery had been her place of refuge for as long as she could remember. After this morning, all that had changed. She couldn't wait to leave.

Once they were back outside in the reassuringly normal surroundings of the gardens, with the usual queue of people waiting for tables outside the café and a group of children playing tag around the mulberry tree, Beth felt a lot better.

'We could sit over there, on the bench,' she said, indicating a spot a little way away from the rest of the visitors.

'Good idea. I'll get us a coffee. Or a tea?' York cocked his head.

'Tea would be great. There's a stall, just past the café. It's much quicker, and they do takeaways.' York smiled at the tip, and set off again.

He always seemed to be in motion, thought Beth, feeling so much better as she settled on the bench, her back against the warm slats of wood, not worrying overmuch about the effect of the lichen-coated seat on her worn jeans. It had been a while, now, since she'd dressed up for work. Though the teachers at Wyatt's always looked like corporate apparatchiks, who could easily have doubled as lawyers or city whiz kids, no-one looked askance any more at her own distinctly casual take on work wear. At first, she'd been able to justify jeans and simple tops because she was leafing through dusty old documents. Now, people had just grown used to her look. They saw what they expected to see.

With a jolt, Beth wondered if that was why the girl had been left in the Gallery. Where would you hide a body? With other bodies, surely? Though there was no question that she was going to be found, and found quickly, there was a certain logic and tidiness to the thinking that, she had to admit, appealed at a bizarre level to her own OCD leanings. Plus,

66

Margaret Devereux's tomb made a perfect platform. Even the slightly pitched lid of the tomb had only helped to emphasise the position of the girl's hands – the most disturbing aspect of her pose, as they had so obviously been placed, by a third party, in that mock-pious cross on her chest.

It made Beth wonder if the person behind it all was really another teenager – in many ways, it seemed the most likely scenario – or whether it was actually someone closer to the thirty-stone Milwaukee truck driver paedophile, after all. Would a teenager have enough background knowledge these days to know that crossed hands were such a motif, from crusaders' tombs to kings and queens lying in state?

The two pictures that the girl had reminded Beth of – the Millais *Ophelia* and the *Lady of Shalott* – didn't feature the hand motif at all. Ophelia's hands were apart, breaking the surface of the waters she'd drowned in, seeming to be supplicating, begging the world to save her, rather than praying or making the sign of the cross. John William Waterhouse's *Lady of Shalott*, meanwhile, was holding her boat's chain in one hand, showing that she had set herself adrift, while the other hand lay uselessly in her lap, failing to steer her course.

One of her favourite poems, Philip Larkin's *Arundel Tomb*, suddenly popped into her head, in the way that poetry quietly invades a contemplative mind. She remembered the knight and his lady lying peacefully entombed in a country church. To Larkin, the shocking twist was that their stone hands are clasped together over the centuries, not crossed meekly at their breasts at all.

Where had this person, who'd left the girl in the Gallery for her to find, got the idea of the crossed hands from? Beth sat and frowned, barely conscious of York until he'd almost reached the bench, carrying two tall cups of tea. It surprised her, until she realised that the clipped sound of his usual determined stride had been muffled by the grass.

One look at his set face pushed the thoughts of hands and history from her head. She took the tea, plus one of those stirrer sticks and a handful of sachets of sugar, before she asked, 'What's happened? That call that you took just now in the Gallery, it was important, wasn't it?'

York looked at her, the usual bland evasion dished out to members of the public on his lips. Then he shook his head slightly. Beth knew he was weighing up what to say to her. She seemed to be developing a lamentable knack of getting herself involved in these things, which she knew drove him mad, and which she wasn't too thrilled about herself. But on the other hand, her information could be crucial, to identify the girl – and find whoever had done this to her, before it was too late. Find the culprit, find the mix of drugs that had been administered, and they had a chance of saving her life. But the clock was ticking. She sensed that, in these circumstances, York would take any help going.

'What is it?' she asked again, her hand touching his sleeve as he bent forward and perched his tea precariously on the bench between them. They both turned to look at the small hand lying there on his jacket, Beth in shock at her own temerity – were you even allowed to touch policemen on duty? Then she relaxed. He'd taken her arm, just now in the Gallery, hadn't he?

York reached for the notebook in his jacket pocket, dislodging Beth's tentative fingers, and she clasped both hands firmly in her lap, out of trouble. York propped his notebook on his knee, then reached for his tea again, prising the plastic lid off, essaying a sip to see whether the temperature had dropped from scalding to merely red hot, trying to get the lid back on and then giving it up as a bad job. Finally, he spoke.

'The thing is, a girl has now been reported missing.'

'At last!' said Beth. 'I couldn't understand why that hadn't happened already. It's not like anyone would lose track of their children here. I mean, no-one runs wild.'

At that moment, a group of whooping small children careered past the bench, shouting and shrieking, their high-pitched voices splintering the summery air.

'Ok, well, they run *that* sort of wild,' said Beth with a smile and small shrug. 'But that doesn't mean there's no-one watching them. I mean, look over there.'

York followed the direction of Beth's head. Out on the grass close to the café was a table seating four women, of a type he was starting to recognise as Dulwich Yummies. They were all somewhere in their thirties, even at this distance conspicuously well turned out, with the sunlight glinting off shiny hair, tasteful jewellery, large and complicated-looking sunglasses. Although the women were chatting determinedly, occasionally throwing their heads back in laughter, and all sipping away at their cappuccinos, every now and then one would raise a head, look around, and zoom in on the gaggle of children. Though much prettier – and a lot less wrinkly – the women were like the velociraptors in the Jurassic Park films: hyper-vigilant; alert to every threat; and presumably, every bit as deadly if anyone dared threaten their young.

'I see what you mean. And yes, the radio silence on missing children was already one of the oddest aspects of this case. *One* of the oddest aspects,' he stressed, as Beth's eyebrows rose. 'But even now, the weird thing is that it's not the parents who've reported the girl missing. It's the school.'

'Which school is it?' Beth asked. It was not the right question, she realised as soon as she'd opened her mouth. That would have been, '*What's the girl's name?*' But hey, it was the Dulwich question. What could she do? A lifetime in the place had left its mark.

York answered, with a tiny upward lilt that betrayed the fact that the answer meant nothing to him. 'The College School.'

'No!' Beth was stunned. If she'd had to take bets, she would never have plumped for the most fiercely academic and rigorous school in the area; a place which made the polished Wyatt's look a tad ramshackle round the edges, and which trounced the results of all other girls' schools in the area – and most in the country.

'And of course, the really important thing – who on earth is the girl?' Beth said quickly, a little shame-faced.

'Look, I wouldn't normally tell you the name. I mean, we don't know if it is *this* girl, for a start. We have one girl reported missing, and one girl we haven't yet identified who's been found. And for some reason, the girl's parents themselves aren't the ones sounding the alarm. It's possible that, somehow, they don't even realise she's missing yet. So, I wouldn't want to have a position where you know more than the actual family... But... On the other hand, maybe you will actually know the girl?'

'Maybe,' said Beth, not wanting to put York off confiding in her. Privately, she highly doubted it. When Ben reached his teens, she'd be bound to know a lot more teenage girls, and develop plenty of views on which were suitable companions for him to hang around with... or even fool around with... Though she still couldn't quite believe there would soon come a time when he'd opt enthusiastically for the company of girls over boys. His little primary class was mixed, but he didn't really rate female footballing skills – despite having been taught much of what he knew by his patient and long-suffering mother – and none of them were as interested in gaming as he and Charlie were.

Long may his current obliviousness continue. But she wasn't going to tell York that teenage girls, apart from Zoe Bentinck, were practically a foreign species to her little household, and even more so after her frightening internet research earlier. Not when he was on the brink of breaking one of his cardinal rules, and was actually going to give her useful information about a case in progress.

Beth fixed a helpful expression on her face, which she hoped hinted that, beneath her floppy fringe, there lurked total understanding of modern teenage ways, and looked enquiringly at him. After an obvious struggle, he balanced his tea on his knee, wincing slightly as the heat of the liquid seared through the inadequate container, and said simply, 'Well. The missing girl is Sophia Jones-Creedy. Do you know her?'

Beth was about to shake her head ruefully, when the welter of images she'd looked at on Facebook earlier danced before her. The giggles, the silliness. And, rising above them all, the uncrowned queen of the sidelong glance, the cheeky knowing smile, and the most seductive of dresses. The girl that everyone had tagged in photos, the one whose pictures had got the most likes and endless streams of comments. The one who popped up as everyone's mutual friend. *Sophia Jones-Creedy.*

And, amongst the jumble of shots she'd seen of Sophia Jones-Creedy that day, one picture in particular floated to the forefront of Beth's mind. A pale, pale dress, a dark background, and a small slight girl. There were huge differences. In the picture Beth had seen, the girl's eyes were alight, like a mischievous, knowing pixie, and the wide mouth quirking upwards at one corner hinted at secrets only she knew, but might be willing to share because you were her *best friend.* The girl in the Gallery, on the other hand, was a cipher that wasn't so easy to solve. But her build matched, and so did her pallor. And was there was a connection, too, in the innate theatricality that ran through both the Facebook preening, and the artificiality of the posture at the gallery?

The look she darted at York was full of dawning horror. 'I have an awful feeling that, yes, I do know her,' she said slowly, and looked down as she felt something splash her lap. Her hand was shaking. Tea was going everywhere.

By the time York had run to the stall and back again, proffering wodges of paper napkins, Beth had got herself under control – and slung out the remnants of her tea onto the grass.

'Sorry about that,' she said ruefully, swabbing away at her jeans with a thick handful of tissue. 'It was just the shock. Making the connection. The girl on Facebook – well, she's so alive, she looks so, you know, *naughty.* And the girl from this morning. She was so… inert, crushed.'

'Show me what you mean,' said York, and Beth stabbed away at her phone, cursing the perennially unreliable Dulwich wi-fi signal. Eventually she got Instagram to load and there was the torrent of shots of Sophia Jones-Creedy, available to more or less anyone who wanted to gawp.

York stared. It was hard to make out the detail on Beth's frankly rather crummy phone – she was lagging a few models behind the bandwagon on this front – but he soon got a flavour.

'It's not proof positive, but…'

Beneath her fringe, Beth's brow was crinkled. 'The school reported her missing? Not her parents? Surely that's odd?'

York shrugged a little, his large shoulders rising and falling. 'I'm not a parent, of course…' The 'but' was certainly there for Beth to hear, though York forbore to judge. 'It sounds like an unusual situation. Well, maybe not for these parts. Her father's a surgeon and has been operating since the crack of dawn, it seems. Her mother is on her way back from a work trip to the Middle East. Not a nice surprise waiting for her when she lands.' York looked down briefly. He wouldn't be doing the intercepting, but the poor PC whose job it was to tackle the jet-lagged mother would be in for a hell of a time.

The mother had a cast iron alibi, so there was no question of scrutinising her reactions for signs of guilt. But it was still going to be the PC's task to note down any behaviour at all that was outside the usual remit of shock, grief, horror, dismay… and they weren't going to be able to give the woman any details. Just the basic outline: that the school had reported her daughter missing, because she hadn't turned up that day. That would be enough to get all hell breaking loose.

'And the mum's a lawyer. Well, she would be,' York said, sighing heavily.

'That's a problem?'

York grunted. 'She's going to be frightened and angry, and she'll want someone to blame. I'm willing to bet that's not going to be her husband or son, at least initially, though the au pair might well get it in the neck. No, I think she'll be threatening writs left, right, and centre before the night is out. Whether it's me or the school, I wouldn't like to bet.'

Beth, who felt nothing but sympathy with the mother, turned the subject. 'Where does the father work?'

'Ironically, at King's – and that's where his daughter is. If he hadn't been doing back-to-back operations, we'd have fished him out, but his underlings insist he can't be interrupted at any stage of the list today. He's in orthopaedics. I suppose you can't just wander off halfway through reconnecting somebody's spinal cord. And some of these jobs take eight hours in themselves.'

'I'd have thought they could send in a note, or something,' said Beth.

'Yes, but what if his hand slips as a result? Bad enough that his daughter's hanging between life and death. I suppose his team don't want to be responsible for some poor bugger ending up in a wheelchair. And, to be fair, she's been unconscious the whole time. Her entire family could be crowded around her, singing her favourite song at top volume, on repeat, and she wouldn't take a blind bit of notice.'

'But they say hearing is the last thing to go, don't they? If there were someone with her, holding her hand, talking, then maybe she'd sense that, feel less alone,' said Beth. 'It's certainly what I would want, if I'm ever in a coma.' She tapped the bench as a reflex, and noticed York's smile. 'What? Don't you ever touch wood?'

'I can't say I've noticed it working that well.'

Altogether too solid and down to earth to be superstitious, thought Beth a little crossly, as York went on speaking.

'In fact, you were saying exactly what I was thinking earlier, when I left the hospital. She needs her family there.'

'So, what's going to happen now?' Beth said heavily.

The fact that they had established the poor girl's identity, somehow made everything a lot more concrete. When the girl had been nameless, finding her had seemed like a horrible dream, something that might melt away at any moment. But, as ethereal as she had been, stretched out on the cold marble, she had turned out to be a real flesh-and-blood Dulwich girl. Beth had probably even shrunk away from her as she moseyed around the Village with a pack of other young, privileged, and lucky children, loud and entitled as they settled themselves in the best seats in all the cafes, or hogged the pavements walking four abreast. No-one could say that Dulwich kids were *rude* exactly – their schools did everything they could to inculcate good manners, as these were essential for making your way in life. But no amount of polishing could take away the certain knowledge this generation had that they were the most important people in the universe, deserving the best of everything.

Now, one of these golden children had been brought low. All right, the girl that Beth had stalked today on Facebook seemed shallow as a puddle and silly as a sausage, but she was *young.* In the normal run of things, she'd get great A levels, go to a good uni, and end up a useful member of society. She'd help to pay for the NHS and state schools out of her lavish wages, even if it was more than possible that she'd choose BUPA herself and then send her own kids to private schools in their turn. She certainly didn't deserve to be on life support, after being made into a ghastly public display.

If Beth hadn't chanced upon her almost the moment the Gallery opened, it could have been a party of schoolchildren who'd come across her lying there forlorn, or a clutch of pensioners.

For Beth, the conclusion was inescapable. Someone evil was at work in Dulwich, and had preyed on one of their young. She couldn't allow it. She had to do everything she could to stop it. Silliness should not be punishable by humiliation and the shadow of death.

'Who do you think has done this?' Beth turned to the man beside her. He wrinkled his forehead and shrugged.

'That's just what I've been wondering. What is all this about? And what the hell are they playing at?' His phone rang. He took a quick look at the display and shot off the bench, saying over his shoulder, 'Sorry, got to take this.'

Beth watched as he paced the Gallery garden, skirting the sharp edges of the building, turning around and retracing his steps, his hand frequently going to his hair, grabbing handfuls of the thick blond thatch. Though there was no-one remotely within eavesdropping distance, his shoulders were hunched around his ears and he frequently glanced around, as though expecting to see locals earwigging in the bushes.

Beth had begun to think he was never coming back to the bench, and was wondering whether she should wander over to Katie's and pick up Ben. Doubtless, though, he would be furious at being removed from his best friend, and his best friend's state-of-the-art gaming equipment, not to mention Matteo as well.

Just then, York strode back, making short work of the wide lawn.

'Hospital,' he grunted, with a sidelong glance at Beth. Immediately, she sat up straighter.

'Is it Sophia? Is there any change?'

'There's been another… episode,' York said flatly. From his unwilling tone, she could tell he really didn't want to confide any more. She was a civilian, after all, and could not have any legitimate involvement in the official police investigation. On the other hand, she had managed to get caught up in this mess right from the beginning.

'*Another* episode? What do you mean?' said Beth. Immediately, she knew she'd made a mistake. He was going against protocol telling her anything at all, and here she was complaining that he hadn't filled her in completely. He tutted, and inwardly she kicked herself. How could she persuade him to tell her more? She'd just have to lay her cards on the table.

'Look,' said Beth reasonably. 'If you're going to tell me anything at all, you might as well give me the full picture.'

York gave her a level look, then sighed. 'I suppose it won't hurt to tell you this much. She had a flutter this morning – the machines went mad. The doctor said it happens a lot in these cases. Could mean everything, could be nothing, but usually… Well, let's just say it *isn't* nothing. Now they're saying it's happened again.'

'So, some sort of crisis?'

'I suppose you could call it that.'

'But she's still alive.'

'She is. For what it's worth. Every time this happens,

they say there's less chance her brain has escaped intact. They're called "insults", I believe. They want to start testing for brain stem activity.' York didn't look at Beth as he said this. But she knew exactly what it meant.

'They want to turn the machines off.'

'Well. We're not there yet,' he said.

They both stared out across the wide lawn. It was a beautiful day in Dulwich. The bright lushness of the grass contrasted with the mellow, yellow-grey brick of the Gallery. The laurel bushes on either side of their bench were strewn with scarlet berries, like bright red drops of blood. They could hear the chatter of the café clientele, the very English chink of china teacups, and the occasional muted yells of the children. It was all so normal. But there was a girl lying in a hospital room close by, who yesterday could have been here – but today was about to be ripped away from all this. Beth shook her head. It wasn't right.

'Do you have any idea yet how she got into the Gallery? Has CCTV turned up anything?'

'CCTV isn't always the be-all and end-all.' York turned to her wryly. Beth knew that all too well from her previous case – well, she could call the whole business that in her own head if she liked, couldn't she? Either the cameras weren't in the right place, pointing directly at the murderer at the crucial moment, or there was some other kind of SNAFU and the film was missing, wonky or inconclusive… You name it, the supposedly fool-proof way to catch most criminals was as fallible as anything else humans got their hands on.

'What we do know is that there was a reception last night, for St Christopher's Hospice, and we've got some of it on camera,' York continued. Beth nodded. Everyone in Dulwich knew the great work done by St Christopher's, which ran a palliative care centre in nearby Sydenham and also helped out in the community. All the schools raised money for the hospice with bake sales and sponsored cycles, runs and swims. Beth dimly remembered getting an invite to the reception at the Gallery with her last Friends' mailing, along with details of upcoming exhibitions, talks and children's classes, all of which looked great but which she couldn't persuade Ben to have anything to do with.

The reception was the sort of thing she'd have gone to, if James had been alive. They would probably never have been in the position where they could drop a few thousand for a good cause, but they'd have donated what they could. And it would have been hard to resist a crystal glass of something cold and bubbly, an excuse to make the effort and wear something pretty for a change, and the chance to see her beloved paintings after hours, beautifully lit and with that special secret atmosphere that galleries had when closed to the general public. But as a lone parent, it was the kind of thing that was anathema to Beth. An entire building jammed with well-heeled married couples, smugly discussing their second homes and exotic holiday options? That sort of occasion left her feeling an utter failure. *No, thank you very much.*

Beth was puzzled, though. 'A reception? That'd be adults only, not teenage girls...'

'They get the local teenagers to act as waiting staff. The older kids take the drinks round, the younger ones organise the coats and so on... The CCTV footage is grainy, but there are a number of kids around who could be our girl... I need to sit down and pore over it, but there's too much going on at the moment and I'm so short staffed.'

'I don't suppose I could?' Beth began hopefully.

'Are you crazy?' York's eyebrows disappeared into his thatch of hair at the very idea. 'It's bad enough sitting here telling you *anything*. Getting you involved in the enquiry would be madness.'

'It's such a pity. I've got the time – well, I haven't, technically, I've got a hundred things to do at work, but somehow I don't seem to be there – and I'd love to help. But it's your call.'

'The thing that *would* really help me would be if you could go through everything you saw this morning. There could be something, anything, that could make a difference.'

Beth sat and pondered. There *was* something eating away

77

at the back of her mind. Something she'd seen while she'd been sitting here – something amongst the standard sights and sounds of a Dulwich afternoon – which had jogged a faint but important memory. What was it? For the life of her, she couldn't quite remember. It was as though a favourite jumper she'd been searching everywhere for was dangling, just out of sight, at the back of her mental wardrobe. It was maddening.

She rested an elbow on the arm of the bench, and pressed her fingers to her temple, willing the thought to surface again. She remembered having taught Ben how to hold his breath under water, years ago, and then having to watch anxiously as he spent the afternoon disappearing for longer and longer moments under the choppy turquoise waters of the swimming baths at Forest Hill. Now, she was holding her own breath, as the memory stubbornly stayed submerged and threatened to drown itself in the useless trivia of her subconscious. Beth cursed herself for knowing where their library tickets were, for remembering the dates of the key Napoleonic battles, not to mention the names of most of Thomas the Tank Engine's colleagues, and for even having tried to follow the plot of *An Unfortunate Series of Events*. If she'd had less rubbish crammed in her one poor head, she might have been able to delve into a mind as tidy as a freshly-sorted filing cabinet and fish out this one, elusive fact, which turned out to be all she really needed anyway. She groaned. York turned to her in concern.

'Look, I'm not going to say don't fret, because that's all we can do for her at the moment. But you did everything you should have done. We got her to the hospital as quickly as we could, and everything that can possibly be done is happening right now,' he said kindly.

Beth took her hand away from her face, touched at his worry. She was concerned about the poor girl, but she had faith in the NHS. During the two great medical crises of her life – Ben's birth, and her husband James's terrible death – it had been magnificent. 'Thanks, but it's not that. There's something I've just remembered I've forgotten, if you see

what I mean. Something that could be really important...
And it's just *gone*. Does that make sense?'

''Course. Happens to me all the time. Just be patient. It'll
come back when you least expect it.'

'Well, that's all well and good, but I really think we need
it now. If Sophia could be dying... that makes it all the more
urgent. And whatever it is that's nagging away at me... well,
I feel it might give us a lead. We don't have a lot, do we?'

A wince from York reminded Beth not to say 'we' too
much. As far as he would be concerned, there wasn't any
'we'. He was police; she wasn't. All right, he'd blurred the
boundaries by telling her the little he had. But she'd do well
not to remind him of that. It was better to concentrate on
trying to coax this bit of information out of her unhelpful
head. Maybe it was nothing, but she had the feeling that it
was *something*.

'So, it's just occurred to you again now, but you actually
first thought of it earlier today?' York asked.

Beth nodded.

'To do with the girl, I'm guessing. So, was it those
photos you were looking at? Facebook, Instagram?
Something in the background, maybe a person, a place?' He
scanned Beth's face as he spoke. She thought hard, but there
was no spark of recognition. The trail seemed cold. He
shrugged and turned back to the gardens in front of them,
leading up to the austere planes and angles of the Picture
Gallery. 'Something to do with the Gallery itself? One of the
pictures there reminded you of something, someone you've
seen, the girl, maybe?'

This seemed a bit more promising. Beth considered for a
moment, flipping through her personal database of the
Gallery's pictures in her mind's eye. She'd visited so many
times, she knew the pictures almost by heart. Did Sophia, or
one of her friends, perhaps remind her of one of
Gainsborough's beautiful Linley sisters, for example? Beth
loved this picture. It was another sweeping, full-length
portrait, like the one of sad Mrs Moody. This time, it featured
sisters Mary and Elizabeth Linley, at the peak of their youth

79

and beauty. Beth loved the story behind the picture almost as much as the canvas itself.

Elizabeth Linley, in blue, was painted with a saintly look in her eye. In real life, she was anything but. First, she broke off a promising engagement after a fling with a family friend, then she electrified society by bolting to France with the playwright Sheridan. Two duels were fought over her hand. Appropriately enough, Sheridan was the author of the smash hit of the times, *School for Scandal*, and the escapade gained her the kind of international notoriety, across Irish, English and Parisian circles, that a girl like Sophia Jones-Creedy could only dream of.

Beth felt disloyal to the Linley sisters, as she'd always loved their portrait, but had to admit that Sophia had the edge when it came to beauty. She could understand why Elizabeth might want to look a little aloof, given her all-action private life, but to today's tastes she appeared a tad frosty. Her sister, Mary, had drawn the short straw on the dress front, getting the drab brown gown instead of Elizabeth's shimmering blue silk, but her bold gaze invited the viewer to draw closer, sit down, and listen to the beautiful singing she and her sister were famed for. There was sheet music open on her lap, and it wasn't a stretch to imagine her bursting into a heavenly aria.

The Linleys were definitely the 'It' girls of the 1780s, and if Beth had been reminded of anyone in the Gallery, it would have been them. But that wasn't it. She shook her head. 'I just can't think. It's driving me mad.'

'You were here on the bench when you suddenly thought of it again. Is it to do with where we're sitting, something you can see from here?'

Beth sat up a little straighter, and shot a look at York. He was good at this memory game – presumably because he spent so much time trying to jog the reluctant recollections of various hair-raising criminals. Though she doubted he'd coax them quite so kindly. She tried to concentrate. She could feel the warmth of the sun still on the back of her neck, hear the familiar sounds of Dulwich snacking and chatting, see the

Gallery in front of her... It was all a lot nicer than being locked in an interview room, facing hostile questioning, but she felt almost as much under stress. This was so important, and she just wasn't getting anywhere. It was *so* frustrating.

She shook her head from one side and the other, about to declare she'd drawn a blank on all fronts, when the laurel bush at her side caught her eye. Peeping out here and there from the mass of glossy, racing-green leaves were those startling berries, as red as the drop of blood from Sleeping Beauty's finger when the spindle did its worst. It was the colour she remembered. With a shiver, she was back in the mausoleum, only that morning, though it already seemed like days ago, catching her first sight of the prone form. But what had she glimpsed just *before* that horror?

'The backpack! The red backpack. Where did it go?'

'What backpack?' said York. It was his turn to sit up a little straighter. Piercing blue eyes met intelligent grey ones. Beth's gaze widened and out came a torrent of words. 'It was bright scarlet, it had long straps, it was lying there by the bench in the mausoleum. It was what I saw first. Sophia was out of sight from anyone just passing by from the main gallery. You had to go right into the mausoleum itself to see her. And the reason I went in was because of that bag – the colour, you know. It reminded me of... last time.'

York could sense her revulsion as she remembered what they'd both seen that spring. The last thing he needed now was for her to go off-track. He put a warm hand on her arm. 'Concentrate on this morning,' he urged, not realising that the grip of his fingers was now distracting her almost as much as the bad memories. She shook her head a little.

'Tricia was there, she was frozen, I rang you... we stayed until the paramedics got there, they shifted Sophia out... I don't know what happened to the bag, I don't know! I just wasn't thinking about it; I was only hoping she wouldn't die...'

'Look, don't worry. It's not your job to keep track of everything at the scene, for goodness' sake. What usually happens is all the belongings go to the hospital with the

81

patient. I bet it just got swept up with her and shoved into the ambulance – simple as that. I'll quickly ask at the front desk here, in case it did get left behind, then we'll go to the hospital and find it.'

'We?' Beth was struck again by the pronoun.

'Well yes, if you don't mind. After all, you saw it – you can identify it. We wouldn't want to make a mistake over what could turn out to be our only clue.' With that, York was off the bench and striding away.

Beth hurried to follow, then remembered. Ben! She couldn't just take off like this, tempting though it was to keep York believing she was free to help him out with the investigation. She had responsibilities. Her heart sank a little, and then she chastised herself. She should never see Ben as a burden. Hard though it was being a single parent, it was also the most enormous privilege – and she loved it. She felt a backwash of guilt, but also a devout wish that she could be in two places at once. It wasn't even as though Ben would want her to come and drag him away from Charlie's. There was nothing for it, though. She'd ring Katie and arrange to pick him up and just go home.

'I need to make a call,' she said, to York's rapidly retreating back. He raised one hand in acknowledgement and strode on. How lovely to be that unencumbered, that determined, able to do whatever you felt was right, she thought fleetingly as she dialled. 'Katie? It's me,' she said.

Five minutes later, Beth caught York up as he was leaning over the ticket desk and charming Tricia's replacement. Although it was hardly appropriate, she had the bubbly feeling you get when you wake up in the morning and realise it's a Saturday, not the drab weekday-workday you were expecting. Katie had let her off the hook completely.

The three boys were immersed in some sub-Game of Thrones-style cyberworld, busily collecting coins and wands and slaying dragons left right and centre. Katie said Matteo had picked the game up incredibly fast. Charlie had even been nursed through his piano practice and two pages of tutoring, while Ben and Matteo – apparently – had diligently

82

studied the spellings for their usual test on Friday. Beth found it hard to believe of Ben, though she was intrigued that her son seemed to be developing great acting skills. Every week she struggled to get him to go over the spellings, and every week he told her he knew them already, despite plenty of red-penned evidence to the contrary when the book was marked. Maybe this Matteo boy was a good influence? Maybe three heads were better than one? Well, if so, Beth was thrilled and ready to put her qualms about the interloper to rest.

The upshot was that Katie, hearing that York wanted Beth to help him with his enquiries, suddenly became extremely keen for Ben to stay the night. Maybe it was because she didn't have the heart to interrupt their game. Maybe her matchmaking antennae were twitching like a dog scenting sausages. She wasn't letting on. Matteo only lived round the corner and was being picked up by his mother, but Katie said she would drop Ben at school in the morning. Then she and Beth would try and meet for a debrief coffee if they had time – at Jane's, the price she was exacting for the not very arduous task of keeping Charlie happy all evening by having his friends round. Both women finished the call wreathed with smiles – though Beth immediately tried to tamp hers down a little. After all, her prize was to go off to hospital to see a girl suspended between this world and the next. It was hardly a jolly.

But, Beth realised, a part of her would always be like this, relishing the challenge of the puzzle and the chance to slot some pieces into place, so much that it was a struggle to remember the human dimension – the girl. Though it sounded as if she was now so far adrift from the world that she wasn't far from floating free. Beth thought about the girl's unknowing family, so far apparently oblivious to the crisis. Beth didn't have to try too hard to imagine the pain they'd feel. She just had to picture Ben, for one second, in the same situation. She shook her head fiercely. Unbearable.

York, cocking his head towards her, having drawn a blank on the backpack as far as the Gallery was concerned, led the way quickly to his car. It was plonked right outside the gates, in flagrant disregard of all the Dulwich parking by-laws. Beth stood and gawped. 'It must be so great, never having to worry about getting a ticket,' she said, sounding rather awed by his job for the first time.

York chuckled. 'Usually it's the idea of racing round at top speed with the siren and lights that takes people's fancy. In a place like this, it's the parking perks that impress people.' Beth slanted a glance up at him through her fringe, and smiled.

'Did you ever think about joining the police?' he asked her.

'It didn't cross my mind. The idea of chasing villains – I'm not sure I'm built for it.'

York gave her a sidelong look. 'You can run, can't you?'

'Well, yes, if I have to. But aren't there, erm, height requirements?' said Beth, shifting uncomfortably in her seat. It was as clear a signal as a big red neon sign hovering over her diminutive head, shouting 'five feet nothing!'

'No height restrictions at all in the Met, and they've gone in all the other forces, too. In fact, it's now a bit of a thing to be the smallest police officer in the country. There's a PC in Wiltshire who's about 4ft 10, I think.'

Beth snorted.

'No, really,' insisted York. 'Every year they have a picture of the tallest and shortest officers in the press – sort of little and large.'

'I don't know, I'd be a bit worried about some huge villain just picking me up and carrying me off,' said Beth.

York smiled at the image, but said confidently, 'Oh, stick you in a stab jacket, give you a taser and a Glock, and I think you'd acquit yourself ok.'

'You don't have a gun, do you?' Beth said in alarm, shrinking away slightly in the confines of the car.

'Not on me,' said York. It was funny, firearms in the UK were still a source of fascinated revulsion for the public. Though people were more used to seeing armed officers in airports and at the main stations, where automatic weapons were the norm, there was still great faith in the Dixon of

Dock Green school of policing, where a village bobby kept perfect order simply by finding stray cats and saying, 'Evening all.' If only the world were still that simple.

York set off down Wyatt Road into the village. The rush hour was by now in full swing. Though most of the mummies had already been out and back to pick up their charges, there was a second wave of massive 4x4 cars on the streets as after-school activities finished. Some lucky children were now going home; others were being ferried to yet more improving appointments. York, stuck behind a massive Lexus SUV with tinted windows that would not have looked out of place getting a rapper from gig to gig in downtown LA, was beginning to lose patience. When a Volvo the size and shape of a cruise ship cut in front of him at the intersection with Calton Avenue, he'd had enough. Reaching over to Beth's side, he scrabbled in the glove compartment with his left hand, plucked out a domed plastic light, flicked the switch, opened the window, and jammed the magnetic device onto the roof. At the same time, an unearthly wailing sound started up and he yanked the steering wheel to the right. For a second, Beth thought they were giving way to a police car behind them – then she realised. *They* were the police car, giving way to nobody. They were, in fact, now sailing past the rest of the traffic, while the mummies scurried to turn their huge vehicles into the left side of the road and leave a clear path for them.

'Is this legal?' said Beth, raising her eyebrows and clutching the side of the car door with a nervous hand.

'Of course, it is. We're in a hurry. That girl is dying, and we need to get there before it's too late,' said York.

Beth couldn't argue with that. She hunkered down in her seat, surreptitiously checking that her seat belt was a) fastened and b) sufficiently sturdy. Then she stared straight ahead, trying not to see the red lights and Give Way signs that loomed in front of her, only to be swerved around or simply ignored. After five minutes, she decided it was probably best to squeeze her eyes closed.

Just when she was about to ask if she could get out and

walk and meet him there later, they came to an abrupt halt and the siren was turned off in mid-wail. Once the sound was no longer there, filling her head, Beth realised how loud it had been, and how much energy she'd been expending in blocking it from her hearing. She opened her eyes, gingerly, and found that they were parked right outside the hospital, and that York was looking at her, the usual amused smile in his eyes.

'Ok?' he said.

'Oh, absolutely.' She lowered her head over the seatbelt buckle, hoping he couldn't see quite how terrified she'd been. If he'd ever needed a demonstration of how unsuited she really was to the police force, that had definitely been it. Her hands were still shaking so much that pressing the simple red button to release her belt was a major achievement.

York laughed. 'You didn't do too badly. I've known new recruits to be sick as dogs after their first full-speed chase through London. All right, we weren't actually in pursuit this time, but I had my foot down. It was the right thing to do,' he said, springing out of the car. Beth fumbled with the door and he came round and held out a steadying hand as she stumbled slightly on the pavement. 'Let's get going. Something tells me there isn't a moment to lose.'

Chapter Six

Sophia Jones-Creedy, finally happy with the face she saw in the mirror – and more than happy with the stream of slavish likes rolling in for her off-the-shoulder pic on Instagram – clicked her mascara shut, dropped it into the sparkly evening bag she'd pinched from her mother's wardrobe, and left her room. She didn't feel any qualms about swiping her mum's clutch. It wasn't like her mum ever even used it; stuff like this was totally wasted on her. The door slammed on clothes drifting across every surface from her try-on session, with enough make-up littering her dressing table to deck out the cast of Cats. No time to think about tidying now – or ever. Laters.

But after a moment, the door opened and she reappeared, and took up her favourite stance again in front of the mirror, her weight on one skinny hip in the way she'd found really emphasised the switchback curve of her tiny waist, one eyebrow pulled up high, as usual, as she blew her reflection a kiss. 'Good luck, darling,' she said softly. It was the sort of thing a doting mother would say to a beloved child, off on the threshold of an exciting new venture. But there was no-one here at her side, to wish her well. Sophia shrugged, her little face becoming hard for a second, before she remembered – sad thoughts made sad lines. She hoisted her bright smile again. Would anyone even notice if it didn't reach her eyes? It was too bad she was on her own. But, for God's sake, she was used to it. She'd just have to do it all by herself. As-per-bloody-usual.

87

***

Beth sat by the girl's bedside, holding a small pale hand in her own, much warmer one. In fact, she was uncomfortably hot all over; the heat of the day seemed to have coagulated in this airless, cheerless, determinedly blank room. Her gaze flicked away from the still features of the girl to the three walls, painted in the uninspiring dead lettuce tone that hospitals seemed to buy in bulk. The window dominating the fourth side of the room was no more inspiring. Dusk had fallen, the traffic was muted, and all she could see were eerie reflections from the room she was in, played out on the dusty pane of glass.

She started trying to take off her thin cotton cardigan, but realised she'd have to let go of the girl's hand to do it. While she knew it couldn't actually matter – and what on earth was she doing, holding hands with a stranger? – she knew that physical contact was important. If it were ever, God forbid, her own child lying there and she was unable to be by his side, she would want anyone with an ounce of compassion to do what she was doing now. She squeezed the inert fingers encouragingly, though by now she'd lost her first, initial, totally unrealistic hope, that the girl would sit bolt upright in her bed and open her eyes as soon as Beth, with her magical mummy powers, had walked in. Meanwhile, she was stuck with her cardigan at half mast, feeling not a little ridiculous, but still determined to do whatever she could.

***

She was chatting away in a soft voice, when York sauntered up outside. He passed a plastic cup of coffee to the PC sitting on guard, and peered through the small window in the door. He could see that Beth's cardigan seemed to be slipping right off her shoulders, but she was oblivious, leaning in close to the bed. If it hadn't been for the preternatural stillness of the girl lying there, it would have looked like a normal girly gossip in progress. York wondered what on earth she was saying. As soon as he pushed the door, though, she clammed up, as he'd known she would.

He smiled down on her, as a nurse bustled in, her unflappability and sense of purpose somehow making the atmosphere of the room less rarefied. Yes, a potential tragedy was unfolding here, but the nurse, in her sensible blue tunic trimmed with white at collar and cuffs, black machine washable slacks, pens in her top pocket, security lanyard swinging round her neck, seemed the very embodiment of a safe pair of hands. Her slightly harried air, her dry-looking dark hair coming adrift from a scrunchy, her broad snub nose shiny as the ancient air conditioning system failed to get to grips with a warm day, and even the sense that this girl was just one of many patients under her care, helped to normalise what was happening.

'Now then, time to do all my checks. Family, are we?' she said, a broad smile beaming across pleasant features and lighting up big brown eyes, showing her approval that people had finally turned up for this poor child.

'Not exactly …' Beth began, but York broke in.

'Any change since this afternoon?' Something about his tone told the nurse straight away that this was business – well, that and the PC on the door, of course. She looked over at him, got his measure, stood a little straighter, opened the notes folder she was carrying, and scanned the last page quickly.

'No change at all since I took over. Poor lamb. I'll be looking after her till morning. And I'll be saying a prayer for her, that's for sure. She needs her mum,' she said, casting a compassionate glance at the still figure.

'Poor girl,' echoed Beth, her hand clasping the girl's. 'Do you know if she's likely to wake up, any time soon I mean?'

The nurse looked from Beth to York and shook her head very slightly. 'I'm thinking you should talk to the doctors about that.'

'You must have seen things like this before,' Beth said pleadingly.

The nurse sighed, approaching the bed and checking the

monitors, writing in her notes, scanning a professional eye over the girl's blank features. She put her folders down on the bedside table, then came round and gave the blue covers a professional tuck over the girl, smoothing out every crease from the faded blanket. There was little enough she could do for this patient, but she could show this care at least.

'Of course. People are all different, though. The ones you think are going to make it, pah... then a little girl like this can sometimes surprise you. Sometimes they can be stronger than you think. You never know, until you *know*,' she said with a shrug. Her eyes flickered again across the girl, and slid to Beth's hopeful, pretty face. 'See you later, guys,' she said, padding away with a beaming a wide smile at Beth and a more circumspect glance at York.

'It's so frustrating,' said Beth, once the door had closed again and the atmosphere in the little room went back to tense expectation. She stared at the inert girl. 'She's locked in there; with everything she could tell us. She knows what happened. If only she'd *speak*.'

York dragged the other plastic chair round so that he mirrored Beth's position on the other side of the bed. They looked, more than ever, like anxious parents, bookending their sick child, he thought. No wonder the nurse had initially made that mistake. 'The worst thing is I've checked with the paramedics. No-one remembers that backpack.'

Beth sat up, shocked into dropping the girl's hand. 'You're kidding! We were relying on that. How can no-one remember it?'

'Well, it was quite a scene. Tricia was pretty much out of it, from what you've said...'

Beth tutted at the memory. She shrugged out of her cardigan, while she could, and then took up the girl's hand again as though she were drowning and clutching at a rope. 'This is dreadful! I should have taken the bag myself, I don't know why I didn't,' Beth said, looking towards the silent third party in the room again. 'Oh, this is so awful, I was pinning everything on it.'

'You don't have to tell me,' said York, his head bowed.

He looked up. 'Ok, just let's just go through everything about the moment when you found it. Did you look inside? Was it full of stuff, was it heavy? Anything at all.'

Beth looked distraught. 'I know it was only this morning, but it seems like years. Ok, I'll try.' She squared her shoulders. 'So, seeing it was initially such a relief. It was bright red, you see, and that flash of colour... well, I thought it explained what I'd seen that was so out of place. But just as I was thinking, yippee, just a bag, nothing awful – no blood – Tricia saw *her*. And that really pushed everything else out of my head.'

'I know,' said York as patiently as he could. 'But you're the only one who can help us with it now. Well, Tricia might remember something – but I wouldn't put money on it, would you?'

Beth looked at him and dropped her eyes. It was all down to her. And could she really remember anything at all? So much seemed to have happened since. She sank her head onto her hand, resting on the small wheeled bedside cabinet, which held a plastic jug of water and a cup. She looked down at the scuffed, unloved surface of the table, its varnish clouded by hot drinks and spillages she didn't want to think about – and an idea came to her.

She settled the girl's hand back on the bed, as though positioning a holy relic, and scooted her chair nearer to the cupboard, then pulled on the handle. It was stuck. She clasped the metal knob with both hands and tugged for all she was worth. Nothing. York looked over at her, understanding dawning on his face. 'Locked?' She nodded.

He leapt up and ran into the corridor. The PC quickly sat to attention, but York ignored him, staring up and down the corridor. Sure enough, their nurse came into view, coming out of a side ward. 'Can you help us?' York yelled, waving his arms.

The nurse broke into a lumbering trot, and collected a couple of colleagues along the way. York realised, too late, that she thought it was another cardiac incident. He was shame-faced by the time she'd burst into the room, mob-handed, with a mobile defibrillator machine bringing up the rear.

'Sorry, we just need the key to this cupboard,' he mumbled, rattling the handle uselessly. There was an audible *tsk* from a junior doctor, but the rest ambled away without complaint. There'd be another life or death situation along in a minute. Their nurse grimaced a little, but squeaked over and unfastened the offending cupboard with a master key fished from her pocket.

The door swung open, to reveal a completely empty, slightly dusty interior. 'We usually put belongings in a plastic bag and hang them *here* these days. People kept leaving their stuff behind,' said the nurse, motioning to the side of the cupboard.

Beth's heart leapt again for a moment, but the hook on the outside of the cupboard was bare, too. She and York exchanged a hopeless glance. They weren't having much luck.

Then, with no warning, the door crashed back on its hinges. A powerfully built man in his forties stood there, visibly exhausted but crackling with nervous energy. For a second, Beth wondered if he was going to do some Incredible Hulk-like transformation; he seemed wired enough. His short brown hair was covered by a surgical cap, which he whipped off and threw on the floor, and his scrubs were rumpled, one leg daubed with a stain that looked suspiciously like dried blood. His tired eyes, beneath capacious pouches, took in York, Beth, and the nurse, then his gaze went irresistibly to the still figure on the bed.

Behind him, the PC popped up, looking apologetic, 'Sorry sir, he just dashed past me…' he said lamely to York, who shot him a glance as scary as a major tongue-lashing, then jerked his head to tell him to wait outside.

'They told me Sophia was here. They said she's been here *all day*.' The man's voice was rigorously controlled, his ferocious anger all the more palpable as a result. Someone, somewhere, had decided that a full list of patients took precedence over his sick child. Beth was glad she hadn't been the one to give him the news. Though she understood that rescheduling operations was a logistical nightmare, things weren't quite so bad that this man was the only surgeon in south London. She wouldn't want to be that decision-maker now.

The doctor strode forward, his face intent. He got within a foot of the bed and stopped dead.

'I don't understand. Is this some kind of sick joke?' he hissed at York.

York and Beth looked at him, baffled. The nurse, perhaps more practised in the way of the top ranks of the medical profession, busied herself by bending over her folder of notes and avoiding everyone's eyes.

'What do you mean, sir?' said York. His manner wasn't exactly deferential, but it was definitely designed to be conciliatory. There was clearly not much length left on this man's personal tether. It was not the moment to rebuke him for abusing the Metropolitan Police, let alone blameless members of the public.

'I *mean* this isn't my fucking daughter, *is it*?' the man yelled at top volume.

Chapter Seven

Once calm had been restored, and Mr Jones-Creedy, consultant orthopaedic surgeon, had taken himself off home after a disastrous case of mistaken identity, Beth and York were left looking at each other blankly once again.

There were more questions facing them now than there had ever been. Who on earth was the girl in the bed? She might not have been Sophia Jones-Creedy, but she was *someone*. And someone's daughter, too. Meanwhile, according to the au pair, the real Sophia Jones-Creedy was yet to return home.

Beth scrutinised the pale face of the girl on the bed, opened the Facebook app on her phone, and dredged up the picture that, in her mind, had linked this poor waif with Sophia. She showed the shot to York. He studied it in silence, then returned the phone to Beth. Yes, there was a strong resemblance, anyone could see that. But Beth now realised the Jones-Creedy girl had so much more animation. Like her father, whose presence had crackled through the room, Sophia seemed to have the ability to light up and dominate any space she was in.

Beth flicked through her endless parade of Instagram snaps. In a group shot, the eye went straight to her, skipping over her contemporaries, though on the face of it they were every bit as pretty and winsome. The only reason she looked a bit like the girl in the bed, in that one particular photo, was because it was a rare picture showing her quiet, still, and – maybe – actually asleep.

'They look very similar. But at the same time...' said York.

'I know. There's no real comparison, is there? I'm sorry,

I was so sure…'

'Don't apologise. We had almost nothing to go on.'

'Thanks to me not keeping an eye on the bag.'

'That was not your responsibility. Don't go blaming yourself. No-one's put you in charge of every aspect of this investigation – yet,' said York. Beth met his eyes with a small smile.

'So, who on earth *is* this girl, then?' Beth looked down once more at the wan little face. The girl looked even more washed-out and insubstantial now, compared with the images of Sophia and the live impact of her Mr Jones-Creedy's restless anger. Beth felt a tug at her heartstrings. There seemed to be no-one who cared about the girl enough to notice she was missing. No-one, that is, but Beth.

York, meanwhile, was thinking, too. 'So, where on earth can this Sophia have been all day? And all night? She doesn't strike me as the truanting type.'

'Doesn't she? We've never met her, though. We're just making assumptions based on her background, the fact that her parents have responsible jobs, she's middle class so she must be a nice, hard-working girl. But she could be a total slacker, for all we know,' Beth reasoned.

'The College School, though? Don't tell me that's the type of place that tolerates truanting,' said York.

'Hmm, you've definitely got a point there.' Beth was impressed at how quickly he was picking up Dulwich nuances. Though it was hardly a secret that parents would kill – more or less – to get their boys into Wyatt's and their girls into the College School. If any student started to cut classes, there were plenty more on the waiting lists ready to fill their places. Beth couldn't see the College School's headmistress giving anyone much leeway and, judging from her Facebook profile, Sophia Jones-Creedy was already an enthusiastic boundary-pusher.

***

Little did Beth know it, but Miss Douglas was pondering

95

exactly the same matter, alone in her office at the College School. She liked the place best when it was empty. Much though she enjoyed the girls, there was no question that the school at night was a much more restful place – perfectly still, classrooms standing ready for the next day's lessons, floors polished, chairs tucked under desks just so. She loved the peace, and the sense of expectation and promise it held. So different from the days, when the girls and their endless demands – and the teachers and their complaints – seemed to fill her days with alarums and excursions. Even the street, which she could survey now without worrying about random delivery men popping up, was quiet and tranquil, the behemoth cars of the parents safely squeezed into tiny parking spaces on Dulwich's narrow roads. She sighed a little and turned back to the matter in hand.

Spread before her were Sophia Jones-Creedy's academic records. She'd been at the school since the age of four: in pre-prep where she'd been obstreperous and controlling; then into the junior school, where she'd started exerting her influence on her peers in a less obvious, but infinitely more manipulative way, devising endless games which had the aim of excluding whoever in the class had fallen out of her favour. Her contemporaries then had seemed like deer caught in the headlights of her peculiarly commanding stare, falling in with whatever she suggested and adopting her chosen pecking order without question. Really, sometimes it was too easy for these strong personalities, thought Miss Douglas.

She wished she could say that all that had changed, that the girl had mellowed. And certainly, now that the girl was in the senior school, there was little Miss Douglas could put a finger on. There was nothing, for instance, that she could write to the child's parents about. They were a daunting couple, even by Dulwich standards, but that would not have stopped Miss Douglas. Yet, though there was no obvious sign that Sophia Jones-Creedy was the instigator, whenever there was any sort of disturbance in Year 9, she was there, in the thick of it, with that smile that so many found beguiling. Miss Douglas certainly itched to slap it off her face. But that was a thought that could never make its way to the light of day, and an action that would put paid to her hard-won career in an instant.

Miss Douglas thought back over the most recent crop of incidents involving Sophia Jones-Creedy's cohort. As early as Year 6, there had been the first rumblings of concern over weight. As usual, no-one could blame Sophia for planting the seeds of worry, but suddenly a group of girls started weighing each other relentlessly on the school nurse's scales at lunch time, and teasing the larger members of their gang. Of course, the nurse had reported this immediately, and the scales had been removed forthwith, but it was disturbing to see girls of that age – nine and ten – suddenly so concerned about who weighed what. Sophia, the slim and active daughter of lithe and super-busy parents, had no worries. Others had more sedentary lifestyles, puppy fat, and more indulgent mothers – and had become targets for ridicule.

Anorexia was a huge worry in girls' schools, particularly competitive, academic establishments like the College School. Girls who felt under pressure with so many deadlines and exams, flexed their muscles where they could. Food was one of the few areas where they could exert some control. It happened all over the country, with or without the likes of Sophia Jones-Creedy to stir things up.

Still, reflected Miss Douglas, she did not feel happy *at all* that five of that early weigh-in group had gone on to have recurring troubles with the illness. Two had since left the school – one to be admitted to a private clinic; one to be treated at the nearby Wellesley NHS facility. Though they were out of sight, and no longer Miss Douglas's problem in many ways, she couldn't avoid hearing on the grapevine how the girls fared. Neither would be going to university at the proper time, exams having been dropped by the wayside as the obsession with weight grew and the girls shrank. One of them would be lucky to survive. Sophia, of course, despite having been overheard saying self-deprecatingly that she 'had thighs like an elephant', 'was never hungry at lunchtime', and 'always burned off her supper with a workout', had never been in the slightest danger of succumbing to anorexia at all.

Then, there had been the outbreak of self-harming. The group of girls was a little different, though Sophia was never far from its centre. This time, the fetish was shorter lived and seemed to cut – if she could permit herself to use that term – less deeply. Though it was meant to be a secretive business, one girl had slashed her arm at school with some scissors from the art department and been seen dripping blood. A series of stern chats from Miss Douglas herself, a psychologist from King's College Hospital, and a psychiatrist parent, had shed so much light on the subject that it no longer held any shameful secret thrill for the girls, and the Monday morning excuses that kittens had swiped their arms or rose bushes had snagged the skin seemed to vanish overnight.

In the midst of all this, Sophia had achieved a phenomenal set of results in every test she'd ever been set. She was off the scale, with an exceptional memory, she was highly numerate, and she turned a phrase neatly. Her reports were full of teacher euphemisms – 'makes a very positive contribution in class' (*never shuts up*); 'not afraid to back up her opinions' (*argumentative*); a leading light in the class' (*ringleader*); 'always ready with a view' (*nightmare*); 'full of energy' (*nightmare*); 'always shows an inquiring mind' (*nightmare*). But all agreed, she was 'very able' (*clever as a cartload of monkeys*). She would garner a rich harvest of A*s for the College School, and they would all be extremely relieved when she trooped off to Cambridge to make some poor don's life hell.

Miss Douglas shut the folder with a sigh. Many of the mysteries about Sophia Jones-Creedy were illuminated by a whisk through these pages. But not the central puzzle facing her headmistress now. Where on earth *was* the blessed girl?

***

It was getting on for 7pm when Jo Osborne struggled home with Lewis strapped into the buggy, the handles festooned with the cheap thin carrier bags you got these days since the 5p charge came in. That was 20p she'd wasted just on plastic bags, she was kicking herself, but where was she supposed to keep spare bags at work all day at Debenhams in Oxford Street? Her handbag was small – she was trying to look as though she was on top of things, she didn't want stuff bulging out everywhere. She wasn't wearing a big coat now the weather had turned nice at last, so no pockets to stick bags in. Oh well, 20p wasn't the end of the world. Not quite, anyway.

Lewis was happily chewing away on a Peperami. She'd read in the *Metro* paper the other day that processed meat was going to kill them, but what wasn't? Kept him quiet, anyway, on the bus ride back from the childminder's. It was a trek, but he loved it at Tracy's and that was worth gold. She'd look for somewhere nearer their new flat, but it was going to take time – something she didn't have. She could feel the clammy chill of the battered fish she'd brought for their tea swinging against her leg as she powered up the street. She was worrying now that it would have defrosted itself by the time they got back. Was that going to kill them, too? It always said, 'best cooked from frozen'. Oh well. There were worse things. Like, why did they never sell meals for three? It was either two or four, and two wasn't really fair on Simone. She liked a bit of fish, and she was at that fussy age. Fourteen. God, Jo remembered it well. Boys. Parties. That had been the start. Well, it wasn't going to be like that for Simone. Thank God, she was a good girl – and it was going to stay that way.

Christ, Lewis was heavy enough, but with the bags layered on as well, she felt as though she was shoving a tank up the hill in front of her. Nearly old enough for a nursery place, then it would be school… it went so fast. And he'd be her last. She was determined about that. No more mistakes – not that either of her kids were *that;* she loved them more than her life. But if she wanted to give them a proper start, she couldn't be distracted again by a load of promises that she half-knew were crap, even while she was taking off her clothes.

No, they were sorted now, with Simone in her good new school, with a full bursary. Could you believe that? Jo'd always known she was a clever little thing, but this? She'd aced that test they set her, then flown through the interviews, too. And now the school were paying for everything. Over fifteen grand's worth of education – and Jo still couldn't get her mind around all the people at the school who could actually shell out that much, *every single year*, to get their kids taught. Where did they get that kind of money? It was a different world.

Well, now it was their world, too. For her bright-as-a-button Simone was sitting pretty with all the rich kids, even getting her uniform and all the school trips paid for and everything. The idea, as the nice Bursar lady had explained, was that Simone should feel every inch a member of the school community. That meant she had everything the rest of them did – as far as the school day went, anyway. There weren't going to be any skiing holidays… or probably any holidays at all, for that matter. And if she brought friends back, well, Jo would do the best she could; the place was always clean, but it was what it was. They weren't nobs, and there was no use pretending. But they'd sort that out when it happened. Simone hadn't asked anyone back yet. Jo knew she should press her, try and help her make friends… but the truth was she did feel a bit daunted. These kids would have big houses, probably second homes, certainly cars and fancy phones, and all the gear that Simone wanted but knew better than even to ask for.

Still, there were more important things than *stuff*, Jo told herself. They all loved each other and that was key. It was the three of them against the world, and they were tight. Things were good. Lewis was happy as Larry at Tracy's, and she was doing well at Debenhams, they'd said so in her last assessment. Life was on the up.

She bumped the buggy backwards up the endless steps to the front door. Theirs was the little second floor maisonette – not much, but it was cosy and she could afford it. As long as she didn't go mad with the plastic bags. Her key rattled in the door. Usually that was enough to get Simone running to give her a hand with the buggy, with Lewis.

The door swung open. Dark. Silent. The flat had that empty feel. Jo looked around, could see straight into the kitchen, the dishes by the sink, from her and Lewis's cereal. She had to get him off so early, then get to work herself. She always let Simone sleep in. Well, she needed her zeds, teenagers always did, and the walk to school only took her minutes. But usually Simone tidied up the kitchen, bless her, before she got off for the day.

Jo looked at the pool of milk on the plastic tablecloth, the cereal box with its untidily torn corner, a few Cheerios lying there, stuck to the surface, shrivelled. All as it had been this morning. It wasn't right. Jo started to feel the cold clutch of dread. Thought back to the night before. Then fast forwarded to the morning. Realisation crashed in on her, shivers down her arms.

'Simone?' she called out. *'Simone?'*

Katie had just dropped off Charlie and Ben. She'd waved hello to some of the mums, and had a brief – very brief – chat with the determinedly smiling Belinda McKenzie, and was turning to wander back down Court Lane. Belinda always tried to corner her when Beth wasn't around. It was no secret that Belinda and Beth didn't exactly mesh. Beth worked, and was a single parent, and was not groupie material. But when she was out of the picture, Belinda perpetually cozied up to Katie with little plans to show her what she was missing out on. It was as though she couldn't bear to have Katie outside her herd. Katie, perpetually sunny, deflected the woman so kindly that Belinda always thought it was worth another go.

Katie shrugged it all off. She didn't mind Belinda, but she didn't want to spend all day being held to ransom by her stories, which always seemed to be on the theme of the marvellous things Belinda had done for other people, and the terribly unjust things that had happened to her in return, with a smattering of semi-evil gossip thrown in. It wasn't really

Katie's thing. Especially not on a day like this.

It was another beautiful morning, the skies above Dulwich as blue as the cute little aertex shirts sported by Wyatt's prep school kids. Yet again, she wondered whether they'd done the right thing, putting Charlie into the non-fee-paying Village Primary. Michael had wanted him to go straight to the prep, which, barring any catastrophic results, would have seen him sailing effortlessly on to a place at Wyatt's secondary school. But Katie had loved the quirky little Village School as soon as she'd seen its Hansel and Gretel buildings. And besides, staving off the fees for a few years meant that Michael's hair could stay on his head, not fall out in handfuls as some Dulwich husbands' did, as they scraped together multiple sets of school fees from toddlerdom onwards.

Just then, she heard footsteps behind her, and turned to see Maria Luyten, her new neighbour. Maria, with her beautifully cut, swingy dark hair, was wearing what Katie recognised as a Euro casual uniform – designer polo shirt with a logo; jeans which clung to her slim form; and a small Prada bag worn messenger-style across her body, which managed to be both eye-wateringly expensive and relatively low key. The only giveaway to its price tag was the distinctive triangular shape of its tiny nameplate.

Katie wondered how Belinda MacKenzie was reacting to the new arrival in their midst. Today, Belinda's own bag had been about the size of a full Moses basket, and screaming as loudly as usual about money and status. And not only did Maria feel less need to show her wealth via labels, she was also a doctor.

Belinda was a bit iffy about working mums. Though she had been something huge in PR before having her babies, she had dropped work like a hot coal as soon as she'd seen a blue line on her pregnancy test. Now she lapped up *Daily Mail* stories about the dire consequences of neglecting your offspring for a career, while her au pair kept the children amused. A doctor would call her bluff, though. Like most Dulwich parents, she'd adore her brood to become doctors –

even the girls.

'Ha! I am glad to have caught up with you. Or should I say, caught you up?' Maria said.

Katie smiled diplomatically. 'Either! Your English is perfect, a thousand times better than my Italian, or French, or Dutch or… well, you know what I mean. Typical English person, here, who just points at things on the menu on holiday.'

'Ah, no, I can't believe that. But English is very kind to foreigners; anyone can pick it up. Spelling it, that's a whole different matter. Don't ask me *ever* to write down borough, thorough, through or throw, please!'

'Promise I won't,' laughed Katie. 'Do you have time for a quick cuppa?' She'd just had a text from Beth, putting off their coffee at Jane's but requesting a full run-down of last night's activities, including what Ben had eaten and whether he'd had a good night's sleep, plus how he'd looked this morning, as soon as Katie had time.

Well, he was her one and only, and Katie understood all too well how much love could be poured into one small boy. She also had a 10.30am class to teach at her yoga studio, and she'd been planning on running through some stretches first, so she could help others without her own joints creaking like unoiled doors. But she wanted to be friendly. It would be great to get to know Maria a bit more.

'That would be lovely. I am a little concerned about something, you see… and of course, I wanted to thank you so much for having Matteo round last night. He had a such a great time, he was thrilled to be included. It's not so easy, making new friends, even for little ones.'

'It was a pleasure. He's a lovely boy.' In fact, looking back on it, they'd had a few tricky moments last night. Katie hadn't been that surprised. Ben and Charlie were such partners in crime, it was a little awkward to slot a third party into such a well-established double act. She'd wanted to help Beth out, and knew her friend had very limited childcare options at such short notice – plus she did mischievously wonder what might happen if Beth and York kept being

103

thrown together – but the timing could have been better.

As it was, things had worked out in the end. Once they'd finished Charlie's allotted PlayStation time, they squabbled solidly, until Matteo had come up with a role-play game. He'd been the doctor; the others had been patients. They'd all been happy enough with this for a while, though she'd had to draw the line when she found he was trying to get them to drink cups of shampoo in the bathroom to cure 'stomach aches'. But it had certainly kept them busy, to her relief.

Now Katie ushered Maria in and, a couple of minutes later, she was perched on a stool in Katie's breathtaking kitchen – all sweeping, pristine pale marble countertops, leading the eye past the family dining table, to the green swathe of lawn stretching outside floor-to-ceiling doors. Today, they were cracked open a few inches, but when the weather truly warmed up – if it ever really did; this was England, after all – the doors would be shoved right out of the way and they'd be living the dream, with the garden becoming a greener, tuftier extension of the kitchen. Katie would have to think of a way to ensure that no football, ever, got kicked inside the house. But other than that little wrinkle, it was perfect.

Katie fiddled with the many levers of her shiny chrome coffee machine, then realised whatever she produced wasn't going to be a patch, realistically, on the coffee Maria had been brought up on. She passed over the little espresso cup with a moue of apology. 'This is the best I can do,' she shrugged.

Maria took a sip, and smiled. 'Delicious,' she said generously. 'Mm, Katie,' she said, putting her cup down precisely. 'I must ask you. My daughter, Chiara. She is at the College School. We were very pleased when she got the place. Of course, we didn't really know then that it is said to be very hard to get in. We just applied when it turned out Theo was being transferred here. It was, well, all a big scramble.'

Katie nodded sympathetically. She'd heard from other ex-pat wives who'd been uprooted from homes and lives at a few weeks' notice, and were expected to create some sort of future in a new place without much time, information – or help. It was tough. And when it involved children of school age, there was a whole new side to the problem. It was quite possible for some of these families that they would be on the move again soon, so although the school solution didn't have to be permanent, it still had to be good enough.

Katie, who felt as though she'd spent years of her life trying to get the stars into the right alignment for Charlie's upcoming assault on Wyatt's, could only imagine how much she'd hate to be thrown into Maria's position.

'We were so pleased with Chiara at first. She hasn't done entrance exams before, and the school seemed so good... Miss Douglas, she is a bit, hmm, scary, but it seems she cares for her girls. But it is a big place. It's not easy for Maria. She was in a quite small school in Kuwait; the international population is not huge. And some of the girls here in the UK...'

Katie, sensing they were getting to the nub of the issue, peered over the rim of her coffee cup at Maria. The woman's dark hair shaded her face, her large dark eyes lowered. There was something negative here that she was reluctant to say.

'Chiara is, what? Thirteen, fourteen?' said Katie gently.

'She was fourteen in March.'

'Right. So that's Year 9, I'm thinking?'

Maria nodded, but seemed to hesitate. Katie compressed her lips and thought. Though Charlie hadn't reached such dizzy heights yet, Katie had already scoped out the years ahead. Teenage boys had the reputation of being charmless and monosyllabic. It was hard to imagine any son of Michael's becoming such a tiresome one-way street. Michael was sociability personified, endlessly interested in other people. But she'd heard and seen enough to know it was probably inevitable, at some point, that the cheery, chirpy Charlie she knew would turn into a mumbling beanpole that she'd probably hardly recognise.

She could deal with that. She was even braced for him towering over her. Michael was over six feet tall and Charlie was already taller than Ben, though maybe that wasn't saying much, as Beth, bless her, was so teeny. Had her late husband, James, been tall, though? Katie had no idea and realised she was drifting away from the issue at hand. Teenage girls. They were, basically, from all she'd seen and heard, a mountain of trouble.

'Is she having problems, Maria? With the girls in her class?' Katie's tone couldn't have been gentler. She realised she was being intrusive – she hardly knew Maria, and the woman might well not want to talk about this at all. But Maria seemed to be on the brink of a revelation. Katie couldn't take it as a massive compliment to her proffered hand of friendship. Poor Maria hardly knew anyone in the country. She didn't have a lot of candidates for the position of confidante.

Oh, there would have been Belinda MacKenzie, of course. She always chummed up with the newbies, looking for fresh recruits to her band of followers. But Katie wasn't at all surprised that Maria had thought twice before discussing anything difficult with Belinda. She'd no doubt already heard the woman gossiping for Britain, and probably decided she didn't want her business to be the next item on Belinda's bulletins.

'You don't have to say anything if you don't want to, I'm not trying to pry. It's just that I've heard the College can be quite… pressured. A lot of clever girls, all stuck together like that, and if you throw in hormones and GCSEs and all that, then well, it's not surprising it can get a bit… intense.' Katie smiled.

There was a pause, then Maria raised her large brown eyes. Katie saw, to her surprise and shock, that they were brimming with tears.

***

Harry York sat with his eyes shut, head in his hands. Again. It seemed to be becoming an habitual posture, and he felt the protesting ache in his shoulders and back. A bit more sleep would be good, too, he thought, standing up and stretching his arms over his head, checking first this way and that down the grim green corridor. He didn't want to be caught out by any nurses or doctors waving his arms around like an idiot. He sat back down, and the plastic chair protested with a creak. He knew how it felt. If he sat here much longer, he'd take root.

He didn't blame the PC, who was supposed to be taking a five-minute break, for swinging the lead a bit. The poor kid had been there for hours. It was one of those jobs when you were glad it was boring – except that boring was *boring*. There was a skill in staying still and being patient, one which York knew full well he didn't possess. He'd been lucky that his 2.1 degree in criminology and law from Derby had got him fast-tracked into the Met; a bit of a golden ticket – though achieved via plenty of hard work – that had seen him swerve round some of the duller duties. That made him all the more sympathetic to those ploughing a career path the hard way.

PC Wilson was probably getting whatever was closest to a full English down in the Costa branch downstairs. That, in itself, was a perfect example of NHS double-think. All those exhortations to eat your five-a-day, and yet every single food outlet in this place, packed with patients suffering diabetes, high blood pressure, heart disease or other diet-related ailments, was piled high with tempting arrays of chocolates, crisps, fizzy drinks and pastries, the very thought of which was making him hungry enough to eat this damned plastic chair.

It had been a hard night, not so much for him, but for Jo Osborne. Having got home to an empty flat, and immediately checked her daughter Simone's bedroom, Jo had been beside herself at realising the girl had not slept there the night before. She'd then rung 999.

'She must have sneaked out last night when I was asleep. I fell asleep putting Lewis to bed around 8, I was dead to the world, spark out. I can't believe she's done this; she's never done anything like this before, never. I'm mortified. I can't

107

believe it, I can't,' Jo explained to York, again and again. 'I can't believe I didn't check her room before I left for work. I feel terrible. *Terrible.'*

York listened to the lament, but knew there was nothing he could do to take the edge off her distress. If she'd noticed her daughter was missing last night or even this morning, things might have gone down differently. Jo Osborne would have to spend the rest of her life making her peace with that.

Her panicked call to the emergency services was just the beginning of her nightmare. 'Tell the truth, I was expecting them to fob me off – saying she hadn't been missing long enough, nothing they could do… Instead they was, like, on red alert,' Jo had explained to York, her voice and hands still trembling.

The poor woman, expecting a huge machine to take little notice of the spanner she was trying to lob into its works, was justifiably terrified when a squad car was immediately dispatched to her address, and she and the protesting Lewis were bundled off to King's. Her terror did not lessen when she glimpsed her parchment-pale daughter.

She burst in, shouting the girl's name, and York felt a sense of completion as Jo took up her rightful place by the girl's bedside, head nestling into the girl's unresisting shoulder, sobbing her heart out onto the faded blanket and NHS issue nightgown.

The child had been claimed, and at least one mystery was solved. Here lay Simone Osborne, fourteen years old, a pupil at the College School in Dulwich. For the second time, though, the girl resisted the call to consciousness. She'd been untouched by all Beth's maternal efforts and now, despite her real mother's tears, exhortations and pleas, despite the jammy fingers of her little brother trying to prise her eyelids open, the slight figure on the bed remained impervious, her limbs inert, her mind floating above them in who-knew-what dream world. Whatever Prince Charming she was waiting for, York prayed he'd bring strong magic with him. It would have to be, to break this charm.

Chapter Eight

Sophia Jones-Creedy lay back on the none-too-fragrant cushions of the lumpy sofa and sighed with pleasure, letting her hand fall back limply so that Raf could claim the smouldering stub of the joint. He took it from her, snorting with something that might have been disdain when he saw how little was left, but too chilled at this point even to remonstrate with her.

Her eyes, when she opened them again, were pinkish, the token of a night spent happily stoned, and far from her cosy Dulwich home. She smiled her crooked smile.

'What's up, babe?' said Raf lazily, waiting for her to tell him she was smiling because he was so great. She'd certainly seemed enthusiastic, he thought, wincing a little and running a hand over a claw mark on his arm made by her sharp little nails.

'Just imagining my parents' faces when they realise my bed hasn't been slept in for two whole nights. My mother should be back from her *work trip* by now, unless it's been extended again. They'll go *mental*, that's what. Serves them right. What's the point of even having children, if you spend no time with them and have absolutely no interest in their lives?' she asked Raf angrily.

He shrugged indifferently and started lazily kissing her neck. She was a very lucky girl. If he wasn't too stoned, he might just be in the mood to show her again. He'd found her a few weeks ago, with a bunch of giggling friends, at a club they were transparently years too young to attend legally. It was a while since he'd had that trouble himself – he didn't like to remember it too clearly, but he was pushing 28 now – but a lot of his girlfriends had to be nice to the bouncers, or get themselves fake cards. It was just the way it was.

Soph was the latest girl – or perhaps fairer to say, one of the latest batch of girls – to fall for his mix of still-boyish looks, ripped physique, open-handed way with the drinks and the weed, and his undeniable expertise in bed or, to be strictly accurate, on this stained sofa. There wasn't much in the way of furniture in his flat off Peckham High Street. He'd get round to all that.

Meantime, he had big plans for Soph. She was a looker, anyone could see that. And she was eager to get her hands on life, try everything all at once – the drugs, the booze, and the rest of it, too, he reckoned, once he'd got her needing something every day. These posh girls were easy to break. Used to everything going their way, it was a big shock when the ponies and parties stopped and they needed to work for a living. For the moment, though, the two of them were in the honeymoon phase. He dropped another sloppy, lazy kiss on her neck.

He'd had to jettison his last girl, fast. A bit too fast for his liking, but it couldn't be helped. He just hoped there wouldn't be any comeback on that whole situation. No point worrying about that, though. It was his mantra, and it had got him this far.

He opened an eye and grinned at Sophia, taking in the lithe curves, the perfect skin, the milk and honey look of the pampered child that clung to her, despite everything. She had potential.

'Soph,' he said, nudging her bare bottom with his knee in a way he judged irresistible. 'Do us a favour.'

She flipped over and squinted at him, pulling at the old sheet to cover herself, smoke from his smouldering joint getting in her eyes. 'Do us a fry-up, will yer?'

Sophia looked around, surprised. 'Is there any food here? I thought you were out of supplies, that's why I got the pizza last night.' He winced as her cut-glass vowels sliced through his muzzy head. He didn't really get hangovers, kept his levels well topped up all day, but the dope left him headachey in the mornings and that fucking accent was doing him in.

The sooner he moved her over to something harder, the better. His head would be better, and she wouldn't be talking so much any more.

'Nah. You'll have to pop out and get it, love. You do *know* how to do the shopping, doncha?'

As he'd hoped, the merest suggestion that she wasn't up to the job had Sophia scrabbling for her clothes, eager to prove him and the world wrong. Not for nothing had she been trained by that posh school of hers. He bet she thought she was going to be the best little shopper in Peckham. And then she'd cook whatever she bought so well, it would be like that bird off the telly, Deliciously Bella, or whatever her name was. Soph was going to make sure it was the best thing he'd ever eaten. He couldn't help grinning to himself.

'Right, I'm off then, Raf. Just one thing…'

'Yeah?' he said, opening one eye and squinting at her.

'What's *in* a fry-up, actually?'

He rolled his eyes. 'What, your mum's never done a fry-up for yer dad?' Sophie snorted at the idea and was going to explain, but Raf cut her off. Of all the things he couldn't be arsed with, the intricacies of her home set-up was now top of the list. 'Bacon, sausage, tomato, beans, toast,' he gabbled, and tacked on at the end, 'oh, and get us out another £50 in cash, will yer?'

She smiled, looking like she was floating on air at being treated like a *grown-up* and part of a *couple* and all the rest of that shit, and she dropped a loving goodbye kiss on his well-developed bicep. 'Back soon,' she trilled. Too soon, probably, he thought, as soon as the door shut. He pulled a stained cushion over his head and dozed.

***

York knew he should resist, but he couldn't. He needed to discuss the case with someone. Yes, there was the PC on the hospital door. Yes, there was his guv here at the station. But that was it. He was chronically sort-staffed on this case; it was ridiculous. The awful thing was that, at the moment, it was being classified as just a drug overdose. *Just.* It was an unspoken fact that if the girl died, everything would change. The case would be bumped up to suspicious death and funds would suddenly become available. It was a horrible irony but if there was no longer a girl to save, he'd be in a much better position to save the girl. It was doing his head in, he didn't mind admitting it… but who could he even admit it to? He needed a sympathetic ear, it always helped him get cases straight. He played idly with his phone, scrolling down recent calls. And there was Beth…

He stopped himself thinking about how wrong all this was, and instead considered the fact that she was the one who'd found the girl – Simone – in the first place. Maybe there was still something they'd overlooked, something useful from those first moments of the case? OK, it didn't stand up to any kind of scrutiny but… he was already pressing dial.

'Harry? Sorry, *Inspector?* Any news?'

Beth was at her desk, with the by-products of her labours of that morning in front of her. A cardboard container of coffee and a ravaged bar of Cadbury's whole nut – she reasoned that it was important Ben didn't see her eating too many unhealthy snacks at home. The fact that this gave her leeway to ingest a lot of rubbish at work was… convenient, she had to admit. Oh, and there was also a whole pile of archive stuff that she'd been busily ignoring, while she checked the news on Google every five minutes to see what, if anything, had been reported.

'I still don't see anything about the case online… just wondered…'

'Well, the news is that we have identified the girl; her name is Simone Osborne. Her parents, well, mother, has been informed, she's at the hospital – but there's no change.'

'Oh,' said Beth, and immediately realised just how much she'd been hoping for better news, for a miraculous return to consciousness. 'But it's great that you've found out who she is. Simone? Doesn't ring any bells. And wait, what about the other girl, Sophia Jones-Creedy? Where *was* she all that time? And the bag? Any sign of that?'

'Can we meet?' said York heavily. 'I just need to do some thinking out loud.'

Beth was silent for a beat. He'd never said anything like this before. Previously, in fact, he'd batted off all her attempts to get him to discuss the case. She savoured the change for a moment. 'Of course,' she said. 'I'm due a break,' she added, crossing her fingers. She was actually due to do a smidgeon of work – but this, she decided, was far more important. 'Where?'

'Look, I know there's a pecking order of cafes which I can't hope to understand, but somewhere quiet would be good.'

Beth mentally scanned the places she knew round about. Jane's was out, unless the Met Police wanted to issue a press release direct to all the mothers of Dulwich. She'd already subjected York to Aurora's once before and, though he had seemed to shrug off the experience, she wasn't sure she'd ever want to watch him eating one of their bacon sandwiches again. The lovely tiny deli, Romeo Jones, was too dinky – the other patrons would be virtually sitting in their laps, vacuuming up every detail of the case even more assiduously than Beth herself. The other Italian deli on the other side of the road was a bit too dark inside… And the restaurants? The unwritten rules of Dulwich made Beth think of them as lunch venues only. No, there was only one place it could be.

'How about the Gallery again? That's where all this started. And the café is great. If it's full and you're worried about being overheard, we can sit outside – either on the bench away from everyone, or at the tables if it's not too crowded.'

***

Jo Osborne was sitting at her daughter's side, her hand clinging desperately to the cool, lifeless fingers, which felt like a bundle of strange, delicate twigs now, not like real flesh and blood things any more, not like the useful pair of

113

hands which had fluttered around their kitchen, making a surprisingly good cup of tea, helping out a bit with Lewis's messes, burning the toast of course. But what Jo wouldn't give now, for a piece of toast burnt to cinders by her daughter.

Simone was moving further and further away, and there was nothing she could do to stop her.

Jo put her forehead down on their clasped hands, and a tear leaked out of her eye onto them. She kept thinking she couldn't cry any more, then she'd realise her face was wet and she hadn't even known she'd started up again.

The doctor had already been by that morning, explaining things to her. Tests, and time, and waiting, and whether the waiting should go on.

'It's up to you,' he'd said. And that was the weight on her heart, as heavy as Simone had been in those final days before her birth, when she'd felt her baby low in her womb, dragging her down, making her steps roll like a sailor fresh off a boat, and she'd known then that the two of them couldn't go on in the same body any more. Maybe what she knew now was that Simone couldn't go on separately any more, either.

But what if she was wrong? She wasn't much of a one for reading, but there'd been cases, hadn't there, of people who'd sat up after years in comas? Wasn't there some woman in Germany who'd missed the wall coming down? Or was that just a film? She wished, not for the first time, she'd had a different kind of mind, the kind of cleverness that Simone herself possessed. Because, what if she went along with what they were saying, let them do the tests, turned off the machine, and her Simone could have come round half an hour later if she'd just left well alone?

It was ridiculous, but she kept thinking about that pot plant she'd bought last Christmas. One of those bright red things? What did they call them, poinsettias? She'd bought it on impulse at the check-out, just thought it'd brighten the place up a bit, but no. The leaves had started to drop almost as soon as she'd got it home, then all the bright red petals,

114

too. She'd slung it out, or intended to; just dumped it by the bins outside, really. The bin men were terrible around Christmas; you never knew whether they were coming or not, once all those Bank Holidays threw the schedule up in the air. Two weeks later, that plant was looking as bright as when she'd bought it, stuck out there in all weathers, and she took it back inside, glad the bin men hadn't taken it after all. What if she did that to Simone, though, unplugged her too soon? There'd be no second chance for her.

Doctors weren't always right, were they? She might come back from this, she might... Or what if they found something, in two years' time, say, that could wake people up from states like the one Simone was in? That could happen, couldn't it? If she could just keep her attached to everything, there was hope. If she turned off the machines too early – well, it was too easy to say she'd never forgive herself. She'd never forgive herself for any of it as it was.

All those months she'd dithered when she'd first fallen pregnant, wondering whether to have Simone hoovered out, thrown down a sink in some clinic. All those months after she was born, when she thought she'd just have to hand her over to the Social, worn to nothing by the screaming, baffled about what the tiny red angry creature *wanted* from her... loving her but hating her; sixteen and trapped for life with a baby and no help; her own mother worse than useless; her latest stepdad not safe around a nine-months-pregnant girl, let alone a baby...

What a mess it had all been, and yet somehow, it had turned out all right. They were never going to be rich, but she had her job, Simone was doing so great at school, Lewis was a poppet when he wasn't a little devil. They were ok. Simone – from being that tiny, angry bundle – was her best friend; they had a right laugh these days. And she could see the years ahead, clear as day. They'd be one of those mother-daughter pairs who did everything together, got their nails done, went out on the town, even. When Simone got married, they'd have a hen do with those fuchsia pink sashes and L-plates and plenty of booze, and why not? Even those inflatable willies, and all. She could see it. She wanted it so much. The pain was terrible now, she could hardly breathe for crying.

She raised her head and pleaded with her still, silent daughter, 'Come on then, love, we've been ok together, you and me, ain't we? Come back to us, come back to me and Lewis. Wake up, love, just wake up. *Please,* hon.'

There was no answer.

Chapter Nine

Harry York and Beth were at the Gallery again, this time at one of the wooden tables close to the café. There was hardly anyone around – a feat achieved by picking a *rendezvous* time between early nursery pick-up and lunchtime. So, most of the mummies were occupied at home, possibly slaving over their weekly food orders from Ocado, but more likely planning to buy everything from posh frozen meal shop Cook while watching Netflix like ordinary mortals.

Beth was stirring her cappuccino in slightly desultory fashion, while York outlined the gloomy state of the case so far.

'The trouble is, we don't actually know that this wasn't all an elaborate suicide bid.' He held up his hand as Beth started to expostulate.

'I know, I know, it's hardly the place anyone would pick... but we don't know this girl, Simone Osborne. Maybe she's a highly theatrical type. I mean, for goodness' sake, most teenage girls seem to be on the verge of hysteria half the time.'

Beth contented herself by giving him a short but effective death ray stare, though her own researches over the past couple of days had convinced her that young girls were a very different breed now from the almost cartoonishly innocent kid she had been way back then.

'Was there nothing at all on CCTV?' she countered. 'Why do people even have it? Nothing useful ever seems to get recorded.'

York shot a glare at Beth now. It was certainly a lamentable fact that in both this case and the one that had thrown them together, CCTV had been worse than useless.

'You can't really expect the Gallery to train their security systems on three dead people when they've got priceless art on the walls,' said York, trying to be reasonable. 'It's not a big surprise that the mausoleum itself isn't covered.'

Beth, much though she wanted to raise a pithy objection, realised that if she were running the Gallery's budget, she'd have made exactly the same choice. No-one in their right mind was going to try and shift a solid marble sarcophagus, which must weigh several tonnes and have no resale value – unless you wanted to retile your bathroom in doomy oxblood red, of course. But the thought of half-inching a nice Poussin did cross even the least nefarious of minds, as she could herself attest.

'Even if there's no footage of anyone leaving Simone in the niche, surely there must be some of her working at the St Christopher's event?'

'We have spotted her there – not easy, though, as all the kids were wearing special black St Christopher's T shirts and baseball caps for the do, and the girls with long hair had it tied back. Basically, they all look the same. Every single girl seems to have had a long pony tail. You'd think they'd be trying for a bit more individuality. I thought the teenage years were full of experimentation,' shrugged York.

Beth, swishing her own luxuriant pony tail a little defensively, said quite mildly, 'I expect the organisers wanted them all to look the same, and asked for a simple hairdo.'

York nodded. 'Hmmm. Doesn't get us any further, though.'

'And anything on the bag?' Beth's question was tentative.

York sighed. 'I hate to disappoint you, but yes, it has turned up.'

'But that's great!' Beth sat up straighter on the bench, suddenly radiating energy. 'And?'

'And… it was empty. Nothing in it at all. Just a cheap Primark rucksack, no distinguishing features, no phone, no *anything* that's the slightest bit of use to us.'

'Oh,' Beth's voice was very small. 'Do you think

something could have got lost, while it was at the hospital?'

'Possibly, but we can't search everyone at King's. No, the bag is a dead end. We've just got to move on.'

Beth sat and thought for a while. York was right, there was no point wallowing in disappointment. So, the bag had been empty. There were other leads to pursue. 'Have you asked the Gallery top brass what their take on the whole thing is?' she said suddenly.

'That's next on our agenda. Drink up,' urged York, swigging back the last of his latte while Beth hurriedly slurped at her drink, then ran her finger round the interior to scoop out the pale foam. She caught him looking.

'What? It's the best bit. I don't know why people order cappuccinos then leave the froth behind. They spend ages making it and fluffing it up just so. Without that, it's just another white coffee.'

She sucked her finger appreciatively and York suddenly found himself averting his gaze, looking towards the blank arches of the Gallery instead. 'Strange, the way this place looks as though it's staring at you,' he said.

'I think that was Soane's idea,' said Beth, still intent on scooping out her coffee.

'Soane? Who was he, the first owner?'

Beth looked up, incredulous. 'You've never heard of Sir John Soane?'

York gave her a long, level look.

'Well, I'm sorry but… he designed this place? And have you never been to the Soane Museum in Holborn?'

York continued with the look.

'Honestly, you should go. They have wonderful candlelit evenings… it's spectacular. Just a normal Georgian house from the outside – well, two houses – and inside, it's stuffed with treasures, like Hogarth's *A Rake's Progress*.' She peeped over at York, but he was still doing that look. 'My favourite thing is this amazing Egyptian sarcophagus with a painting inside it, a simple line drawing, of a goddess… it's so beautiful.'

Beth looked rapturous for a second, but then the full

import of that hefty word, sarcophagus, squashed her pleasure. A harbinger of death, like the ones at the Gallery. And it probably wasn't the moment to be swept away by a nineteenth century collector, either. She was disappointed at York's determination not to know more, but at one level it was a comfort. At least he was concentrating on the matter at hand.

York, whose attention had been piqued by the candlelit evenings and a sudden vision of the two of them together in flickering light, shook his head and looked ostentatiously at his watch. 'Finished? We need to get inside.'

Five minutes later, they were installed in a light-filled office in the new wing of the Gallery, much to Beth's disappointment. She'd been hoping that the Chair of the Trustees had some impossibly grand suite of rooms, hidden somewhere in the old building. She looked rather sniffily round at the space-age sheet glass desk, the slanting wall of windows, and the chrome and leather chairs, and thought that they could have been at any big bank or firm of accountants. Only a framed poster of the recent Ravilious exhibition on the wall hinted at a connection with art.

York, meanwhile, was looking round with an open expression of pleasure. Beth darted him a disbelieving look. Then the door was flung wide, and a small woman advanced towards them. Though she was little more than Beth's height, her perfect posture made her seem formidable, as did the severe way her dark, silver-streaked hair was swept into a chignon. She wore a floaty grey silk dress which showcased toned arms, emphatically free of the accursed bingo wings which dragged down half the population after a certain age. Her only accessories were large shiny silver earrings and a complicated matching collar of metallic beads in varying sizes, in the sort of style Beth privately derided as 'fancy-pants', though she automatically sat up a little straighter in her chair and tried to hide her scuffed trainers.

The woman sat down with an elegant economy of movement, laid her phone face down on the desk, and smiled briefly at them both. 'Anneka Baker, Chair of the Trustees of the Gallery. We're all terribly upset at what's happened, and we want to do everything we can to help,' she said, her voice low and confiding. She settled her hands in front of her on the desk, loosely clasped, and smiled slightly at them both.

Beth, thinking crossly there was something rather showy about this woman, had a 'doh!' moment, remembering that Anneka Baker had turned down a career in dance to become an academic, rising to become Vice Principal at the Prince's College, London, part of London University, and, indeed, was the mother of Drusilla Baker, prima ballerina of the Royal Ballet.

York, meanwhile, was gazing unabashed into Anneka Baker's lustrous brown eyes and was beginning to look like one of those nodding dogs you put in the back of your car.

'If there's anything we can do to help, just ask,' said Anneka again, this time spreading the beautiful hands wide, the light catching the finely manicured, almond-shaped nails, just touched with pearlescent polish.

'There are a few questions we need answers to,' said Beth, leaning forward – and breaking the spell. Anneka Baker sat back in her chair, her features looking less gentle and sympathetic by the second.

'Really? Because there's very little that we, as the Trustees, could possibly know about the... events of that night.' Anneka's fine eyebrows arched.

'Oh, well, you must have a guest list for the St Christopher's reception held here, for starters, then you'll know the names of all those who were brought in to help with the event... and we'll need to see any visitors' book that people might have signed.'

This time, the brows snapped together, and even York turned to Beth in surprise. 'Well, it's true, we need that stuff, don't we?'

'We do,' York conceded. 'Absolutely.' But he paused and smiled at Anneka Baker. 'And we really appreciate all your help and co-operation, it's essential in a terribly sad case like this.'

'But the girl hasn't... I understood she was...?' Anneka

121

Baker delicately left the sentence dangling.

'She is still alive, but it's not looking good. There's very little chance of her waking up at this point, so we're going to need to start thinking of this as a possible... Well, a very serious investigation.'

Beth didn't quite roll her eyes at the way York was playing Anneka Baker's tune and avoiding the dirty word of murder, but she did let a small snort escape. Both of them looked at her – Anneka Baker in mild disdain; York in concern.

'If you could arrange to get those lists to me as soon as possible, that would be incredibly helpful,' said York rapidly, and started patting his pockets, making sure he had his phone, then rising to his feet.

'Is that it?' Beth, still seated, was astonished. She'd thought they had loads of ground to go over. But Anneka Baker leapt up immediately, her dress falling into graceful folds as she stepped forward and stood to shake their hands. Beth got up too quickly and lurched as she tripped on one of her trailing trainer laces, whacking her thigh painfully against the unforgiving surface of the glass table.

York shot out an arm to right her, which she shook off crossly. Anneka Baker studied her briefly, then busied herself giving York one of those double handshakes which only the most insincere of politicians went in for, to Beth's mind. When it was her turn, the woman gave Beth the merest touch with fingers that felt impossibly delicate, while Beth knew her own, much sturdier hand was decidedly damp after her embarrassing stumble. It was all most unfair. She was petite too – why couldn't she be dainty with it?

They trooped out of the office together, and made it safely down the glass corridor and back out into the Gallery gardens before Beth exploded. 'Well! What on earth was all that about? Call that an interrogation?'

'Hang on,' said York, wheeling on Beth, making her shrink back and ram one of the café's metal outdoor chairs. 'Why should I be interrogating her? We need to butter her up, get her on our side... without her, we're fighting the Gallery.

Have you seen the names on the list of Trustees? It's practically everyone who's ever run a business or the BBC. Great and good doesn't even begin to cover it. We need access to information from the Gallery, and we aren't going to get it by getting their backs up. They'll just shut us out and make it ten times harder.'

Beth, chastened, looked down at her ratty trainers. She knew York was right. She'd let her personal – and completely unreasonable – animosity get the better of her. It was really silly, and it wasn't helping them, or, more to the point, helping poor Simone Osborne.

'Is there anyone else on the list that's a bit more… approachable? Someone who might give us the inside track?'

York gave Beth a considering look. 'Well, there's one person you might actually have an in with. It's Dr Grover.'

'Dr Grover from Wyatt's? The headmaster?' said Beth, beginning to smile, as most women in Dulwich did when they thought about the flamboyant head.

'The very same,' said York shortly.

'Why didn't you say so, instead of wasting our time with… that old stick?' said Beth, getting a sly dig into the elegant Ms Baker while she could. 'I can get to work on Grover right away.'

York grunted his assent. It was his turn to kick at the grass with his hefty size 12s.

***

Sophia Jones-Creedy looked around at her little coterie of admirers. There was a smile on her face – not her trademark, quizzical, one side-higher-than-the-other grin that always brought in bushels of likes, but a mild expression of approval that was enough to keep her friends twittering away to her, without them noticing that her attention was far, far away.

She still couldn't quite believe she'd got away with it all. Two days she'd been absent; *two days* her bed at her parents' home had not been slept in. Two days missing from school.

She'd been expecting a massive row when she finally

turned up again last night. She'd only gone back because she'd run out of money and Raf had run out of weed. Once her cashpoint card had come up empty, he'd suddenly remembered an urgent appointment on the other side of town. She knew it was just his way, she didn't really take it amiss. He wasn't used to being in a *relationship* yet, but he'd learn. They needed each other, needed to be together. More importantly, he needed her. He'd forget to eat if she wasn't around, she thought with an indulgent chuckle. He'd definitely forget to wash and clean the flat. But she was the ideal teacher.

Ok, so she'd never had an actual boyfriend before, but she'd been reading magazines, checking out websites, watching DVDs her whole entire life, which prepared her for this – being in love – and not much else. Oh, apart from the career in law her mother was always banging on about. Raf was the one, definitely; even though at the moment he was, yeah, a little rough around the edges. But that would soon be sorted out. As well as the endless questionnaires, like 'Ten ways to work out if your man really cares,' – and he did, even if he might not yet know *how much* – there were plenty of sites which promised to whip even the most obdurate boy into shape. No problem for someone really motivated like her.

So, there was that. But there was also the situation with her parents. She didn't like to admit it – it never paid to show weakness – but she was seriously pissed off that *no-one had basically noticed* that she'd been away. Sure, her mother had been in Dubai and then on that endless flight. And her dad had been tied up the whole day with those tiresome sick people. She wasn't going to call them cripples, for God's sake, that was so offensive, but there was definitely something wrong with them all. And great that her dad could fix them. But he was also her dad, and surely that was his most important job?

You wouldn't think so, from all the concern he'd shown. Once he'd got over his outrage at being dragged in to see the wrong person in hospital, he'd just retreated to his study to write up his case notes for the day. And mum, well. She'd just been a jetlagged zombie. The most cursory question about *homework*, a hug, a vague ticking-off about 'late nights', then lots of cross-questioning her stupid brother on what he'd eaten for every single meal since she'd been gone. It was ridiculous.

She could basically have left home for good and no-one would have noticed. Except, of course, for the au pair – she knew her bed had not been slept in. The girl had finally been brave enough to tell her parents. Sophia would remember that, and pay her back in spades. But, after about two seconds' worth of anxiety, when her parents had demanded an explanation at long last, Sophia had lied her way effortlessly out of the hole. Everyone had been relieved to accept her half-hearted excuse that she'd been round at Chiara Luyten's house. There hadn't been a single awkward question. Would they even check up on her story, by ringing Chiara's boring, stressy mum? She seriously doubted it. Honestly, what kind of parents did she have, anyway? They thought they were so smart, but they couldn't see what was happening right under their noses. They shouldn't be this easy to fool, should they?

When she was a parent, she was going to get chapter and verse from her kids on what they were up to 24/7. Because she knew the dangers out there, even if her stupid mum and dad didn't.

You'd think they didn't want to keep her safe. You'd think their own dull lives – which were basically over now, anyway – were more important.

You'd think they didn't even care if she ended up like the girl in the Gallery.

And they didn't seem to have really taken anything in about that anyway, though her dad was still furious that he'd been dragged to see Simone 'on false pretences', as he kept saying. For all the guff he was always spouting about how much his patients mattered – and she knew he always put them first, a long, long, way before *her* and her dumb brother, that was for sure – he hadn't been very caring about

125

this patient, had he? And her mum had been, if anything, even worse. She just kept spouting on about how it was utterly outrageous that anyone would think for one second that it could have been *their* daughter lying there. It was like someone had tried to make them accept knock-off gear instead of an iPhone, or said something bad about their professional reputations. They were cross, but for all the wrong reasons.

Because, as Sophia knew all too well, it could easily have been her lying there. In a coma. Nearly dead. Or whatever.

Her parents were idiots. They just had no clue. Not even the first idea of what she went through, every single day, of how difficult life was for kids like her. End of.

She seriously thought someone should teach them a lesson.

Then she remembered, bitterly, that only a couple of days ago, she'd thought she *was* teaching them a lesson. Unfortunately for them all, it was one they hadn't managed to notice, let alone learn, despite all their degrees, diplomas, and professional laurels. It had been a wake-up call, but they'd slept blithely on.

But this time, *this time*, once and for all, Sophia thought, they would finally *get it.* She picked up her phone and studied it intently.

***

Katie threw her phone down crossly on the marble counter top, then hastily snatched it back up again to check that the smooth rose gold surface wasn't damaged. That was the trouble with these stupid gizmos. You couldn't even make a grand gesture, for fear of damage to their expensive and incredibly frail innards. She was waiting for something from Beth. A call, ideally, but by now she'd have been happy with a text, a WhatsApp, or even the briefest emoji. She had too much information inside her. She had to share some, right now, or burst.

126

The phone chirruped its soothing ringtone – selected because it was the most yogic sound available – and she snatched it up. 'Beth? Where've you been? I've been trying to get you.'

'I'm so sorry, it's been a bit mad... I've been helping Harry, er, Inspector York, and there's been so much going on... and now I'm at work, and I've got to put in a bit of effort... I know we said we'd catch up, but yesterday I was over at the hospital. It's been awful. So, how's it going?'

'Terrible! Look, I need to talk to you. It sounds like nothing compared to what you've been through, but I've heard something... really disturbing. And I think it's actually got something to do with the girl you found.'

There was a split-second pause, then Beth said, 'Can you meet me in the park for a quick lunch, then? We can talk... Unless it can wait until pick-up?'

'No, let's do the park. Lunch. Great. I'll be so much happier when I've got this off my chest,' said Katie.

'This isn't like you, Katie. Is everything ok? Do you want to just tell me now, over the phone? Oh, wait, I've got to go and see the school secretary. Oops, that was supposed to be five minutes ago. Christ! I'd better run. See you at the Summerhouse at 12.30?'

Katie's lips quirked irresistibly as she finished the call. Beth always made her laugh. She thought she was so organised, but actually she was as scatty as anything. Then Katie realised with a shock that her face felt stiff. It was the first time she'd really smiled since she'd had coffee with Maria Luyten.

Sometimes, being the only woman in a male household was hard. She couldn't possibly talk to Charlie, and Michael had been out all night at a work do, only coming home after she'd gone to bed. He'd left again before she was up this morning. She'd resorted to phoning him at the office, when she'd failed to get hold of Beth earlier, but she felt mean, burdening him with her woes while he was at the coalface of work. Instead, after an initial attempt to open the topic which he completely misunderstood, she fell back into her usual

127

pattern of half-listening to his complaints about co-workers, entirely unrealistic authors and their crazy expectations, and the stresses and strains of attempting to churn out saleable books in a fiercely digital age. He was a wonderful man, she loved him dearly, and his anecdotes were always well told – but there were times when her mind did wander. That phone call was definitely one. If she'd had to sit an exam on his current concerns, she would have got an E, while she'd looked at her own worries upside down and inside out, without succeeding in unravelling them at all.

She was so pleased she was seeing Beth. She was just wonderful at that sort of thing. She had a brilliantly analytical mind, loved puzzles, and was great at solving conundrums – as she had already proved. Katie was yearning to drop this whole matter at her feet, like a gun dog with a still-warm kill. Whether Beth would accept it with a happy smile and give her a pat on the head, remained to be seen.

***

Beth gave Janice a long look as they sat in the school secretary's office, just behind the Reception desk at Wyatt's. Time was when Janice herself had spent the long hours on duty at the Reception desk itself. Now, there was a newly-appointed – and pretty efficient – underling there, fielding calls and doing Janice's bidding, and Janice was safely tucked away here in comfort and style, with a large pot plant, swish executive chair, and the pick of this year's A level art work on her wall.

A lot had changed in the few short months that Beth had been at Wyatt's. The large sparkling engagement ring on Janice's finger, for example. When Beth had first arrived, a band from a completely different marriage had shone a little more mutedly on the woman's finger, and Dr Grover, too, had been in an apparently happy, long-running union. But dramatic events can have lasting effects. To the chagrin of most of the mummies in Dulwich, Janice was lined up to be the second Mrs Grover, while her own first husband – and Dr

Grover's first wife – had melted away. Not together, as some Dulwich wags would have had it. But far enough and painlessly enough for the efficient machinery of Wyatt's to run smoothly on, as though things had never been different.

Janice had always had the most wonderfully warm smile, but Beth hoped she wasn't imagining a depth of contentment that was new. And, of course, some of the endless parade of family lawyers churned out by Wyatt's School were also benefitting from a new revenue stream.

'So shocking about the girl in hospital. Can you believe it was a College girl, of all the schools? They used to be so hard working and sensible, didn't they? What's *happened* to that school?' Janice frowned.

Beth, with all those Instagram pictures dancing before her, shrugged a little. She had much less faith in teenage innocence now than she'd enjoyed three days ago, but was the College School worse than any other?

'I'm just so relieved Wyatt's isn't co-ed,' Janice continued. 'We've come under a lot of pressure over the years, but honestly? Can you imagine it? What would we do with teenage girls? How do you even deal with them?'

'Oh, come on, Janice,' Beth felt she had to remonstrate. '*You* were a teenage girl, not all that long ago. It wasn't that bad. Was it?'

'You weren't there,' said Janice with a frank glance. 'Ok, I was out in the sticks in a tiny village in Hampshire, but we got up to whatever we could.'

Beth, remembering those off-licence trips again, nodded. 'I suppose teenagers will just push all the rules they can – boy or girl. The College lot are no different.'

'But trying to get served in pubs when you were 17, that's nothing now, is it? And buying a packet of Players, well, that seems like something out of a Beatrix Potter. Anyway, I'm just glad we don't have to pick up the pieces here with *girls*. Boys can be a nightmare, but in such a different way,' said Janice.

'Fights?' mused Beth.

'Yeah, that's part of it – the easy bit in a way, as long as

129

no-one gets hurt too badly. We've had broken bones in the past – *lot* of testosterone with teenage boys – but nothing like that under Dr Grover, of course,' said Janice with a smug little smile of proprietorial satisfaction. Beth found it touching that Janice still referred to him formally, even among close colleagues. 'No, it's stuff like Muck-Up Day that can still go wrong,' Janice mused.

Beth looked blank. Janice explained. 'It's after the exams, a way for the departing sixth form to let off steam – we basically give them free rein to decorate the school and have a bit of a party. You've probably seen crowds of boys wandering through the village in the morning, end of summer term?'

'Oh yes, I suppose so. I thought they were going on school trips…'

'I wish!' said Janice heavily. 'Unfortunately, it's all on the school premises. Every year we have to impose more rules to keep it under control. It's licence for all the clever, mischievous ones to try and outdo each other – and be more outrageous than the year before, of course. One year, they put the entire school up for sale on eBay. Another time, they let a herd of goats out into the playing fields; God knows where they got them. They ate everything bar the rugby posts, bit a bunch of Year 7 kids into the bargain. That was a huge sketch with the parents, insisted the school pay for a load of jabs. But last year? They only carried Dr Grover's car right out *onto the middle of the lawn.'*

There was no doubt that, in Janice's mind, defiling the Wyatt's lawn, a semi-circle of green velvet perfection in front of the school's imposing doors – and tampering with Dr Grover's wheels – were both equally heinous crimes. Beth couldn't help smiling. This year, the Headmaster's car would be much easier to move. He'd junked his heavy, respectable, sensible, and solidly tank-like Volvo with the first wife, and upgraded to a sporty little Porsche that even the Year 6s would have been able to shift.

'The meeting point has gone to the bad as well. They used to congregate beforehand in Dulwich Park, to have a bit of a feast – stuff they'd grabbed from home or bought specially, sweets, doughnuts, crisps, all the kids' party fare they never really grow out of. Now, it's basically a question of necking vodka until they can hardly stand. For some of them, the first thing they do when they reach the school is throw up. Honestly, the cleaning bill is becoming *astronomical.*' Janice wrinkled her small nose.

Beth nodded obligingly but felt a sneaking sympathy for the Wyatt's leavers. They were going out into a tough old world – grades had to be higher and higher now to get into the best unis, like a curious reverse limbo dance. And although they could look forward to the odd bender and a few good times, student suicide and drop-out rates were rocketing. Then, after three years of slog, they emerged to find a stagnant job market. Even with the current, probably brief, spike in divorce cases in Dulwich, there wasn't the demand for lawyers there'd been five years ago.

Let the poor kids let their well-coiffed hair down for once, she wanted to say. Once they'd left the hyper-efficient machine that was Wyatt's, life would probably never be as well organised again. But then, she wasn't responsible for ironing the dents out of the lawn or repairing goat-ravaged football nets.

'Ugh. Well, I'm not even going to think about that until nearer the end of term,' said Janice, shutting her laptop with a determined flap. 'Now, you came here to see me about something, and I've taken us off at a tangent. What can I do for you?' Janice smiled.

'It's just that, with all this stuff at the Gallery, you know, the girl who was found…'

Janice immediately looked serious. 'Awful. If there's anything I can do, or Wyatt's as a school… Our hearts go out to the parents.'

'It seems to be just the mum on her own – Jo, her name is. She's lovely. Oh Janice, if you could see that girl, poor Simone,' said Beth. She hadn't meant to say any of this, but just thinking of that small, pale child in the bed made her tear up yet again. She squeezed her eyes shut and shook her head

131

a little to banish the images. 'It's just that I found her, as you know...'

'You seem to make a habit of that,' said Janice wryly.

Beth sighed. 'Well, it's certainly one I'm really keen to break. But I didn't realise until earlier that Dr Grover is actually a trustee of the Gallery?'

'He is. He's super-busy, as you know, but he's too good to refuse something like that. And it's a tradition, of course. The original Gallery collection was once housed at Wyatt's. So, the Headmaster is always on the board, if he possibly can be.'

Beth, who hadn't known this quirk of Dulwich history, wasn't surprised, given how intertwined the Endowment schools were with the fabric of the place. There were plenty of parts of Wyatt's which would have made fine galleries in times gone by, when there were fewer pupils clogging the place up.

'Do you think he could talk to me and, well, really to the investigating officer? I'm sure there's a lot he could say that might help to get some background on the sort of events that are held at the Gallery. As it was after one of those evenings that it all, well, happened...'

'Oh yes, it must have been the hospice drinks,' said Janice. 'It was a good evening.'

Beth did a double-take and moved unconsciously to the edge of her seat. 'Wait! Don't tell me you were actually there?'

'Well, yes, Dr Grover always goes, and of course I was with him,' said Janice, a little primly – and a little defensively. With good reason. A few hundred years ago, in a village like Dulwich, Janice's only place after recent events would have been in the stocks, with a large scarlet 'A' for adultery pinned to her breast, or even daubed on her forehead if the elders were feeling really expansive. While now, nominally things had moved on, there would always be whispers about the way she got together with her swain that would dog their relationship. It would either bring them together against a cruel world or, if the weight of guilt got too

132

much for one or other to bear, would break them apart as surely as a hairline crack in the finest bone china.

Beth, who hadn't known the first Mrs Grover – or, indeed, the starter Mr Janice – was firmly on her friend's side, and wouldn't have questioned Janice's right to attend under any circumstances. And she was now positively blessing the change of fates which had led Janice to be present on the arm of a Trustee, on the right night, and at the scene of the crime. She brought her hands together and clasped them in front of her in excitement. With her position now on the edge of her chair, she looked as though she was praying.

'Ok, so no need to bother Dr Grover. *You* can tell me everything about that night. Don't leave anything out. Not one single thing,' she said.

Chapter Ten

Katie was sitting outside the Summerhouse café at one of the uncomfortable wooden benches, having negotiated the ungainly clamber necessary to get into position. The trouble was that the benches were firmly fixed to the large, round wooden tables. It was probably sensible that nothing was portable – people were so light-fingered these days, even in Dulwich – but the furniture seemed to have been designed for giants, not the café's usual clientele of mummies, nannies, au pairs and small children, who had to perform all kinds of gymnastics across the splinter-strewn expanses of wood to get into anything resembling comfortable positions. Add sunshades, which diligently covered only the central portion of the tables, leaving the customers roasting in direct sunlight, and it was a mystery why the place was so popular.

But it was already full, teeming with romping toddlers, marauding Chihuahuas and pugs looking for dropped crusts, and Katie had only secured her bench by dint of turning up twenty minutes early. She was now looking at her phone every few seconds to check the time, and the twenty minutes had seemed like forty, fully ten minutes ago. She'd bought two huge doorstep sandwiches, wrapped in cellophane, which she was eyeing hungrily. She knew well enough to give the coffee a wide berth here, and had instead bought two builders' teas in the café's thick white china mugs. She was trying her best not to swig down her own rapidly cooling brew too fast.

***

Beth trotted towards the café, shiny pony tail swinging,

fringe falling across her face so thickly that it was difficult to imagine how she could see in front of her. Feeling the beam of her friend's attention on her, she speeded up almost to a canter and puffed her way to the table.

'Sorry, Katie.' Beth clutched her side where a stitch was starting up in protest at the steeplechase she had just unexpectedly run, and began to scrabble into position on the huge bench. Opposite them, a couple of mummies with two very subdued pre-school children watched her every move, which of course made her feel doubly clumsy. When she was finally sitting in some semblance of a comfortable position, cursing her stumpy legs and the bench's designer with equal venom, Beth turned to face Katie, preparing to tell all about her meeting with Janice. But for once, her friend's usual placid calm had deserted her.

Katie was pink in the face and leant towards her urgently. 'I've got to tell you what Maria Luyten said to me this morning,' she hissed.

'Who?' said Beth, eyeing Katie, whose normally mirror-smooth hair was sticking up at the back and who was wearing, if Beth wasn't mistaken, old leggings. She normally never stepped out of the house in anything less than box-fresh Sweaty Betty ensembles, knowing that she was her own best yoga advert, moving lithely through Dulwich as though every step was a seamless sun salutation.

'You know Maria, the new mum in the class, mother of Matteo, who was round for a playdate when Ben stayed the night? Remember? She's the Italian doctor, the dad's Belgian,' Katie gabbled.

'Oh yes,' said Beth slowly, remembering cute little curly-haired Matteo, with saucer-sized limpid brown eyes and the faintest twang of an American accent from his international school. It was all coming back. 'Seemed like a nice boy,' she said, feeling that Katie was expecting a lot more from her, but not knowing what to give.

In truth, she knew nothing at all about the lad, only what Katie had already told her and, to be honest, she'd only been listening with half an ear. Ben hadn't mentioned him since the playdate, and therefore she didn't really need to register his existence, did she? Any friend of Ben's was, of course, welcomed with open arms to tiny little Casa Haldane – but she wasn't sure she had time for random children outside that charmed circle. She raised her eyebrows at Katie.

'He's a lovely boy. Well, I think he is. But the point is that Matteo's got a *sister*. Chiara. She's at the College School? Year 9?' Katie was doing that annoying thing of letting her intonation hike itself up at the end, making everything a question. Clearly, there was some large penny that was meant to drop with a thud, when everything would become clear, but for the life of her Beth couldn't... Oh, and then she could.

'Oh my God! You mean she's in the same year as Simone, the girl from the Gallery?'

'Not just the same year, Beth,' said Katie urgently, taking Beth's forearm and shaking it. 'She's in the same class. And she's had such an awful time with those bloody girls. You won't believe it.'

It was the second time that day that Beth had felt herself leaning forward into a mesmerising tale. In many ways, it was a parallel story to the one she'd just heard from Janice, but uniquely horrible in its way.

Janice, it turned out, had seen some of the waiting staff at the Hospice drinks picking on one of their own team – a slim girl who seemed out of kilter with the main gang. 'They just sniggered at her, you know, the way girls do. She dropped a glass and you should have heard them. One girl in particular was really making a meal of it, holding court. The other girl, she just went off on her own, I think she was upset, poor thing. I didn't see her again,' Janice had said. 'That wasn't the girl, was it?'

Beth hadn't been able to reassure Janice. She didn't know. But she could guess.

The story Katie told chimed eerily with Janice's, though it had played out over a period of weeks, rather than a single night.

'Maria didn't realise at first what was going on,' said

Katie. She was talking in a hushed voice, even though the mummies opposite had gone, shepherded by their children towards the playground. 'Chiara just thought she was just being really friendly.'

'*She*?' Beth bent even further forward towards Katie. If this went on, she'd be lying on the table. She made a conscious effort to straighten up a bit. It was ok for Katie, with her supreme bendability. Those who only went to stretch classes when the second blue moon met a month of Sundays couldn't hold positions like this for long.

'Sophia. Sophia Something-Jones. She's the boss-girl of the class. You know there's always one.'

'Jones-Creedy,' corrected Beth automatically. 'God, that name has been cropping up a lot.'

'I'm not surprised,' said Katie. 'She sounds like a piece of work. At first it was all nicey-nice, inviting Chiara to sit at the popular girls' table at lunch, then asking her round to her house – really welcoming and sweet, thought Maria.'

'That sounds kind. It can be awful joining a class in the middle of the year, really hard to find your place. And starting in Year 9!'

'Exactly. Everyone I know who has girls says that Years 8 and 9 are the years from hell. Massive amounts of mind games. Honestly, I wouldn't go back to being that age if you gave me gold bars.'

'Don't tell me you had any trouble then?' said Beth.

'Well, no… but I could see what was going on around me,' Katie said earnestly. Beth could imagine her, gliding like a young cygnet through the turbulent waters of adolescence. She herself, on the other hand…

'How about you?' Katie asked.

Beth sighed. Obviously, she had been a duckling then. She was still one now. 'Well. It wasn't easy, let's just put it that way.' Even with her closest friend, Beth had no desire to discuss the mortifications of puberty, which still smarted. 'I'm with you, I wouldn't go back for anything. But come on, what happened to Chiara?'

'You know, it was just small things. At first, Sophia made

137

a huge fuss of her, was really interested in hearing all about life in Kuwait, was really sympathetic about Chiara missing her friends there… Then all of a sudden, it was all about 'had she tried this great new diet?''

Beth's eyes grew round. 'You're kidding! That's a bit mean. Does she actually need to lose weight?'

'Absolutely not! I've met her, she's a perfectly normal size. She's not wafer thin, granted, but by no means does she need to worry. But it wasn't just that. They were all holding competitions to see who could lose the most every week, organised by Sophia – actual weigh-ins at her house, with prizes. And, get this, these so-called prizes would be dresses that Sophia said she couldn't wear any more because they were too enormous.'

Beth was conscious that her mouth was hanging open. She was stunned. 'But… this is like an invitation to develop anorexia… Do you think her parents know she's doing this? Or the parents of any of the other girls? Or the school?'

'They were all sworn to secrecy; it was a really big thing getting Chiara to make an oath of silence to the group… this huge ceremony… round at Sophia's house, of course. Her parents were nowhere to be seen, Chiara said, and the au pair seemed terrified of Sophia and the friends as well. They shut themselves away in her room, right at the top of the house away from her little brother, and then, well, it sounds ridiculous but they all cut their arms a bit with one of Sophia's dad's scalpels. They mingled their blood and swore on their lives they'd never breathe a word. It sounds like some weird cult thing, candles, chanting, the works. Maria said Chiara was virtually hysterical when she finally managed to make her crack and spill everything. She said Sophia would kill her, no-one would ever speak to her again, and she'd be out of the group for good.'

'Definitely for *good!* God, I can't believe girls sometimes. That's just plain evil. Sophia herself is really skinny, but it looks natural. I'm no expert, but she doesn't have that skin and bone, half-starved look, if you know what I mean. But what about the others?'

'Wait, do you know her?' Katie was surprised.

'I've just seen her Instagram. She's a bit of an Insta-star,' said Beth, rolling her eyes.

'I don't really know anything about the others in the group, and I only know Chiara via her mum. But Maria is in shock. They were so careful, finding great schools for both kids, all that effort to make sure her education wasn't disrupted too much with the move from Kuwait – and then the poor kid ends up in this virtual cabal, with this evil girl in the centre.'

'You know, I think they've actually been really, really lucky. Lucky that Chiara *told* her mum what was going on. I bet none of the others have said a word to their parents. They've been with Sophia since the start of school, I'm sure. They're all totally under her spell, and will just do what they're told. Like you said, there's always a Queen Bee in a class. This time, the 'B' stands for something really nasty.'

'Yes, Maria said that the only reason that Chiara did tell was because she'd sworn on her own life – Sophia hadn't made her swear on her family's lives. She said she wouldn't have been able to break that; she would have been too scared that something dreadful would happen to her mum and dad, or her little brother. She wasn't so bothered about herself, which is heart-breaking, too, in its own way. Don't ask me what she thought was going to happen if she broke her promise; her fears aren't rational. But they're still children, really, and this girl has obviously got them completely spooked. They think she's watching their every move. And maybe she is! In fact, she certainly is, while they're at school.'

Beth shook her head, horrified at the thought of poor Chiara, who'd just moved schools and countries, no doubt trying as hard as she could to fit in and make brand new friends, and going along with this evil rubbish as a result. But what about the other girls? There was much less reason for them to have put up with all this manipulation.

Katie cut into her thoughts. 'But I just don't understand. What's in it for this Sophia, anyway? Why does she want to

139

make other people's lives miserable?'

There was a pause while Beth thought about it, munching as she did so on the thick, spongy white bread of her egg mayonnaise sandwich. It was delicious. 'Maybe just because she can?' said Beth. 'Maybe it's being able to exert all that power. Think about it. No-one is as power*less* as a teenage girl. Their parents have all the control, have done for years and will do for years to come. In the meantime, the girls can see what the world's like – women still not being paid as much as men, stories in the papers all the time about rape and violence. It's not a very nice world we're sending them out into. I'm not saying it's conscious, but maybe she just likes to pull whatever strings she can, while she can.'

'You know what?' said Katie, picking up her now lukewarm mug of orange-brown builders' tea.

'What?' Beth smiled slightly.

'Thank God we had boys! We've got it easy.' Beth nodded fervently, and they clinked mugs.

All the time, Beth was thinking away. 'You know what, we've got to tell Harry all this.'

'Harry?' said Katie innocently, arching her brows.

'*You* know, Inspector York,' Beth rushed on, avoiding Katie's amused glance.

But Katie was suddenly serious. Teasing apart, there were a lot of ramifications to telling a police officer this strange tale, not least bringing more trouble down on the head of her new friend.

'I don't know, Beth. I mean, Maria didn't exactly tell me all this in secrecy, but I'm not sure she's going to want to get the police involved.'

'Ring her and ask,' said Beth urgently. 'Honestly. We can't let this go by. There's a girl in hospital who could die.'

'But that's nothing to do with Maria, and this Sophia girl. Is it?'

'Isn't it?' said Beth heavily. 'How much do you want to bet that she's involved? Everything that's happened seems to be coming down to that girl. She's in the same year as Simone Osborne, I know that much. Do you honestly think it would be at all surprising to find out that she's in the same class?'

Katie looked at Beth steadily, then got out her phone and dialled. 'Maria? Can you come and meet us? Yes, in Dulwich Park, the Summerhouse. Right now.'

***

Raf scratched lazily and opened one eye, bringing his phone up and squinting at it. Christ, only 12. That was, like, the crack of frigging dawn. Something must have woken him. He looked around the grungy room, the warm daylight filtering in unforgivingly on the tangle of belongings which constituted his wardrobe. 'Wardrobe? Floordrobe, more like,' he grinned lazily.

He looked around, waiting for an appreciative laugh, then remembered Sophia was back with her folks. Just as well, really. The state of the place showed she was no housekeeper, and she couldn't cook either. He didn't know why he kept her around, really. Except it amused him to have a bit of posh begging for it. They were always the wildest, when they went to the bad. Raf, with many years' experience now of rebellious teenage girls, scrolled through a long line of mental images of girls he'd known, seduced, and moved on from. Yep, the posh ones were the best – not least because they could afford to sub him a bit, buy the odd can and bit of blow, get the takeaways in, and maybe cough up for a phone or watch if they really *lerrrrved* him.

He scrabbled beneath the old, stained pillow and brought out a wad of notes which he'd extracted from Sophia's bag while she'd been on the loo. Still a couple of twenties left. Ah, he was sorted. No need to contact the girl after all. Not today, anyway. Let her sweat. It always made them keener. Reaching over onto the sturdy old box, which had once contained a microwave of doubtful provenance and now passed for a coffee table, he dug around in the aluminium mince pie case left over from Christmas that served as an ashtray. Among the butts, he selected a joint that had a

141

millimetre or two of smoking still left in it. Just to get him moving, so to speak.

Though, in fact, it had the opposite effect. When he'd got right down to the cardboard filter and was risking burnt fingers, he stubbed it out, turned over on his stomach, drew the greasy pillow over his head to block out the light, and fell instantly into a dreamless sleep. There was nothing on his conscience. There never was. So what, if that other little tart, the friend of Sophia's, was still in the hospital? Yes, he'd read about it, but it had nothing to do with him. He just sold the stuff. It was up to the users what they did with them, and the consequences were on their own heads. Teenagers, adults, whatever. It was all the same to him. He snored on, a slight smile playing across his handsome face. A couple of years ago, his cheekbones had been all hard planes and angles, sharp enough to break a young girl's heart. Now his flesh was like dough, just beginning to puff out of shape.

***

Beth didn't quite know what she'd been expecting, but she knew Maria wasn't it. The woman had beautiful expressive chestnut eyes, olive skin, and lustrous dark hair that flowed in a well-schooled wave around her shoulders – so far, so Italian. But she was also nervy, thin, and pent-up, like a whippet or a greyhound, not quite shivering in the sunshine outside the Summerhouse café where they sat nursing yet more thick white mugs, but certainly very tightly wound. For some reason, Beth's limited stock of Italian stereotypes went more for the bounteous, cheerful mamma type, ladling meatballs onto spaghetti, with a gaggle of small children clustered at her apron strings. This slightly frightening intellectual was more than she'd bargained for. Though, she realised, perfectly reasonable for a doctor.

'…And that's when I knew it was serious,' said Maria, her voice husky with emotion. 'Of course, I blame myself for everything. If I hadn't been so preoccupied with work… but you know how it is when you try to re-establish your

142

working life,' she said earnestly to Beth and Katie, neither of whom had the heart to admit it was something they hadn't quite done. Well, Beth had been making great strides recently, with her new Wyatt's posting – but she couldn't pretend there had been a great powerhouse of a career waiting to be resurrected. She hadn't had a full-time job since before Ben was born. That hadn't been the original idea, but with James's death, a lot had changed. To put it mildly.

She looked sympathetically at Katie, not sure really whether her friend saw her fledgling yoga business as the beginning of an empire, or a little hobby to keep her busy while Charlie was at school. Pre-children, Katie had been something in publishing, which was where she'd met Michael – then, as now, a big fish in the pond she had briefly graced. There were career choices there, all right, but not the sort Maria meant. Katie and Beth exchanged a small, private smile, and both nodded encouragingly at Maria.

'There's the long hours, sorting out the house, and the children. Matteo, he's still the baby of the family. His class has been lovely, really friendly,' she said, with a grateful look at Katie. Beth felt a bit guilty that she hadn't had the boy round yet. But she would, she would. 'He's been anxious, though. And even Theo... it's because of him we moved. The bank, you know. But though we've done all this for the sake of his job, it's not so easy for him either. Just coming in and taking control of his division the way he has done, it's been huge. He's needed my support, too.'

There was a pause as Maria's thin shoulders worked, and Beth realised to her horror that the woman was holding back sobs. She was all over the place. Beth put a hand tentatively out on the table – a feeble gesture, meant to offer support. Katie, meanwhile, quietly put an arm round Maria's shoulder.

'There just hasn't been enough of me to go round.' Maria's head was down now, and Beth strained to hear what she said.

'We understand, don't we, Beth? There's never time, you always worry that you can't do everything, help everyone...' said Katie consolingly.

143

'I really have it easy,' said Beth. 'There's only me and Ben to consider, and still most of the time I feel awful about something I haven't got round to doing. We all feel the same,'

'Yes, but my daughter, only in the country for a few weeks, caught up in this terrible, terrible business,' Maria wailed.

'Well, if it comes to that,' said Katie, practical to the last. 'It could be much worse, you know.'

They all thought for a moment of the young girl, lying somewhere near in a hospital bed, a tangle of electrical cables her only tie to the world.

'Tell us about your work,' said Beth, eager to distract the woman from all these woes, and not nearly as good as Katie at the touchy-feely stuff. If Maria was very into her career, maybe talking about it would calm her down.

Unfortunately, it seemed to have the reverse effect. Maria raised a tear-stained face for a moment.

'That's the trouble. I'm a psychiatrist,' she sobbed, and put her head right down on the table. Quite apart from the sanitary implications – small dogs and pigeons scavenged here constantly, thanks to the enormous crusts of the doorstop sandwiches, and Beth had never seen anyone from the café make even the merest pretence of wiping these surfaces – Maria was now drawing attention in a most un-Dulwichy way. Maybe she was more Italian than Beth had bargained for.

She exchanged a swift glance with an equally stricken-looking Katie and scrabbled off the bench. 'I'll just pop in and get us some refills,' she said, shamelessly abandoning Katie to do the mopping up, with only a quick beseeching glance at her friend.

Katie raised her eyebrows briefly. 'Make ours really strong, please,' she said.

Once clear of the table, Beth managed not to run into the café, but sauntered as though she didn't have a care in the world. She smiled at a couple of mothers she knew by sight who were, of course, agog at the shenanigans at their table.

Inwardly, she was wondering. Maria might be overcome at the moment, but her expert knowledge of the workings of the mind could prove very useful.

It was a point she had ample time to consider. Service, never lightning fast at the Summerhouse, was moving into its languorous after-lunch phase. As she queued up at the counter with a herd of patient mothers, rambunctious toddlers banging into her ankles, she scanned the many familiar notices taped to the café walls, without really paying attention.

When the Summerhouse had first opened with some fanfare, about ten years ago, these walls had been pristine. She wasn't quite sure when the first notice had appeared, possibly during the notorious drain blocking of the summer when Ben had been five. 'Customers are politely reminded NOT to flush wipes down the loos, the Park's drains cannot cope.' Fair enough, Beth had supposed. Unblocking a wipe-gunged sewer could not possibly rank as a pleasant job. But such a specific notice, not far from all the tempting cakes set out behind the glass display cases on the counter? Beth had thought it was a mistake.

That did not stop the author adding another work to the wall a week or so later, containing more capitals, more lurid details about sanitary pads and their effect on the place's pipes and, sadly, missing off a vital apostrophe. In Dulwich, that scarcely mattered – a teacher with a red pen had obviously been queuing for a coffee, and had done a quick correction almost the day it went up.

The next piece of A4 tacked up on the wall declared itself to be a 'polite notice' and threatened visitors with legal action for defacing café property. After that, it was open season. It reminded Beth of Dolores Umbridge's relentless stream of proclamations and prohibitions in *Harry Potter*. Notices went on top of notices, and much fun was had by all the frustrated writers, academics, and comedians of Dulwich in augmenting the words of the increasingly infuriated café owner: 'If patrons were to refrain from breathing, the proprietor would be most grateful' was a favourite, though the one in the style

145

of Samuel Pepys' diary had been fun too: 'To Dulwych, where I did kisse the proprietor in the quiet playe area, where toddleres must sterilyse their handes before touching the bookes provided...'

Things seemed to have settled down now, though there was always an outbreak of waggishness around April Fool's Day. This year's effort had threatened that any toddlers left unattended would be sold to the child-catcher. But as this had touched a raw nerve of parental paranoia, it had been ripped down by customers, not the proprietor, and a stiff editorial was promptly published in the local paper, the *Dulwich Diverter*.

By the time Beth had got to the head of the queue, paid for three strong teas, added milk from an uncooperative flask at the table by the door, and made it outside – two in one hand, one in the other – walking gingerly so as not to scald herself, she could see that Katie had got the situation under control. Maria was sitting up properly again, with a crumpled tissue in her hand, it was true, but most importantly with a smile pinned to her pretty face. Phew. As usual, she owed Katie big time and she signalled this with her eyes as she passed the cups over, managing not to splosh too much on the uneven surface. She hoisted herself over the bench again and settled down.

'Sorry, that took forever as usual. They're lovely, but...' So much of Dulwich life was in those three dots. No-one ever criticised the café *but*...

'Never mind that. Listen, Beth, Maria's got a lot to tell you,' said Katie brightly, nudging the Italian.

Maria gave a slightly wobbly smile. 'Normally, I never talk about my work – and still, of course, the specifics, well, you understand,' she said, spreading capable hands to encompass the Hippocratic oath, the feelings of her patients, and possibly even the inability of laypeople to get to grips with the intricacies of her specialism.

Beth smiled encouragingly. 'In this case, well...' Maria glanced towards Katie for reassurance or confirmation before continuing, Beth wasn't sure which. 'You see, I work at the

146

Wellesley.'

Beth instantly sat up a little straighter. The Wellesley Hospital was just down the road, in Camberwell. Not only did it specialise in psychiatric issues, but it was the largest mental health training institution in the UK. For Dulwich parents, however, it had come to have other connotations. The high-pressure lifestyle that most people enjoyed, with rewarding, lucrative jobs allowing them to pay the College and Wyatt's school fees, had a knock-on effect on their children. Some just didn't perform in the same way their parents had, for many reasons. And every term, a significant minority seemed to be shipped off to the Wellesley for treatment, whether for anxiety, anorexia, or other conditions. Exactly how many were affected, Beth had no idea. It wasn't something people talked about. If their own children were in treatment, people were reluctant to discuss it. And if it was their kids' friends or classmates, then a protective silence also descended.

Falling short of the Wellesley, there was a network of counsellors and therapists who saw children from the Endowment schools – and others. To Beth, who at the moment was in the very fortunate position of having a child who seemed to be coping with life, it looked as though these poor kids were the collateral damage in their parents' assault on the citadels of privilege. Though she was absolutely certain that no parent ever considered their children's mental equilibrium a price worth paying, often they were too deep in the game to change direction – opt for less competitive schools, a smaller range of GCSEs, less ambitious A levels and, ultimately, the consideration of a non-Russell Group university or even *something vocational.*

The awful thing was that private counselling didn't come cheap, while NHS waiting lists for childrens psychiatric services were months' long. 'Getting in' to the Wellesley was almost as difficult as making it to one of the Endowment schools – but it wasn't something that ever got boasted about at dinner parties.

Beth felt as though she'd been hearing about a cult for

years, and had occasionally caught glimpses of it, but always hoped that she would never have to be fully inducted into its mysteries. Now she had accidentally met one of the high priestesses, who knew everything.

Maria's eyes were still wide and beseeching as she started to talk.

'At first I wasn't sure what I was seeing. I specialise in anorexia, you see, so it was very interesting for me to come to the UK. We have an anorexia problem in Italy, but it is not such a big area, for sure. And even in Belgium, where we were living before Kuwait, the incidence was reasonably low. Then in Kuwait, well, the expat community is a very mobile population, and the problem becomes hard to pinpoint. So, you can see why I was excited to come to the UK and take up my work again,' said Maria earnestly.

Katie nodded along, but Beth thought of the many reasons to come and live in this green and pleasant land, this was possibly the saddest.

'So here I was, in this new area, with all this data and many, many patients queuing for treatment.'

This time, both women nodded.

'So, gradually things settle down. And remember, we still haven't been in the country long, just since halfway through this term. A matter of weeks, barely. And yet it becomes clear.'

Beth glanced over at Katie. She, too, was sitting forward on her chunky wooden bench. Maria couldn't possibly have a more attentive audience.

'You know there are sometimes little clusters of incidents in the mental health arena,' said Maria. Her English, always impressive, was even more assured when she was on medical ground. 'There may be, for instance, a spate of suicides of teenagers in the same area… you remember cases like this?'

Katie looked blank, but Beth spoke up. 'There were quite a few suicides at Bridge University recently, weren't there?'

'Yes, though it was thought they were coincidental, rather than definitely linked. They were all very sad cases – one boy had split with a girlfriend, another was struggling with depression. Three of the deaths happened in the first weeks of the new academic year, so we can assume that those are problems the students brought with them and found themselves unable to cope with for differing reasons. The students did not know each other. I am thinking more of what could almost be called an *outbreak* of suicide, for instance like the deaths at high schools in one specific area in California. In this case, the teenagers were highly privileged, the children of high-achieving Silicon Valley workers. It would seem that the first suicide breaks a taboo, and then that makes it easier for others to follow suit…'

'You're not saying that's going to happen *here*, are you?' Beth's glance took in the tranquil park scene – children and dogs playing under a sky which was not far off the duck-egg blue of a Fortnum & Mason carrier bag. Dulwich was an idyll at the centre of London's mad urban sprawl, a small oasis of perfection which existed mainly to show other, less fortunate areas how things should be done. She couldn't help her voice rising in anger and concern, though why she should be reacting so badly to even the suggestion such tragedies could happen here, she didn't know. It was frightening, that was all.

'It is natural to feel defensive about such an idea,' said Maria with an understanding smile which caused Beth's hackles to rise further. 'I'm not suggesting that there will be a suicide pact here; I pray very much not. What I am saying is that there is linked behaviour going on, yes, here, which in my view is dangerous, very dangerous. *Extremely* so.'

Despite the warmth of the sun massaging her back through her thin cardigan, Beth shivered. She had felt the presence of evil when she had looked down at poor Simone Osborne, lying so still in the Gallery. Now, Maria seemed to be confirming there was something malign in Dulwich. Again.

'Linked behaviour. What does that mean, exactly?' Katie asked, with a worried frown.

Maria clasped her hands together and looked down, briefly, seeming to gather herself. Maybe she was marshalling the right words in her second language – or maybe this was going to be difficult to put into words in any tongue. After a beat, she looked up, her brown eyes frank and steady as she gazed at the two women.

'I have not come across this before – and I don't like it. But we are seeing a pattern emerging. Have you heard of the Blue Whale challenge?'

Both women gazed at her blankly. Maria sighed. 'Well, it started, we think, in Russia. In a way, it is mischief, but it is worse; it is very manipulative. There are Facebook groups. You join. You watch other people being set challenges. You start to take part yourself. There are 50 challenges in 50 days. It starts easily, but then the challenges become more extreme. You have to dare yourself to watch a particular horror film right through to the end. You have to do other things which stretch your boundaries, make you uncomfortable, uneasy. Then you have to cut yourself. Then still more challenges. Ultimately, there is pressure – to take your own life.'

'You're not saying that could happen here?' Katie looked pale.

'You don't understand, Katie. I'm saying it *is* happening here. Already. It has spread throughout Europe. There have been no deaths reported in the UK yet, but already there is a toll on the mental health of the children participating. And yes, they are children.'

'But why would any kid from round here want to do something like that?' Beth shrugged.

'It's hard to understand, I agree. On paper, they have everything. But sometimes, things are too, you would say, *cosy*, no? Particularly for teenagers. They need to challenge themselves, this is how they grow. But not like this, I agree. We have to stop these things.'

'How on earth do we do that?' Katie said.

'Yes, it's not easy,' Maria shrugged. 'There are general guidelines if you think your child is on social media too much. There are signs to look out for. Are they withdrawn after using their phone or tablet? Are they secretive? But, seriously? All teenagers are like that. One of the first of the

online acronyms, like LOL, was PIR for *parent in room*. If we had to intervene with every withdrawn teenager who doesn't want to talk to their parents and doesn't want them hanging over their shoulder when they're online, then we would be working on every child in London.'

Beth, who'd fallen silent, piped up again. 'Where is the name from? Blue Whale... it doesn't sound sinister; I suppose they're too cunning to call it Death Cult or anything.'

'In fact, once you know the story, the name is frightening, too. The name refers to a real habit of some blue whales. They beach themselves on purpose and then, well, they die.'

The two women looked at each other, stunned. There was no getting inside a whale's head, but how terrifying that our largest mammals, so apparently serene, could secretly harbour a death wish. Beth immediately worried about the whale music she'd listened to on the rare occasions she'd paid a trip to the beauty parlour in the village – always as a result of getting a birthday voucher from Katie. Maybe their songs weren't quite as restful as people wanted to believe. The whales might well really be wailing.

'But there's no proof that this Blue Whale thing has taken hold here, is there?' Katie, as ever, was clinging to the good news.

'Not that we know of,' said Maria cautiously. 'But there is a group of girls being treated at the moment that is giving us much, much cause for concern. Of course, I cannot really say anything more to you about their names or their situations. There is confidentiality and so on to be respected. But I will say this. There is a leader among them, and *she* is the one doing the damage.'

Beth glanced at Maria, surprised by the vehemence of her tone. The woman's attractive face, framed by the dark-brown bell of shiny hair, was set and her mouth was a determined, angry line. Whoever this girl was, Beth wouldn't like to be in her shoes.

Harry York shoved his hand through his thick hair in exasperation. Usually having a lot of hair was a good thing – his mum, bless her, was always going on about what a lovely head of hair he had. But on a hot day, when he was getting nowhere fast, it was a pain. He felt as though his brain was in danger of melting. If it was this hot now, what was high summer going to be like? Well, with any luck he wouldn't have such a taxing crime to work on. Yeah, *right*, he said to himself. And maybe Catford would finally come up in the world, and he'd win the lottery. And find a parking space outside his flat.

His eyes flicked over to his shabby curtains. His mum had told him a million times to get some nice new ones down at John Lewis, but he never had the time. Or the will, frankly. What did it matter if they didn't quite close? It meant he could keep an eye on his car, parked all the way down the road, if he wanted to. Anyway, this way the curtains matched the rest of his flat – it was all horrible.

The furniture was vintage, all right, but vintage flat-pack, which seemed to age in dog years. It was all either wonky, chipped or broken, or on the verge of it. There was probably an Allen key somewhere that could tighten everything up, but he was buggered if he could find it. Only the bed was functional, and that was all he really needed. He came here to sleep. And read. Kind friends, mostly married, took pity on him now and then and fed him, otherwise it was work, work, work, drinks down the pub, time with his mum and stepdad down in Dartford, joshing on the phone with his younger sister and brother, and reading.

Reading was his passion. Thank God, the bookcases in this place were sturdy, even if nothing else was. They had to be, to withstand the weight of his serried ranks of paperbacks, green spine after green spine glowing in the light of his super-strong reading lamp. York was a devotee of the Golden Age of crime fiction, and had the complete works of the masters, from Margery Allingham to The Z Murders.

It wasn't just a colony of Penguins roosting on his shelves. Like the worst sort of petty criminal, York was indiscriminate about his thrills. Anyone who kept him guessing would do. And for him, the Golden Age definition was ever-expanding. PD James, CJ Sansom, Umberto Eco, he loved mysteries of all types and shades, from grey and grisly to deepest noir.

He'd always have a soft spot, though, for the country house crime, despite the fact that PC Plod was outwitted by a talented amateur every single time he set foot over an ancestral threshold. The way Lord Peter Wimsey or Albert Campion managed to pull off such feats of mental ingenuity, while their police handmaidens struggled to master joined-up thinking, made York smile. A less generous man might have found it infuriating, but York was an indulgent reader. It was escapism he was after, not the grind of evidence-sifting and witness-crunching that he knew all too well was truly at the heart of solving crime. Besides, who didn't love the pirouettes of inspiration and flashes of dazzling brilliance that amateur sleuths always managed?

Perhaps, he thought, struck by a moment of self-revelation, that was the reason that he didn't mind occasionally involving civilians in his own cases – to a very limited extent – and only if they could contribute materially to background information or other aspects of the situation that he couldn't cover to his liking himself.

He could certainly do with a large dash of inspiration in this case. Hopes had more or less faded for little Simone Osborne. With her life support due to be withdrawn tomorrow unless her mother – still praying for her girl – could convince the doctors to give her more time, there didn't seem to be any chance of getting further on in the case. He had no major suspect. No-one had seen the drug or drugs being administered or the girl being positioned. Yes, she had been on the list of waiting staff for the Hospice drinks, but so had a whole gaggle of College girls.

He was surprised their parents allowed them to perform such menial labour – and on a school night, too – but the whole of Dulwich was understandably soft about St Christopher's, as it was a wonderful place that did great things for terminal patients. There but for the grace, and so on. And the idea was that all the waitresses were free by 9.30pm, which was hardly the middle of the night. It was probably a good idea to get some of these privileged kids to see what it felt like, waiting on someone else for a change. York hadn't seen an awful lot of Dulwich, but he'd bet a fair sum that most of them had at least au pairs and nannies picking up after them, not to mention doting parents.

Somehow, though, this public-spirited evening had ended in tragedy. Simone had never left the place, and had ended up splayed on that tomb like a human sacrifice.

If she'd just been found huddled up in a corner, overdosed, then it could have been dismissed as a self-inflicted accident – albeit completely out of character, according to the girl's mother. But then, what mother *really* knew her teenage child? They hid so much. There would still be a question over where on earth she'd got such toxic drugs. But she was living in the middle of south London and, despite her success in getting a leg up in life via the College School, she came from a hardscrabble background. It was certainly not impossible that she knew how to come by the stuff.

As it was, the posing meant that someone else was involved. Plus, the medics' view was that, not long after taking the drugs, the girl would have been completely out of action, incapable of walking, let alone of arranging herself so artfully.

York gritted his teeth as he thought of her, still between life and death, but not for much longer. Either her organs would give out, the doctors said, or her mother would finally consent to pull the plug. Either way, her hours were numbered.

After having that thought, there was no way York could sleep, he thought crossly, even if his flat hadn't been a furnace. He crossed to the window, yanked it up still higher in the hope of catching a breeze wafting somewhere down from Catford High Street, snapped on his reading light, and attempted to get comfortable on the lumpy sofa. He picked up his copy of *The Crime at Black Dudley*, and sighed. A sinister English mansion, a group of armed hoorays, and some desperate foreign baddies who richly deserved killing. Those were the days.

He was half-expecting a bad news call from the hospital, so when his phone rang he answered reluctantly. In a second, he was on his feet. 'What? Another one? You're *kidding* me.'

***

Beth sat at her desk and tried to concentrate. It felt like the first time she'd even switched on her school computer for weeks, but only a handful of days had passed since that horrible morning in the Gallery. Still, there was no doubt that she was now seriously behind with her work. Not for the first time, she blessed the fact that she had so much autonomy. Though she'd been appointed as an assistant, events had conspired to ensure a pretty rapid promotion and she was pretty much her own boss, though technically line-managed by the school's Bursar. Since they'd had several run-ins just after she started, he was careful to leave her to her own devices as much as possible.

She had too much freedom, Beth realised. She really needed someone to crack the whip, tell her to get on with curating items for the permanent exhibition on slavery, not to mention catch up with a project on the centenary of WWI that her predecessor had signally failed to get off the ground. At this rate, the war anniversaries would be over and done before the school got round to celebrating the sacrifice and achievements of its old boys. And all that was without the day-to-day archive tasks of keeping the files up-to-date, and deciding which materials would be of use to her successors in years to come.

She liked to think of someone, in a century's time, sitting here or even somewhere grander, sifting through the artefacts she'd chosen to represent the school in this moment. It was quite a responsibility. Not for one second did she doubt that there would be a Wyatt's in a hundred years' time. While there was a Dulwich, there'd be a Wyatt's School.

It was easy enough to start thinking about the legacy she would be leaving, but Beth found it a lot harder to concentrate on the stuff piling up in front of her here and now. She listlessly leafed through her in-tray and replaced everything in exactly the same order – something she remembered doing only a couple of days ago with a similarly pointless outcome. Surely, she thought, it would be better if she gave the matter that was distracting her some proper thought? If she could only make some headway with the conundrum of the girl in the Gallery, then she could get it off her books, as it were, and settle back down to the archives with all the diligence and concentration that even the most demanding of taskmasters could wish for.

But achieving anything with the mysterious Gallery business was much easier said than done. Every time she thought about it, she got precisely nowhere.

Well, maybe it was time to go right back to basics. What did she know about what had happened, and what could she piece together from what York and others had told her?

Start right at the beginning, she thought. That would be the drinks reception in the Gallery, the night before her macabre discovery. There had been a gaggle of teenage girls there, acting as waitresses, handing round drinks and snacks to a group of invite-only guests. The guests, surely, were above suspicion? But no, it was probably a mistake to assume that. Just because they were the do-gooding type who'd turn out to an event in aid of St Christopher's Hospice did not mean that one among them didn't have murder – or mayhem – on their mind. York must have a list of everyone who'd been there that night, adult and teenager alike. Nothing can have jumped out at him from that. But maybe Beth should glance over the list? Something, or somebody, could ring a bell for her.

Beth stopped short for a moment. She was always implying to York that she knew absolutely everything that went on in Dulwich. This was partly because she did know an awful lot, and partly so that she'd become an indispensable part of his investigations, and he'd stop giving her that terribly dull lecture on why civilians had to keep their noses out and how he couldn't divulge anything interesting to her. She sighed. She hated that.

She looked up, seeing the caretaker wandering across the path with a hoe, bent on eradicating a weed that had the temerity to raise its head in the sanctified flowerbeds that were one of the eight wonders of Dulwich. It was the job of Jeff, the head gardener, to cosset the bejewelled beds flanked by the emerald perfection of the lawn. But it was understood that if anyone else saw an obvious weed while Jeff was held up elsewhere, then they could act independently. They had to be competent, however. Beth had heard tell of a junior secretary who'd ripped out a prized aruncula, and of course had not been at the school for much longer.

The caretaker straightened up, saw Beth through the window, and waved the weed victoriously at her. She mimed a round of applause and they exchanged a conspiratorial smile. It was well known that Jeff was a bit bats, but that didn't mean that they weren't all in the weed war together.

The truth was that Beth did understand the funny little ways of Dulwich, and if there was something outside her own ken, she knew someone who could fill in the blanks. She should stop feeling that she didn't quite merit her involvement in this whole business, and instead decide that York was jolly lucky to have her around. Belinda MacKenzie wouldn't have any doubts. But then, thought Beth, York would probably have some niggling doubts about Belinda MacKenzie. Well, he certainly *should*. But maybe, like most men, he wouldn't see much beyond the very attractively filled-out, regulation-issue, white Dulwich jeans.

Beth snorted a little and realised that all her daydreaming was just, for some reason, making her very cross. Where had she been before her mind had taken a day trip? Oh yes, the hospice drinks – somewhere among either the guests or the waiting staff was someone with evil on their mind. Beth suddenly wondered if Maria, by any chance, knew about the event. Had Maria been present as a guest? Had Chiara been working there, along with her classmates? That might be too much to ask, but she might well know who else, among her circle of new friends, had been involved. She picked up the phone to Katie.

'Hmm, I've no idea whether Chiara was there, but I know a way you can find out,' said Katie, an impish note in her voice.

Beth was instantly wary. 'Yeeees?'

'I said I'd have Matteo after school today, so that Maria's got a chance to have things out a bit with Chiara. But, well, Michael's got tickets for that Benedict Cumberbatch play at the Barbican... one of his colleagues has passed them on because his wife's got acute IBS.'

'Yuck!' said Beth.

'Well, yes, IBS would be TMI if it were true, but Michael says the guy is just desperate to do him a favour, wants him to reconsider dropping one of his midlist authors...'

'Wouldn't he just come out and say that, then?'

'Noooo, that would be *much* too transparent. Because they're dealing with all these novelists' fiendishly complicated plots all the time, these people can't do anything in a straightforward way. It would drive me crackers, but Michael loves it. Says half the time you can legitimately pretend you had no idea what people were up to because it's all so full of twists. Anyway, this guy is hoping Michael will remember he owes him, while Michael is doing his best to forget. Meanwhile, I get to watch Benedict Cumberbatch! Win-win, I say.'

'Lucky you. Yep, no problem, I'll pick up Charlie and Matteo this afternoon, then drop Charlie at school tomorrow morning. Will Matteo need to stay, do you think?' Beth didn't want to sound unwelcoming, but space was at a premium in Ben's bijou little room, and she wasn't sure if she could fit in another mattress. There was a small truckle bed under Ben's own that she wheeled out when Charlie stayed, and they were both used to that drill. Anything else would be like playing sardines.

'I shouldn't think so. It's not like Maria is going to be out as far as I know, but I'll ping over her number to you, so you can check. Thanks a mill for having Charlie. I know he'll have a ball.'

'Are you ok about no piano practice?' Beth said it seriously, but Katie could probably sense that there was the teensiest bit of leg-pulling going on. Luckily, she was so flexible from all that yoga that it didn't cause a twinge.

'I think he'll survive. Obviously, he'll miss it,' Katie joked back, though Beth was pretty sure she really believed Charlie actually did enjoy his piano.

Beth snorted gently. '*Course* he will. Ok, I'll talk to Maria. Enjoy Benedict.'

'Oh, I will.'

Two seconds later, there was the ping of a text arriving, and Beth scrolled down to look at the contact details for Maria Luyten.

Beth somehow made it through a whole day of work, though for her that meant finishing at the not-desperately-arduous hour of 3.30pm. Much of her time had been spent making a string of personal calls, which she convinced herself had been strictly necessary. First, she'd rung Maria to set up the revised playdate, and found out that Chiara had, indeed, been one of the drinks party waitresses. Keen for Chiara to make friends, Maria had suggested the group gather at her house before setting off to the Gallery. She had been working in her study all evening, but had assumed they'd all had fun as she'd heard plenty of shrieks of laughter.

Then Beth got through to her brother's answering machine. She hadn't seen or spoken to him in ages, and Ben missed his uncle, so she'd wanted to chat. Lastly, she'd called her mother, to give a brief and heavily edited outline of her doings in the week since they'd last had a proper catch-up, and find out where her brother was. Josh was still as free as a bird, even though he was now more than halfway through his third decade and had dodged, by her count, six or seven women trying to get him to settle down and acquire trappings of grown-up life, like children, a mortgage, and a lovely wife.

It turned out he was off in the Greek islands. For anyone else, this would be a holiday, but Beth knew Josh better. Her mother confirmed it. He was documenting the human tide of refugees from Syria washing up – or heartbreakingly attempting to do so – on the shores of tiny islands which had not seen so much tragedy and controversy since the heyday of the Gods.

By the time Beth slipped her handbag off the back of her chair, grabbed her light cotton cardi, locked the office door and sauntered out of the school – waving at the porter as she went – she was definitely feeling the virtuous fatigue of the worker who's done a good day in the salt mines.

As soon as she stepped outside and saw the first of many signposts pointing in the direction of the Gallery, recent events flooded back, and she wondered for the millionth time how that poor girl, Simone, was getting on. One more call to be made, she decided, liberating her phone from the tangled recesses of her bag and pressing the number for York. This time it wasn't exactly personal, though it wasn't business either. Nor could she call it a hobby. An obsession, maybe? She was saved from thinking too deeply about the ramifications of it all when the connection clicked, and she heard York's terse 'yes?'

'Just wondering where we, erm, *you*, are on everything? Any news from the hospital?'

From the sound of heavy plodding and the traffic noise, she could tell that York was marching along meaner streets than those in leafy Dulwich. To her, it sounded like the dull roar of one of the snaggier bits of the dreaded South Circular, but it could have been downtown Peckham or even Catford.

She thanked her lucky stars she was strolling through the village, which was looking particularly pretty today in the still-warm sun. Cotton wool balls of cloud bobbed in skies like those in the Gallery's Aelbert Cuyp landscapes, and the shops along the high street were putting their best foot forward for the approaching summer. The pricey boutique was already showcasing gauzy wisps of holiday outfits that would soon make the bankers, hunched over their terminals in the City, blench when they received their monthly credit card statements.

Beth strained her ears to hear York's mumbles, but it was hard against the sirens, muffled shouts, and the constant drone of cars. '…not good. And nor is the other.'

'Other? Other what?' said Beth, knowing she was doing that annoying thing of shouting into the phone, disturbing the mothers who were drifting into position to pick up their offspring from the various schools. She stopped dead, sticking her other hand over one ear and craning into the phone, hoping it would make a difference to the reception if she really concentrated. '…mother is devastated, of course.'

'Mother? Which mother? *Simone's* mother?' Beth was desperate to hear now. Had the final hour come for the Osbornes? She hoped and prayed not.

'the same drugs… two of them…' Then, with a triumphant crackle, south London's killer combination of rubbish phone reception and constant heavy traffic overwhelmed Beth's ancient handset and the connection cut out.

Beth stood stock still. Two of them? Did that mean… another victim? Though she knew she should be at the school gates already, and she really didn't want to be late to pick up three boys – it was bad enough when she kept poor Ben waiting – Beth still stabbed the redial button. She had to know. But, after a few seconds when she hoped against hope the connection would take, the phone went to voicemail. Either York couldn't talk – or he knew he'd already said too much.

She said a bad word under her breath, causing a nearby mummy of a toddler to shy away skittishly lest her child's ears be sullied, then stuffed her phone crossly into her bag and sprinted for the Village Primary. She'd just have to ring him back later, when she got a quiet moment. As she entered the school, and saw her three charges engaged in an exuberant, high-speed tag battle, she wondered when, exactly, that was going to be.

161

Chapter Eleven

It was many hours later, and not until Maria had come by to pick up Matteo, that Beth finally got a second to herself. Instead of immediately turning to her phone, she switched on the kettle, threw a peppermint teabag into a mug, and then sat, gazing into space, while the brew cooled in front of her. She really wanted to get up and swap it for a large glass of red, but she didn't have the energy.

She was going to have a hell of a job reinstating the party line on rules about midweek playdates next time Ben asked. But he had been exhausted by having not one but two chums over for the evening, and had thankfully seen himself and Charlie off to bed for once with hardly any prompting from her. She couldn't hear a peep out of them, which suggested they'd tumbled headlong into sleep – in itself pretty unprecedented, but it had been an odd evening. She'd look in on them when she got her own thoughts in order. Though that might be a while.

Beth had long mastered the art of being present in body if not in spirit when Ben and Charlie played together. It was partly that their games held very little interest for an adult woman, and partly that – much though she adored her son – she did cherish time to herself, which was in very short supply when you were a single parent. This evening, she had tried to zone out as usual and leave them in their highly complex imaginary world of knights, defenders, battles, whatever was the favourite of the moment. But she had soon been brought up short, much though she wanted to disappear into prolonged contemplation of the mess currently besetting Dulwich. For something was off-kilter tonight.

At first, she had just thought it was the dreaded number.

Two was company, three was none, went the adage; and so it had proved all evening long. But was it the fact that there was another boy in the mix – or was it the boy himself?

As she was called upon, time after time, to sort squabbles and right wrongs, Beth decided this was one of the most tiring evenings she'd had for ages. Worse even than when Belinda MacKenzie had unaccountably invited her to dinner, only for Beth to discover that she was a very last ditch blind date for a racist banker chum of Belinda's husband, who'd just got to the other side of an all-guns-blazing divorce. Beth would have thought it was kind of Belinda, who was the sort of woman who thought it was preferable to be married to anyone – no matter how bigoted – than be a single mum. But statuesque blonde Belinda had made so many jokes, all evening long, about how Beth was the *only* singleton in the Village, that she managed to make her seem like a plague carrier instead of a widow, and scuppered any chance she might have had with the awful man, if Beth had actually cared.

And now here she was in a situation that was almost as exhausting. Every time she left the room, after playing UN peacekeeper to a knot of fighting boys, the scuffles broke out again. She decided there was nothing for it but to plonk herself down and make up the other pair, so that there were four of them playing each game. It was no better. Somehow, whatever was going on, and no matter how closely she supervised, it always went awry. It was astonishing. Ben and Charlie had spent so many happy hours here, blowing each other to smithereens on screen while co-existing perfectly peacefully in the here and now. But tonight, everyone was riled.

It would be tempting to put it down to Matteo – after all, he was the new element in the mix. But Beth honestly couldn't identify him as the lone perpetrator. Rather, it was as though his very presence had mixed up the elements of a previously harmonious relationship and rendered it, well, not exactly toxic, but certainly taxing. Beth studied him carefully, the corkscrew dark curls massing round his little pixie face,

163

his large eyes usually mostly hidden behind the curly hair. Finally, after almost an hour of close scrutiny, Beth caught the ghost of a smile flitting across his face as Ben took one of the sofa cushions and thumped Charlie with it. Hard.

'Right, that's it. It's going to be spelling practice round the table now,' said Beth in her sternest voice. There was a chorus of 'awwwws' from the boys, but they were soon settled round the kitchen table with sheets of A4 and sullen expressions, while Beth got on with the not insubstantial clean-up operation demanded by the aftermath of spaghetti Bolognese for four. That was where they still were, kicking each other surreptitiously under the table every now and then, when Maria finally rang the doorbell.

Beth almost ran to throw the door open to her deliverance, wreathed in smiles. Maria, who had thought her quiet compared to Katie's perpetually sunny glow, was taken aback at the warmth of her welcome.

'Come in, come in, the boys are just finishing up. I'll just help Matteo pack his schoolbag,' said Beth, shoving Matteo's stuff away into his still-pristine bag, evidence that he was very much the new boy. As she put in his pencil case, she felt something rubbery at the bottom of the bag. She pulled out a stethoscope. Not a toy; a real one, if looking well-used. How odd. But then she remembered Katie saying Matteo had got the boys playing doctors the other night. Obviously, a bit of thing with him.

Beth felt a twinge of guilt. Maybe she should have encouraged that this evening. Or maybe she just hadn't been welcoming enough? Maybe that's why the boys hadn't been playing nicely.

At that moment, Charlie kicked out under the table and caught Ben on the ankle, and he wailed in distress. No. This kind of malarkey had just never happened before between them. She didn't want to point the finger of blame too quickly – but she was not going to be sorry to say goodbye to this kid.

To her surprise, Maria trilled with laughter as she heard the commotion between the boys. 'Ah, boys! Always fun and

164

games! I can tell Matteo has really enjoyed tonight. I want to thank you so much. It has not been easy for him, the move. And with his sister so upset…' Maria made a little moue of distress. Beth hoped she wasn't going to get emotional again.

Although Maria spoke in a low voice, it was clear to Beth that Matteo was following every word. She wasn't sure she'd have laid it on with such a trowel if Ben had been in the newbie position. Nothing like a lot of emphasis on the negatives to make a child feel like an interesting victim. But then again, Maria was a trained doctor, a psychiatrist. She must know what she was doing.

Maybe Beth herself was too repressed? Was she bringing up a withdrawn child? She looked anxiously at Ben, who was at that moment laughing uproariously at something Charlie had said, their usual bonhomie restored. Well, he didn't look too damaged to her. She shot a look back at Matteo, and saw a rather hunted look on his face, as he watched the other two boys. He was a complicated one, and no mistake.

Normally, she would have invited Maria to stay for a glass of wine, made a bit of an effort to get to know her. But the evening had been frankly exhausting, and the grating of nerves and relationships only seemed to be dissipating now that Matteo was on the point of leaving. Beth could do with a large glass of red, all right, but she'd rather have it alone. She shut the front door on the pair of them with a feeling of unalloyed relief.

Beth wondered if Katie had had a similar experience with Matteo. He'd been round a few times to play with Charlie. But Katie was all the things that Beth wasn't feeling tonight – forgiving, open-hearted, generous-spirited.

Beth was making herself sound like a monster, but there was no escaping the fact that she was more guarded. She blamed it on the shock of James's death, still reverberating down the years. She'd been as open and loving as they came, then fate had blundered in and taken away her future. And Ben's. And, while she'd never tell him that he was a victim of that day all those years ago, when his daddy had suddenly and unaccountably died, it was nevertheless the truth. Neither of them had been left unchanged by that disastrous quirk of fate. Beth knew, in a way that most didn't, how easily and irrevocably life could be turned upside down. She supposed some people reacted by doing all that seizing-the-day stuff, and lived life in the moment. She had built a fortress around her boy, and her heart. It had worked for her.

Realising the tea in front of her had gone stone cold while she'd been mulling over the odd evening, she stood up and trudged the little staircase to her son's room. He was spark out on his bed, his feet poking out from under the navy blue cover emblazoned with stars. Charlie was on the little truckle bed, right next to his friend, but for some reason with his feet on the pillow and his head round the other end, his duvet crumpled on the floor. Beth shook her head and covered him up. She was pretty sure neither of them had brushed their teeth. Damn, another few bad mother-points added to her tally. She'd been too deep in her reverie. She should at least have yelled up the stairs to them. Katie, she was sure, would have hovered over them until every last molar was gleaming. Oh well, she wouldn't tell if they didn't. She couldn't reach Ben without disturbing Charlie, but she blew both sleeping boys a kiss. At least Ben's duvet was tucked in round his shoulders, the way he liked, even if his tootsies were open to the elements.

She started picking up a few of the bits of Lego and the books that had been strewn around during all the horseplay this evening, then she gave up and just kicked a path clear to save them tripping up, in case either boy needed the loo in the night. She wouldn't put Ben's nightlight on. He still liked its reassuring glow, but he had said the other day it was a bit babyish. She didn't want him to be mortified in case Charlie was already big and brave enough to do without these days.

Once she'd flipped off the main light on the landing, she lingered for a moment, listening to two sets of untroubled breathing, allowing her own breath to slow as well. That made her realise how fast and shallow it had been up to now – a result, she supposed, of the stressful evening. Katie, with all her yoga skill, would have diagnosed an unquiet mind from that; and she would have been quite right.

Returning to the kitchen, Beth chucked away the unappetising tea, which now had an oily film on its surface, and got a glass out of the cupboard. She sloshed in a goodly dose of red. It was nothing special – the remnants of one of those Marks and Spencer 'dine in for two' offers that she sometimes picked up for their supper if she felt lazy. She felt she definitely deserved it tonight.

The house phone trilled. Surely it was too late for the double-glazing salesmen, PPI merchants, and other annoying junk callers? The only other person who used her landline was her mother, and Beth had spoken to her yesterday. She picked up gingerly.

'Beth! It's Katie. Just got back. I tried your mobile, but it went to voice. How are the boys?'

By boys, Katie, of course, chiefly meant Charlie. Beth happily gave his doting mother a full run-down of everything he'd eaten, confirmed he was sleeping peacefully, and glided past the tooth-brushing part. 'But listen, Katie, you've had Matteo to play before. How did that go? Did they... get on?'

There was silence for a beat. 'What happened?' said Katie.

'Don't get alarmed, nothing bad. It was just... so much less easy than it usually is. You know how Charlie and Ben are. They're in their own little world, they just get on with it... Tonight, well, it wasn't like that.'

Another pause. 'Katie?'

'I'm here. Just thinking. I'm not sure. I put it down to them not knowing each other so well... but there's sometimes more... *friction?* I don't know how to describe it exactly,' said Katie.

'It could just be that they're getting each other's measure,' said Beth, playing devil's advocate.

'Yes... But Matteo's been over three times now and, well... Maybe it's just that he's a complicated little chap.'

'"Complicated". Funny, that's exactly the word that came to my mind,' said Beth, taking a quick swig of wine. 'Well, I hope Maria's had a chance to talk things through with her

167

daughter, at least.'

'We can find out tomorrow. I said I'd meet her for a coffee after drop-off. Well, you're doing the drop-off, but we can all have the coffee,' Katie laughed.

'I'll have to make it a quick one. I've still got mountains of work to catch up on,' said Beth, with a guilty flashback to her bulging in-tray.

'No problem. See you tomorrow then, and thanks again for having Charlie.'

'That reminds me – how was Benedict Cumberbatch?'

'Mmm, dreamy. I'm not sure how he does it, with that long face like an otter, but he's gorgeous despite being so… ottery.'

'Ottery? Is that a word?'

'It's not only a word, it's a whole meme. Google otters and Benedict.'

Half an hour later, after double-locking the front and back doors, Beth drifted off to bed, still giggling to herself at the deluge of images of the distinguished actor alongside mugshots of otters, looking incontrovertibly alike. She forgot to check her phone. In the depths of her bag, it jolted into life. The screen flashed urgently, but the ringer was still off.

***

York, back in his bedsit, with his copy of *The Crime at Black Dudley* spine-down on his sofa, flicked the phone off in irritation. So much for amateurs. Beth might pretend she wanted in on the investigation, but where was she when it mattered? He needed to discuss the case. Every Sherlock needed his Watson. Granted, Beth – knowing her – probably saw herself as a Harriet Vane in her own right, and not some subordinate sounding-board to his infallible detective genius. But she was falling at the first hurdle as a detective sidekick. No matter how pivotal or otherwise their role in bringing things to a neat conclusion, they had to be *available*.

He sighed, and shifted to try and get more comfortable. On his next days off, he'd definitely get another sofa. But even the thought of what was involved in replacing this lumpy monstrosity overwhelmed him. The trip to Ikea, or the pig-in-a-poke purchase over the internet, all involved time and decision-making skills that he'd rather devote to something – anything – else. Luckily, he wouldn't have a day off any time soon, so there was no need to worry overmuch. Anyway, by slinging his long legs up onto the sofa and adopting a semi-reclining position, he was now avoiding the most spiteful of the springs.

In the meantime, he should probably cultivate one of the DCs at work, get a proper partnership going on a more professional level. Another copper always picked up the phone whatever the time of night, single mother coping alone with a young boy and a job or not. York frowned. He hoped she was ok. She was usually good about getting back to him. It wasn't that he really needed her help. In fact, she was going to get quite a shock when she played her messages in the morning. He almost wished, now, that he hadn't called her at all.

***

Beth made the mistake of starting to replay her messages as she was waiting at the school gates for Katie. There hadn't been a moment earlier, though she'd been startled when she checked through her bag to make sure the phone was actually there, and saw the two missed calls from York. She kicked herself, belatedly remembering she'd meant to ring him back last night. The one from Katie she knew she needn't worry about; they'd already caught up. From that point on, she'd been dying to replay York's messages, but the usual breakfast chaos was doubled this morning by having Charlie with them. Both boys always woke up full to bursting with beans, and this bright sunny day was no exception. Getting them to sit down long enough to shovel some Weetabix into them was a major feat.

Luckily, both were now having school lunches, so she no longer had to face the ghastly job of stuffing two lunchboxes

169

with delicacies that squared the circle of appealing to small boys yet ticking all the no-nuts, icing-free, gluten-avoidant guidelines with which the school attempted to protect the increasing number of pupils with allergies and intolerances. Even if your own offspring could eat anything, woe betide them bringing a peanut onto the premises and causing someone else's child to go into anaphylactic shock.

She just popped a couple of apples into each schoolbag for snack time, and filled up their water bottles. She wondered if Charlie really ate his snack time fruit. She was used to emptying out the equivalent of a greengrocer's shelf of bruised and battered offerings from Ben's bag every week. Occasionally, she made a crumble with the results, but usually they were beyond salvaging. She couldn't abandon tucking the apples into his bag, though. It was an act of faith. One day he'd be hungry enough at break time to remember. Probably. The best yet had been when they'd had to bring in an avocado each for a life drawing project. Three months later, she had discovered brown puree zipped away in a little-used pocket – and Ben had had a lovely new bag the next day.

By the time they got to the school gates, Beth was thanking her lucky stars that Ben was an only child. The boys had had a splendid time, laughing uproariously over arcane in-jokes, seeing who could walk backwards for longest without banging into something (Charlie), and generally messing about in infuriating small-boy ways. The walk, which usually took a few carefree minutes, seemed to stretch like chewing gum as Beth tried to corral the boys away from innocent passers-by and keep the noise down to under ten billion decibels. It was pointless even trying to hear a word of the voicemail messages.

As soon as the boys had been let loose in the playground, Beth had a pang of regret for her grumpy attitude. They were just full of the joys of spring – well, early summer now, with the lilacs starting to come out – and she shouldn't be so churlish. Just then, Ben looked over for a second and she gave him a beaming smile, which he just about had time to return before bombing over to join another game. She sighed, happiness restored, and pressed play on her phone messages.

No sooner had she heard York rasping out a few words than her face fell again. Funnily enough, the slight hint of an Irish brogue was more apparent than usual in the clipped, harassed tones. But the message he had to pass on was grim.

Simone Osborne was dead.

And Lulu Cox, another girl from Dulwich, was in Intensive Care.

Chapter Twelve

Raf was deep in a dreamless sleep, a surprisingly innocent smile on his boyish face, when the annoying thumping sounds from outside finally penetrated his consciousness. Sounded like someone was going to kick the door in. For a moment, he paused. Better to ignore it, maybe? Quickly, he rattled through faces in his mind's eye, wondering who he'd pissed off recently and how violent they might be as a result. Nah. Came back empty. Sure, not everyone was his best mate, but he didn't owe any money – thanks to Sophia having dropped her bank card down the sofa. He'd been searching for coins when he'd found it. It had been like Christmas Day. She'd given him her PIN code a while back, though she'd resisted at first. He'd had to give her the big eyes, the speech about trust. Silly bint, she actually fell for it. No way he'd ever give her any of his PIN numbers; that went without saying. Not that he usually had any money to protect, but still. It was the principle.

He shambled to his feet and went to the door, where the thumps continued, but more sporadically. Whoever was out there was tiring.

'Yeah, wassup?'

'Raf! You *are* there! Let me in,' Sophia's cut-glass tones seemed to cut through the fug in Raf's brain. He did a quick scan of the room for signs of other girls – he could do without a slanging match this early in the morning – and then reluctantly unbolted the door.

'Babe, wassup?' he said feebly, expecting female diatribe number one, 'where have you been?', followed swiftly by 'why haven't you called?' The where-have-you-been bit was easy, he'd been here, hadn't he? Just partying. Well, what

172

could she expect? He kept telling her to cut school and, if she wouldn't, there were plenty of girls who would. And the calling part, well, she could have called him, couldn't she? In fact, she probably had, he couldn't remember. But he didn't have much credit on his phone and he wasn't going to waste it listening to her whining voicemails. So, it was her fault, really. He braced himself, as best he could, and glared at her.

Instead of letting fly with the accusations, Sophia threw herself into his arms and burst into noisy sobs. If anything, this was much worse.

He tried turning the hug into a clinch, making hay while the sun shone, but she pulled away. Not like her. She was usually up for it. Now she'd found a tissue and was honking noisily into it. Raf turned away in distaste, finding the display seriously at odds with his Victorian notions of ladylike behaviour. There were no reciprocal standards for men, it went without saying. He idly scratched his belly, which remained temptingly taut despite his five-a-day Margherita diet, then moved on to root in his crotch for a loving moment. Then, stumped, he subsided back onto the sofa, pushing a heap of clothes out of the way to make room for the waif-like Sophia.

Instead of obediently taking her place next to him, Sophia darted him devil eyes and started to pace up and down, twisting the sodden tissue as she went. There was not far to go in the bedsit without coming up against a wall, a pile of clothes, a pizza box, or the door. So, she stopped, and stood in front of him.

Raf, who'd gratefully zoned out during the pacing and reached for his phone, felt her scrutiny but tried to carry on for as long as possible without acknowledging it. Her mood was clearly not good, and he didn't want any of it. Eventually, he made the mistake of flicking a glance upwards. She stood there, shivering with some feeling or other, and looking down on him with an expression he didn't know and definitely didn't like. She was reminding him of one of those bug-eyed dogs that celebrity bints dragged around with them in bags. Chipolata, was it? Nah, that didn't

173

sound right, but he couldn't be bothered to think further on it.

'Wassup, then, babe?' he drawled again, already bored, not bothering to meet her eyes.

'You know what it is. One of my friends is dead, and another's in the hospital,' she shrieked, and as usual her perfect enunciation, even at this high pitch, *really* irritated him. All those consonants jabbing at him, brittle little knives, while her vowels pounded him round the head.

'You know me, I don't know nuffin' about any of that, babe,' he said, with the megawatt smile that usually had her knickers off. Today, all he was getting was a mean red glare. It was getting him down. For real.

'If you think I'm gonna ask again, why you think it's my problem, you don't know much,' he said, mulish now and hauling himself to his feet. 'I got someplace I got to be,' he said, turning over a pile of clothes in a desultory attempt to find the cleanest T shirt. 'Hey, didn't you bring no washing for me?'

He dimly remembered her stuffing some of his kit into a bag, bustling away with it. That was when she was in wifey mode. Despite all the evidence pointing to the fact that that phase of their relationship had passed, he couldn't suppress a puppyish hope that she would somehow produce a neatly-laundered and ironed pile of clothes.

'You have *got* to be kidding me,' she said, all knives again.

'Whatever, babes. Like I said, I'm off out. You stay here if you like,' he said magnanimously, gesturing round at the ruined furniture, dirty dishes, and telly that no longer worked now the Netflix free trial period had expired. He pulled on some tracky bottoms and the least malodorous T shirt.

'You're not going anywhere until we've talked,' she said, ominously, her fists clenched, her little jaw set, and those once-beguiling eyes set to mean little slits.

Now it was Raf's turn to pace, but when he got as far as the door, he triumphantly flung it open, muttered, 'Yeah, fuck that, man,' over his shoulder, and disappeared down the ratty corridor at – for him – a spanking pace. The further he got from his own front door, the more fluid and graceful his lope became.

He'd had it with Soph, she was more trouble than she was worth. It was a shame, he thought resentfully, with all the hard work he'd put in. Still, best to quit while he was ahead, especially with two of her friends OD'ing.

He tossed a greasy old chip packet from his pocket on the street, and kicked at it ineffectually as he strolled by. Yeah, now he came to think of it, he was finished with this whole area. Time to move on.

Sophia, deflated and defeated now, subsided onto the sofa with tears streaming down her face – and ice in her heart. Her hands, with their stubby, freshly-bitten nails, came up to cover a face that was turning red and blotchy with crying. This was one pose she wouldn't be Instagramming.

***

Leanne sat at her desk and admired the gold swirls on her nail extensions, their blunt tips making them a tiny bit more practical, yet still probably the least helpful accoutrement a secretary could have. Filing, typing, even picking up the phone, were activities fraught with danger, as far as Leanne was concerned. Managing to avoid them, while not giving the gimlet-eyed Miss Douglas or any of her posse of teachers a single cause for complaint, made Leanne's job ten times harder than it would otherwise have been. But oh, she loved her nails. The morning sunlight glinted off one of the inset rhinestones in this week's gorgeous pattern – a symphony of golden filigree that rivalled anything a rococo master could have devised.

Angela Douglas, emerging from her office that moment and seeing the full ten nails held up to the sun in glory, was forcibly reminded of the complexity and beauty of the ironwork of Wyatt's school gates.

Normally, she was tolerant of Leanne's nail fetish. She'd had secretaries in the past with complicated love lives, some with pets and some, God forbid, with children who got ill and

175

needed collecting at the most inconvenient moments. Leanne's nails, though a nuisance, were definitely less bothersome than most alternatives. But today's pattern was unfortunate. She was bitterly aware that the College School's bog-standard frontage bore no comparison to either Leanne's nails or Wyatt's glorious entrance and, though she had more pressing troubles aplenty, the corners of her mouth tugged down as she beheld the fiesta of gold before her.

'Leanne, *if* you have a moment, could you find Miss Troughton for me?' said Miss Douglas, in tones which could have started the nuclear winter unaided.

But Leanne was no amateur. She immediately moved her hands as if to frame the view. 'Just thinking about them blinds we got on order, Miss D. Quote still hasn't come in.'

Miss Douglas, not fooled for a millisecond but appreciating the girl's effort, sniffed, said nothing, and clicked her door shut again. Leanne sighed and levered herself up from a chair so ergonomically padded that it resembled a womb. If it had been any other teacher Miss D had wanted, she would just have rung through to the staffroom and put the wind up them. But if it was Miss Troughton, then Leanne had to personally hunt her down and bring her back here. It usually meant a crisis, and Leanne knew full well that something was up. Everyone in the school had been walking on eggshells since the news came in about poor Simone Osborne being in the hospital.

Leanne had been astonished. She knew all the worst offenders in the school – her position, right outside the Headmistress's door, meant she saw them troop in, cocky as you like, and saw them slink out, chunks torn off them and put right back down in their places. Simone had not had a whisper of trouble in her short career at the school. She remembered the discussions the Headmistress, the Bursar, and the old Trout had had about taking her on in the first place. There'd been other candidates, but they'd all wanted to take a chance on the bright kid with the mother who'd clearly worked all hours to keep her two decently shod and out of trouble.

She was a nice sort of girl when she came – smiley, cheerful, grateful, but trying not to show it too much – and the full bursary meant she got everything the others did, the works. No-one knew the difference. Except, in a school like this, stuffed with smarty-pants girls, everyone knew everything. Simone may have looked the same as the rest, but there was not one girl in the school who didn't know she was this year's charity case.

Leanne remembered with a guilty pang that she'd passed her in the corridor last week. Some of the girls didn't trouble to give her the time of day. Who was she kidding? Most of them. But Simone had always smiled and said hello. But that day, you could tell she was a million miles away. And that nice new uniform? Hanging off her.

Leanne had wondered, then. Had the girl got in with the pro-anas? There was always a bunch of them in the school. No getting away from it, these days, with girls. Leanne thought it was ridiculous. She was happy in her own skin, she thought, her thighs rubbing comfortably together as she walked the endless corridors to fetch Troughton. But there was something about these posh girls. They all lost it, round about the same time. Year 8. They'd start to go feral. Things usually escalated in Year 9, before settling just as the work piled on for GCSEs.

Hormones were terrible things; Leanne knew only too well. She tended to pick a little too much at the carbs at her time of the month. Well, at most times of the month, really. But these girls, getting their first taste of the complicated soup of conflicting desires that made up a woman, well. They just went AWOL for a couple of years; that was the only way to describe it, really.

The skinnies were the worst, unless you counted the cutters. The cutters were fairly new; there hadn't been any when she'd first joined the school eight years ago. Then there'd been the first – a real Emo with dyed black hair. You could get away with that – just – as the regulations said 'natural' colours were ok. Morticia Addams-black was hardly natural in her book, but it was better than pink. First, this girl had taken to wearing long jumpers all summer, even on the hottest days, even insisting on wearing one in PE when the rest were in short sleeves. Then she'd just sat around weeping.

The matron had been on it. She accidentally-on-purpose spilled a cup of water on the girl, got the sweater off and saw the fine network of scars – ruby red for the recent ones, silvery spider's webs of old marks. Parents were dragged in, straight off to the Wellesley for a term, then she was back with a load of plasters and talk of a skin graft. Miss Douglas was that relieved when the girl transferred to a sixth form college for A levels. Her parents had come up with that limp old excuse that she needed a bit of freedom, wanted to mingle with boys. But she and Miss Douglas had known that the girl couldn't cut it at the College School. Which was ironic, when you thought about it, Leanne thought with a smile at her own cleverness.

You'd have thought that would be enough to put anyone in their right mind off the whole cutting business, but these girls weren't, were they? Some of them were so clever they'd left normal far behind. Worse, it had turned into a team sport, with little clusters of them daring each other and egging each other on. Parents were the last to cotton on. 'She said her little brother scratched her.' 'Oh, she said it was just a paper cut.' Honestly, for a lot of clever dicks, they were blimmin' idiots, these parents, that was for sure.

But what the girls got out of the business? That Leanne didn't understand at all. She'd even asked one, a weedy little thing by the name of Amber. Well, these troubled girls spent so much time waiting to go into Miss Douglas's room, she kind of got to know them. And she was curious.

'Release,' this Amber had said. 'I feel all this pressure, all this tension and I've got all this *stuff* just crowding in on me. Then I cut, and it seems to take everything else away.'

What kind of sense did that make? None at all, as far as Leanne was concerned. She wasn't into pain, no thanks, and the idea of seeing blood running down her own arm? Well, it turned her stomach. She knew people who liked a bit of suffering – there were enough friends of hers, as full of piercing holes as colanders, her mum said. They did it for a reason. But this? You didn't even get a bit of jewellery at the end. You had to hide yourself and feel shame. Nah, not for her, not in a million, and why it was such a thing for these rich girls she couldn't fathom. She supposed everyone wondering why they did it made them feel a bit special. But it was plain stupid.

Leanne snorted to herself, and a Year 7 girl slinking along to the loos, hoping not to be seen, instinctively ducked. Leanne took no notice. She should be sympathetic to these girls, she knew, but they had parents, counsellors, and the school to do the caring bit. She just thought they were twits. They had all this, and they risked chucking it away before they'd even got started.

If she were an employer, she'd be looking at any jobseekers, making sure they had no marks on their arms and were a decent size. Why would you want to get lumbered with someone who was only going to get signed off sick and spend all their time mooning about being 'sensitive' and 'troubled'?

No, a normal girl with a balanced outlook on life was the way to go, thought Leanne, swinging her arms slightly as she ambled down the corridor. Then she caught a nail on a doorpost and stopped stock still for five whole minutes, cursing with every ounce of her concentration and every swearword in her not-inconsiderable lexicon. The little Year 7 girl, cowering in the entrance to the loos, too scared to come out and reveal herself yet desperate now to get back to class, learned a whole lot of new vocabulary that definitely wouldn't be in her next spelling test.

***

By the time Miss Troughton settled her comfortable bulk into an easy chair in Miss Douglas's room, her friend's patience was more or less exhausted. Somehow, it was much easier to get exasperated at Leanne and Bernie Troughton than it was to face the potential disaster that was threatening to engulf them. But Miss Douglas, still outwardly calm in today's serene royal blue dress, knew she had to hold it together.

She clutched the pearls in the double rope round her enviably unlined throat, and took a deep breath. Against her inclinations, she'd been on a mindfulness course last year to see whether it was suitable for the school, and found herself liking it enough to insist that any nervy girls breathed deeply before telling her their woes. Every now and then, she even remembered to apply some of its counsel herself. Today was just such a moment, with thoughts spinning out of control, anger firing off in irrelevant directions, and even the concerned face of her dear friend annoying her so much that she itched to slap those doughy cheeks.

Another careful breath, and she let go of the pearls and brought her hands together on the desk, closing her eyes briefly. She was just about to speak when Miss Troughton broke into her thoughts in that impetuous way she had when she'd had an idea.

'What about an assembly? For the whole school? For Simone?'

Miss Douglas compressed her lips for a moment. It *was* a good idea, there was no denying that – but she'd already thought of it herself, and had knocked up a version of her address first thing this morning.

'There are wider issues here,' she said, her voice arctic.

'Of course, of course, but just to show some sense of community...'

'Yes, yes, we'll have the assembly, that goes without saying. But the real question is what the hell we're going to do with Year 9.'

'Year 9?'

Now Miss Douglas was exasperated. 'It's not just the one girl any more, is it? Yes, Simone is gone; that's very, very sad.' Her face compressed, and for one terrible moment she thought the tears were going to come. But it would have been like the Statue of Liberty weeping, instead of just looking permanently aghast. She couldn't do that, to her friend looking on – or to herself. After a spasm of feeling, and yet another breath, Miss Douglas mastered herself and went on. '*But* it's not just one girl. There are others affected, and we've got to stamp on this now. There's Lulu Cox in the hospital already, and who knows what else is going on amongst that group? Do you have any idea?'

Miss Troughton blinked. She might be many things, but no-one would see her as a natural confidante for fourteen-year-olds.

'I've talked to Matron, we've identified the group…'

'Well, that's not hard, now, is it, given that two of them have been hospitalised? There aren't that many of them left.' Miss Douglas was at her most withering.

She suddenly got up and started padding round the room, her high heels abandoned under her desk. Miss Troughton was one of the only people in the world who knew just how much her shoes pained her. Like the Little Mermaid, every step in heels was like a knife. But the shoes were part of her official persona, and that had to be maintained. She wore flats on the drive to and from school, and kicked off the heels every moment she could. Some days, she scarcely needed to walk in them at all. But today was going to be tough on all fronts. Feet, body, and soul were already aching – and it wasn't even break time yet.

'We've got to get control back, show the parents this isn't going to happen again, and it goes without saying that we need to emphasise that unfortunate friendships have been forged *out of school* and that's the root of the problem…'

'You mean… pretend nothing's been going on here?'

'Pretend? *Pretend?* I think you'll find it's no *pretence*,' said Miss Douglas, raising her eyebrows at Miss Troughton. 'The girls simply don't have time to work up whatever strange business has been going on while they're within these gates. We keep them busy every minute of the day, with a timetable crammed with activities designed to stretch young minds and keep them fully occupied.'

Miss Troughton's lips moved as she tried to memorise what she recognised as the party line. 'Fully occupied, yes,

yes, of course.'

'We support the parents in their quest to find out the root of this… problem. And we, as a school, will do everything we can to *stamp out* whatever the hell has been going on, but we are not, repeat not, taking responsibility for it. Do you understand, Bernie?' Miss Douglas halted in her pacing in front of her friend, who was still filling every inch of the easy chair with her bulk, and frowning with the concentration required to internalise the school's message.

'Yes, yes, I see, Angela… But…' Miss Troughton mumbled, head down, avoiding her friend's steely gaze.

'But what?' said Miss Douglas stiffly.

'But the girl is *dead*, Angela. The poor child. She was so sweet and so bright. It's so out of character. Of all the girls to be experimenting with drugs, I'd never have picked Simone. She had so much to lose. Her mother… It's just unbearable. She was so thrilled when Simone got the place. Now, think of her.'

It was too much. Suddenly, Miss Troughton collapsed into the sobs that Miss Douglas was rigorously holding back. Tears ran down the scarlet cheeks and disappeared under the tightly-buttoned collar of her shirt.

Miss Douglas breathed deeply yet again, yanked some tissues from the box on her desk, and brought them round to her friend, pressing her hand onto her shoulder. It was all Miss Troughton needed. Her sobs receded, and her own pudgy hand moved up to rest on Miss Douglas's, ingrained with chalk dust from her years of teaching, the nails short and sensible, the skin weathered by weekends in the garden and their years in the North.

Miss Douglas stood as still as a statue. Miss Troughton's hand was hot and clammy, but she knew she couldn't withdraw her own, however much she wanted to. Bernie needed this moment. Stealthily, Angela Douglas moved her other hand up to pinch the bridge of her nose in a vicious grip. Oh God. She could feel a migraine coming on. That was all she needed.

***

'That poor woman, can you imagine?' said Katie, as they sat over lukewarm coffees in the Aurora café. It was definitely a moment to be as far away from the wagging tongues of Dulwich as possible. The awful news of Simone Osborne's death and Lulu Cox's overdose would be spreading faster than a blood stain on a silk blouse, via Jane's café round the corner and every other spot in Dulwich where you could get a hot beverage and exchange a word with neighbours. Beth was pretty sure even her cat, Magpie, would be well aware of every nuance of the story in the next few minutes. That ginger tom round the corner from their house was a shocking gossip, and the two always had their furry heads together.

'That's the pitiful thing,' said Beth. 'By all accounts, Simone's mum did a great job bringing up two kids alone, making ends meet, keeping them on the straight and narrow, doing her best for them. Simone had done so brilliantly, getting the scholarship; she was a really clever girl, must have been. And now the irony is that her poor mum must be thinking, *if only she'd left her at the other school*. She would probably have been fine. She might not have got the best exam results, no great uni place or amazing career ahead – but she would have been alive.'

'Plus, the way everyone will be judging her,' said Katie absently.

'Judging the mum? What for? None of this is her fault.'

'Yes, well, come on, Beth. You of all people should know how it is. She's a single mother in Dulwich. She's going to get judged.'

Instantly, Beth was fuming. 'This is nothing to do with her being on her own. You must see that.'

It was Katie's matter-of-fact tone that made Beth see red. 'Of course, *I* know that, but that's not going to stop people thinking that if it had been a stable home, with a man around, then none of this would have happened.'

'Excuse me! A home can be stable without a man around.'

183

'I know that, Beth. Christ, I'm not the one you should be losing it with. I'm just saying. People think someone like Simone's mum has made a choice to go it alone, or can't sustain a relationship for some reason, and that makes the kids act up. You know, in some cases, it's not an unreasonable assumption,' Katie finished.

Beth stared at her, and shook her head. 'So, would you judge me if James had walked out on me, instead of just doing the decent thing and dying?'

Katie had the grace to look abashed. 'I'd judge *him*, that's for sure. He'd have been mad to leave you. Look, I didn't make these rules, and I don't play to them – or at least, I hope I don't – but that doesn't mean I can't see what they are. Other people will assume that one of the reasons Simone is lying dead is because her mother couldn't cope at some level. You know that's true. Whenever something goes wrong, people blame the mother.'

Beth sighed. 'You've got something there. Serial killer? Mum didn't stop him torturing hamsters. Evil dictator? Didn't get put on the naughty step enough.'

Both women smiled, but their accord felt more brittle than usual. Beth relied on her friendship with Katie; it was the rope that lashed her ship together as she sailed the uncertain seas of single parenthood. Today, she had felt the boards creak beneath her feet and she didn't like it.

She knew she was outside Dulwich norms, bringing Ben up alone and earning her own keep. In the 21st century, it was ridiculous that she was an anomaly here, but in many ways this place made Agatha Christie's fictional St Mary Mead look like Sodom and Gomorrah. On the surface at least. As she had cause to know, nasty secrets could lurk beneath the most placid of exteriors.

Beth felt a sudden surge of solidarity with Jo Osborne, Simone's mother. From that momentary meeting over the moribund girl's hospital bed, Beth had felt the strength of Simone's fierce love for her daughter. Now she, in turn, felt protective of the woman. Katie was absolutely right, her reputation was about to be casually and thoughtlessly trashed by all the smug middle-class mamas, keen to tell themselves that such a fate could not befall their own daughters because this luckless single parent family had brought it on themselves. Well, Beth was going to get to the bottom of this, and prove once and for all that what Jo Osborne had, or hadn't, done was irrelevant. This crime was rooted in Dulwich today, not in whoever had fathered Jo's baby fourteen years before.

Though, no sooner had she thought this, than a big red warning sign went up in Beth's brain. It didn't happen often, but when it did, she knew it meant a large clue had come her way.

'Hang on a minute. You know, you might have some sort of a point,' she said excitedly.

'Well, thanks a bunch,' said Katie in mock umbrage.

'No, I mean – the father. Who's the father? What if it's somebody big in Dulwich? And what if it was all about to come out? Don't you see? They could have a motive.' Beth found herself leaning forward. Katie, her jaw dropping slightly, leaned in, too.

'Oh my God! You're right. But how can we find out who he might have been?'

'I'll have to ask Jo,' said Beth, grimacing at the thought of cross-questioning the bereaved mother about something so delicate. It would take all her not-particularly-well-developed skills of tact and diplomacy – and then some. 'Wait a minute. Maybe I can just get York to do that. It's a job for the police, right?'

Katie nodded, relieved. 'That's a better idea. I hate it when you do the dangerous stuff.'

'I'll let you into a secret,' said Beth, with the glimmer of a smile. 'So do I. Meanwhile, what *can* we get on with? I think the school angle is one of the best.'

'We don't know it's anything to do with the school yet, though, do we?' said Katie.

'Weren't you listening to Maria: all that stuff about the Blue Whale challenge, the Emos, the anorexics, the cutters? That school is riddled with girls who can do the schoolwork with their hands tied behind their backs, so they fill the time by thinking up ways to torture themselves – and their friends.'

'Beth, that's harsh! They're just schoolgirls, after all. We have no idea what happened. Maybe Simone took the drugs at that party, maybe she *was* into all that stuff…and this Lulu girl as well, for all we know.'

Beth hunched her shoulders defensively for a second, then relaxed. 'You know what, Katie? You're absolutely right. I think that's one of the most frustrating things about this case. There are suspects, sure, but it's everybody at the College School, or everybody at the Gallery party. Or yes, it's just Simone, getting hold of the stuff and taking it for some reason that we just don't understand and will probably never get to the bottom of. It's either too wide a field, or too narrow.'

'But hang on. If Lulu Cox has taken the drugs as well, or been given them or whatever, surely that makes a big difference? Don't you just have to find out where she's been and who she's friends with, and things should start to make sense?'

Beth, lost in gloom, took a while to absorb her friend's words. Then she looked at Katie in wonderment. Her sunny and beautiful friend was quite right. It wasn't a case of *cherchez la femme*, but *cherchez la schoolgirl*. 'You're amazing, you know that?'

Katie smiled. 'All part of the service. Now, are you coming to my stretch class?'

'Sorry,' Beth shook her head. 'I've got a million things to do.'

'Are any of them part of your job?' Katie asked, head on one side.

'Well… maybe one or two.' It was Beth's turn to smile.

Just then, the door jangled, and York loomed in the doorway. Katie glanced at him and got to her feet with hurried grace. 'I see what you mean. Don't work too hard now,' she smiled, then edged past York with a quick hello and was off round the corner to her exercise studio above the dress shop, head full of musings which she didn't plan to raise with her friend.

'All right for coffee?' York asked. Beth looked doubtfully into the dregs of her cappuccino, which had managed to be simultaneously bitter and yet still over-milky. Maybe she'd be luckier with another? 'Could I have a flat white?' she asked, tentatively.

'I'll see what I can do,' he said, strolling up to the counter, where the waitress had gone on auto-simper, her mode when dealing with male customers.

Beth tried to marshal her thoughts and block out the sound of inane girly giggling while York put their order in. By the time the waitress had pirouetted, blushing, into the kitchen to throw their coffee around and York had finally plonked himself down opposite her, she was more than ready to plunge into speech.

'We need to look into this friendship group; it all comes down to that. These girls hunt in packs at that age. There's got to be something going on in this group that will explain who did this, and why.'

York kept his counsel while patting his pockets for his notebook and pencil, and got out his phone as well for good measure. Beth, watching rather sourly, wondered if he could possibly do it all any slower. 'Do you know for a fact that these girls were even friends?' he asked eventually.

'You can't tell me it's coincidence that something like this would happen, in one of the best girls' schools in the country?'

'I don't see what the calibre of the school has to do with anything,' said York in reasonable tones.

Beth tutted. 'Well, you wouldn't. You don't know Dulwich. But the thing is that these schools are hothouses. The girls at the College School aren't like pupils at any other place around here. They have huge expectations put onto their shoulders from a really young age.'

'Who by?' said York.

'Well, *everyone*. Their parents, their teachers... *themselves*. If you think about it, there are what, 300 places at

187

the College School in Year 7? Most of those will already be taken by parents who've been paying thousands of pounds a year for their daughters' educations since they were four years old. That's quite an investment, but some people consider that it's worthwhile to get them into the secondary school without having to do the exam. You've got to remember that the College School is in the top 20 schools in the UK. So, when exam time comes, the pressure, the grooming of those girls is quite incredible…'

'Grooming? That sounds dodgy,' said York. It seemed to be an attempt at levity, but Beth frowned repressively. She was serious about all this.

'I just mean extra tuition. Almost every girl that sits the exam will have been tutored, even if they come from the private prep schools. No parent wants to leave it to chance. I'm not saying any of this is good, it is just the atmosphere that surrounds the College School.'

'I'm still not really with you,' said York, large hands pressed palms together on the table, and taking up a good deal more than half the space. Beth drew back slightly and tried again.

'By the time a girl has got into the College School, I would imagine she's elated, but she's also under no illusions. It's not going to be easy. She's surrounded by clever girls, all of them ambitious, focused on success. It's not a relaxing atmosphere,' she said heavily.

'Well, OK, I see that. Are you saying all this pressure warps the girls?'

Beth thought for a second. 'I suppose I am. Sad, isn't it?'

'Yes, it is. It really is. But would it warp them enough? Enough to make sense of whatever's going on?'

'I think so,' said Beth sadly. 'I think we need to talk to Simone's friends. And Lulu's. We need access to Year 9.'

Just then, the waitress emerged from the back room with two cups and saucers. York's was placed daintily before him – a cappuccino with, for once, quite a reasonable head of foam and even a wobbly, smiley face marked out in cocoa powder. Beth's flat white was just that – an uninspiring brew, the colour of dishwater, and without so much as a trace of foam on top.

She looked up at the waitress, but the girl's face, body, and whole attention were turned to York, and Beth gave up the attempt to remonstrate. With a final simper, the waitress wandered back to her station and lounged, chin propped in hand, on the counter, quite obviously trying to overhear their conversation.

York gave a quick glance in her direction, then edged his chair round so his substantial back was facing the girl and he was at right angles to Beth.

'I've told you before what I think about "we" in these matters,' he started sternly. 'But in this case, it is quite useful to have someone on board that I don't have to pay. Guards sitting outside hospital doors round the clock don't come cheap; the overtime has been coming out of my ears.'

Beth smiled slightly at this unlikely vision, and at the news that she had, yet again, managed to inveigle herself onto the investigation. Only in a small way it was true, but who knew what she'd be able to winkle out now?

'I think our first port of call should be Maria Luyten at the Wellesley,' she said decisively.

'Wait a minute now, I thought we were going straight to the friendship group? I thought you said that was the key to this whole thing?'

'I think it is. But I'm not sure you really understand teenage girls, and I think she can really help us. Plus, I think she's probably treating a few girls from Year 9. She probably knows them better than anyone,' said Beth, taking a mammoth sip of her flat white, and then nearly choking. Her regrets were nearly as bitter as the coffee, as York thumped her back and her eyes streamed. The waitress even wafted out, proffering some tissues – to York, not to Beth – to help mop up.

Beth grabbed them and did her best, then gathered her things, as York sipped his own drink without any sense of urgency. She was fidgeting away and perching on the edge of her seat when she suddenly remembered her other brainwave of the morning. 'Also – Simone's father.'

'Mmm,' said York, raising his eyes from the coffee, which he was showing every appearance of enjoying far too much. If this went on, the Aurora would lose its hard-won reputation as the worst café in Dulwich, and Beth would have to find another corner to conduct her quiet discussions. Mind you, her own coffee had been as disgusting as ever. Her bolthole was probably safe.

'Well, who *is* he? Don't you see, he may well have a motive? Maybe the secret was about to come out and he had to stop her.'

York sat there stolidly, seemingly unmoved by Beth's breakthrough.

'Oh, come on, you have to admit it's a great motive for murder,' said Beth, exasperated.

York took yet another swallow. 'Maybe. But don't you think if it was the father, and he didn't want the truth to come out for some reason which we have no idea about, then he'd probably turn his attention to Jo, rather than his own child? Men don't usually kill their kids, but they might want to shut up a blabbing ex. We have no proof that Simone even knew who her dad was. But Jo certainly does. Or I would hope so, anyway,' said York off-handedly, carefully putting his notebook, pen and phone back into their individual pockets at precisely the same unhurried pace by which he'd produced them in the first place.

Beth, who'd felt on the verge of cracking the whole business wide open, subsided slightly in her seat. 'Oh. I didn't think of that. Well, I suppose it saves me having to have a very difficult conversation with Jo, anyway. Or asking you to do it,' she said, pinning a smile to her face.

'Look, we can find out who the father was, but I'm not sure it will push us any further on, are you? And I think we have bigger fish to fry at the moment,' said York.

The waitress, pricking up her ears, stepped forward. 'You'd like the fish? I'll just talk to the chef.'

York held up a hand. 'No thank you, not today. Lovely coffee, though,' he said with a smile that made the girl's

190

sallow cheeks blush peony pink. Beth scowled and scraped her chair back loudly, scraping up her bag from the floor, flinging it on the table and searching for her purse.

'I've got these,' said York, his hand coming down warmly on hers for a second.

Startled, she met his eyes and smiled, then inwardly cursed herself. She wouldn't be as silly as the waitress. She just wouldn't. She stumped off to the door and tried to pull it back. As usual, it stuck and squealed a protest on the tiled floor. York, throwing down some money for their coffees, hastened over and gave the door a gentle yank that sent it flying backwards.

'Wait outside. I'll bring the car round,' said York, and Beth emerged blinking into the Dulwich sunshine. As usual, the café had begun to feel very small when they'd been standing there, together. At least there was room to breathe on the pavement. She trotted past Village Books, the window piled high with all the latest releases. It had been ages since she'd had a good read lined up for the evenings; she'd spent much too much time of late on all her freelance assignments. She made a mental note to pop in and stock up as soon as she had a minute.

A board outside the shop advertised a signing with a local author on Saturday. That could be fun, and there might be a drink in it, too. She'd see if Katie would like to come with her. Michael would be fine to watch the boys for an hour or so; it was the weekend, after all. Their slight falling-out this morning had been worrying, but this would be just the thing to heal the rift, get them back on their usual footing.

There was something about being out of doors in Dulwich on a bright, sunny day that lifted even the gloomiest of spirits. Beth looked around appreciatively at the busy street scene. The chemist was doing a roaring, though discreet, trade in nit shampoo and mean metal combs as the temperature climbed. The deli's tables were already filling with nannies having post-post-breakfast coffees, and mothers ordering pre-pre-lunch lattes. There was a young mum herding her toddler into the shoe shop, where you took a numbered ticket and waited your turn, like in Harrod's deli, while the eternally patient assistants wrestled with tiny chubby feet the size and shape of Dairylea triangles. Beth remembered sitting there with Ben aged three, and getting him fitted for sandals that would last three months and cost £40, while she tried to hide the fact that the soles of her own shoes were flapping open as widely as a Labrador's smile.

As she was musing, York drew up in his car and parked blithely on the double yellow lines. While the traffic wardens, who once circled Dulwich as persistently as wasps at a picnic, were now nowhere to be seen, someone, somewhere was watching them all on a computer and firing off penalty notices into the ether. To everyone except policemen, of course. Beth opened the door and slid in. York smiled. 'So, the Wellesley, then, eh?'

Beth briefed York as they drove, so by the time they glided into a parking space right in front of the long, neo-classically designed redbrick façade of the hospital, he knew as much as she did about Blue Whale and a shoal of other teenage troubles.

'You don't seem surprised at all this stuff. I was horrified when I heard about it.'

'Surprised isn't the word. We see a lot in this job,' he said shortly. 'But that's not to say I'm not saddened and concerned by what you've told me,' he said, glancing at her. She noticed that the tiny twinge of Irish in his voice was always stronger when emotions were in play. Then he cracked open the driver's door decisively and the moment was gone. 'Right. Come on, let's get to it.'

As usual with hospitals, there seemed to be a game of hide-and-seek going on. Signs that were irrelevant to their quest were large and obvious, but anything pointing in the direction they needed was in a tiny font, and usually hidden by a member of staff who appeared to have been sworn to secrecy or was on their first day.

Eventually, they wound their way along a last pastel corridor to what seemed like the only door they hadn't already tried. 'Dr Maria Luyten', said a small plaque. Eureka.

A tap on the door elicited a faintly harassed 'Come in', and they peered into a small, square treatment room, with a bed covered in paper sheeting pushed against the wall, a folded screen, and a desk and three chairs crammed into the remainder of the space. A high window looked out onto bricks, and a 2015 calendar was turned to September, with an illustration of white horses thundering through a meadow. Beth envied them the freedom and space. There was a white clock on the wall, its bold numerals shouting the wrong time, though it was ticking loudly. Beth supposed it was still right twice a day.

Maria was deep in her computer, pushing this button and that in obvious frustration. 'I'll be with you in just a moment. Oh,' she said, then threw up her hands. 'No, I'm giving this up. I'm supposed to tick off my last patient, otherwise the central desk thinks I'm still with them. According to this, I have been with the same girl since 2pm yesterday. Even she doesn't have that many problems. They will just have to work it out and send the next when she comes.'

She stood up to shake hands, her curtain of glossy hair swinging around her shoulders, her tall, slender frame reminding Beth once again of an elegant racing dog, vibrating with stylish energy. She smiled briskly at York and warmly at Beth, who to her surprise was drawn into a rapid kiss-on-both-cheeks.

'Matteo has talked so much about his lovely time with you. This is not the moment, but we must arrange for Ben to come to us? We would like that very much. Now, do sit down, both of you, and tell me what it is I can help with.'

Beth had been expecting some sort of casual acknowledgement, but the enthusiasm of the woman's welcome had disconcerted her. She sat down, allowing her fringe to flop forward over her face a little while she collected her thoughts. Just because Maria had greeted her like a long-lost friend didn't mean she couldn't ask the woman hard questions. They'd only met a couple of times. They weren't bosom buddies.

But, as ever, the good mother within her rose. If there

was a chance that Maria's son was going to enter the charmed circle of Ben's friends, then the two women would have to get on. She wouldn't soft-pedal the interview, of course not. But she might just let York get on with it for the moment, see where he got to. She turned and looked expectantly at York, who blinked in surprise. From the way she'd been lecturing him in the car, she guessed he was expecting her to plunge in and drag as much as she could out of this expert on the foibles of teenage girls. But, on taking a breath, he seemed to accept the new balance of power. After all, thought Beth, he'd surely never complained about being given the lead before.

'Ah, Dr Luyten. You probably know why we're here.'

'No,' broke in Maria, looking from one to the other with a bright smile. 'I have no idea what this is about.'

'Really? No idea? When a teenage girl has just died of an overdose in a hospital down the road; when she was in the same class as your own daughter at school; when another is in the hospital as we speak and when you are an expert, or so I believe, on the mental issues of adolescent girls?'

York's tone was even and non-accusatory, but it was still quite a litany he'd recited. Maria continued to look politely interested, but her hands started to toy with the NHS lanyard dangling round her neck.

'Sorry, I'm not sure what the question was there,' Maria responded. 'But yes, you're right, I do know about issues with teenage girls, absolutely. And I am very happy to help, if I can shed any light on the underlying problems which may have caused these girls to experiment with drugs.'

'You think they took the overdoses themselves?' said York.

Maria looked from York to Beth, obviously confused. 'Well, yes. I thought that was the case. Very sad, of course, but still these things happen. Even in the best schools.' She nodded and shrugged her shoulders slightly.

Beth didn't quite understand why, but she felt anger rising. Maria seemed to be making a very neat assumption that Simone, and now Lulu too, had taken a decision to end it all. The overload of emotions Beth had seen in the park, when she and Katie had had coffee with Maria, seemed now to be tucked deeply away. It looked as though the woman had thought better of her outpourings that day, when she had all but accused one of the College girls of targeting her own daughter and driving others, including Simone and possibly Lulu, to experiment with things that were way beyond their comfort zones.

'Are you really saying both girls were just suicidal? That this is all deliberate?'

Maria turned to her politely. 'I am not sure how you infer that from the little that I have said, but if it were the case, then Simone would not be the first troubled teenage girl to have taken her own life in this way, surely? And the other girl, this Lulu, as well, I suppose.' Her hands were spread wide now, the fidgeting forgotten. She was on surer ground. Immediately, Beth wanted to backpedal, to see what would make Maria nervous again. All her radar was beeping frantically. There were secrets in this room.

'Of course, you understand that I can never break my patients' confidentiality.' Maria had turned to York with her large beseeching eyes – eyes that reminded Beth of her unsettling son, Matteo.

'Was Simone actually a patient here?' Beth asked abruptly.

'Well, no, she wasn't…'

'Or Lulu Cox?'

'No.'

'We can hardly breach their right to privacy, then,' said Beth, then realised she'd sounded harsh. She started again, in more conciliatory mode. 'You seem to be misunderstanding the reason we're here, Maria. We want to get some background on teenage behaviour, the kind of dynamics that go on in these friendship groups that girls have at this age.'

'You sound as though you know a lot already.' Maria favoured Beth now with one of her lovely smiles, again tinged with relief, and Beth wondered what that meant they were missing.

'Of course, when we were at the park, we did discuss this a little and I talked in general terms about teenage girls,' Maria continued. Beth noted the way that Maria was emphasising the general. Surely their chat had been quite specific? But Maria was carrying on.

'As we have said, things can become exceptionally intense. When girls of this age form a tight bond, it can become almost like prisoners of war or survivors of a particular trauma.' Maria gestured with her hands, interlocking the fingers. 'They consider themselves to be surrounded by hostile forces, they turn inwards, and their own value systems become reinforced. They may develop codes, systems of behaviour, that we outsiders would consider abnormal.' Beth could see that Maria's knuckles were turning white now, so tightly were her hands pressing together.

'You mentioned hostile forces,' said Beth. 'What would those be exactly?'

'I'm afraid that's us.' Maria smiled deprecatingly. 'Their parents, their teachers, definitely any doctor trying to look into their state of mind. Any authority figure, really. Teenagers are caught between the powerless state of children and the power*ful* – or possibly I should say potentially powerful – state of adulthood. It is never easy to be in transition. For a brief period, there are no clear rules, and that is difficult for everyone.

'On the one hand, you cannot put them to bed when it gets dark any more. But what time should they go to bed? In any class, you will find a wide variation, which they will discuss amongst themselves and start to resent. That is just one example of the huge variety of adjustments and discrepancies any teenager will be measuring themselves against. And puberty itself is a lottery. There will be girls in Year 9 who are at the same height and stage of development as a Year 7 child, but the girl sitting next to them may already have the body of the Venus de Milo. These differences are hard on everyone. Girls are not always kind, as I'm sure you will remember yourself,' said Maria, with a searching look at

Beth.

Beth tried not to react, but her eyes widened and inwardly she squirmed, as excruciating memories flooded back. Yes, she'd had a hard time of it as a teenager. She remembered the rest of the class becoming curvier by the day, while her own two sturdy stumps and solid body seemed as determined to remain unchanged throughout the years as Stonehenge.

Soon, her former best friends had started collecting in small gaggles to giggle over boys while she, as uninterested as she was undeveloped, was baffled and bored. She had an older brother, so males were very far from being intriguing creatures. Josh, at that age an angular amalgam of smelly socks and stupid jokes, had no mystique and his friends were equally uninspiring. So, her flock of classmates had morphed into birds of paradise overnight, flying away to parties and snogging while she remained earthbound and bereft. The only plumage she'd developed was her enormous fringe, which she still hid behind to this day. Bloody psychiatrists, she thought, trying hard to maintain a neutral expression, and even a faint smile, while she wanted to glare hard at Maria.

She told herself that Maria couldn't know how accurately her dart would hit home, scoring a full 180 humiliating points – though the woman was trained to infiltrate people's psyches, and she did have the evidence of her own eyes. Beth was still tiny, and in many ways had carried on representing the 'before' picture in the puberty manual. And had Maria ever met any short people who weren't sensitive about their height? But still, she didn't want her anger to derail the interview. That would make things altogether too easy for the doctor, and there were things they needed to find out.

'Sometimes women aren't that great either,' she couldn't resist saying, with an ironic twist. 'But if we could come to Simone's case in particular?'

'But I know nothing of Simone,' said Maria, spreading her hands wide. 'I thought we had established that.'

'You treated some of her group, though, didn't you?' said York, who seemed eager to get back in the conversation.

Well, he was welcome to it. She'd had just about as much of Maria's focus as she wanted.

'I did, yes, and indeed some are still coming to sessions. I treat them individually. We occasionally offer group sessions, but I find with the teenage girls that they unfortunately swap ideas. There is a lot to be said for openness, but they are extremely suggestible at this age. We don't want those who are anorexic to make it seem appealing to those who are already vulnerable.'

'Really? That happens?' York leant forward, hands on his knees.

'Oh, absolutely. Peer pressure is very strong at this age and with girls who are already at risk, one word out of place can trigger the most unfortunate trains of thought.'

And you'd know all about that, thought Beth sourly.

'There are many websites, for example, that feed on this interest of teenage girls. And of course, now Instagram, Snapchat, and so on. They call it "pro-ana" or "thinspiration". And there is "pro-mia" too, supporting bulimia. These sites are very popular. There was a study recently... I was sent it.' Maria started searching her in-tray but soon gave up the fight. 'It said that something like twelve per cent of girls between thirteen and seventeen have visited pro-ana sites. Meanwhile, one in three girls from *six* to seventeen have Googled diet tips.'

'Why aren't these websites stopped?' Beth couldn't resist butting in.

Maria spread her hands. 'They position themselves carefully. They suggest they are offering a forum for sufferers, allowing them to find support on their journey back to health. Then they post galleries full of pictures of girls who are little more than skeletons. The girls take the pictures themselves and upload them, supposedly to show their progress, but in fact to gain praise for their emaciation. And there are many on these sites that deny anorexia is a medical condition and seek to redefine it as a lifestyle choice.'

'Surely that should be illegal?' Beth turned to York, who shrugged. He didn't need to tell her that the Met Police had enough trouble dealing with grannies being mugged on the streets without venturing into teenage girls' headspace.

'It is so hard in this age, when models are venerated and celebrated. Kate Moss, for instance, once said that "nothing tastes as good as skinny feels", and there are a lot of websites that take that as a mantra,' Maria continued. 'There are a lot of conflicting messages in the culture. To an extent, we promote the view that self-denial and exercise are good, but then we swing to the other extreme and demonize those who, in our view, go too far with this. It is not surprising, perhaps, that the young – and boys can be sufferers too, we should not forget – become very confused,' said Maria.

'And at the same time, we attack those who are obese, we "fat-shame" them, and the papers are full of stories about the perils of overeating; diabetes, heart disease, and so on,' Maria continued. 'Girls can see this and feel, to some extent logically, that they are doing the right thing.'

'We've got on to anorexia – do I take it that some in the group from the College are suffering from it?' As ever, York went to the heart of the matter.

Maria, who had been leaning forward expansively, abruptly sat back in her chair.

'You know our confidentiality issues. What I can say is that we deal always with a *mixture* of issues here. But perhaps you have heard of Wellesley family therapy?'

Both Beth and York looked blank. Maria seemed much more comfortable talking in generalities than skirting around their specific case. Her duty to her patients' privacy loomed large, but Beth wondered if there was more to her reticence than the usual concern for confidentiality.

It was something she kept in mind as Maria spoke. On sure ground now, and with her shiny helmet of hair gleaming under a neon strip light that Beth was certain was doing nothing for her own English pallor, Maria explained the system. 'It was developed here, in fact, and it has been found more effective than individual therapy, for patients who are under eighteen and who are within three years of developing the condition.'

'The condition? Just to be clear, we're talking about anorexia here?' York interjected.

'Yes, anorexia, that's right,' said Maria, hurrying onwards, and again Beth wondered what it was she was so keen to leave far behind. 'There are three stages, which hopefully help towards a positive outcome, that is, to lead to the patient "growing out" or certainly growing away from, the disease, if you will.' Maria ticked them off on her fingers: 'Weight restoration; returning control to the adolescent; and establishing a healthy adolescent identity. One of the keys is that the parents do not blame or chide the child. They take over responsibility for feeding the child initially, and the condition is seen as an external disease. We treat it like any other illness that can befall someone, and there is no blame of any sort attached to it.'

'Even though these girls are flirting with "catching" anorexia, by visiting these websites and developing the obsession?' said Beth.

'Yes, despite all that. For, if someone becomes obsessed, is it really their fault? And, more importantly, does it *matter* whether it is their fault or not? Could we not say that the obsession with bodies is society's fault, after all, and the girls' only misfortune is to be part of such a society and perhaps too susceptible to its pressures? Dr Susie Orbach, for one, published research showing that girls' self-esteem plummets after three minutes of looking at retouched photos of other women in magazines. We are all exposed to these images all the time, in adverts, on television. It is no mystery why teenagers, whose own sense of self is not yet robust, are so badly affected.'

Everything Maria was saying made perfect sense to Beth, but she still wondered what was *not* being said.

'Do you think the Wellesley system, with these three targets, actually works?' she asked.

'*Stages*, not targets,' Maria corrected with a quick on-off smile which left Beth feeling like the slow kid at the back of the class. 'We have a lot of empirical evidence showing good results from this method. I have to tell you that anorexia is recognised to be the deadliest of all psychiatric disorders. The effects of starvation on the heart and other organs, not least the brain itself, can lead to complex medical conditions, frequent relapses, and fatalities, even when the patient finally seems to be recovering. But, if all goes well, the outcome is positive and the family is often closer as a result of their struggle.'

There was a moment of silence. Beth had never realised how serious the disease could be. There had been a girl at her school – there was probably a girl at every school – who had mysteriously stopped eating and spent all her break times running round and round the playground. She wasn't in her year and Beth hadn't known her to speak to, but she'd been pointed out as a curiosity. She was universally considered 'weird' in that cruel way girls have of categorising those outside the mainstream. But then she had apparently recovered. Beth remembered that, ten or even fifteen years later, this same girl had died of a drug overdose. Had she been more vulnerable because of the strain she had put on her body as a teenager? Or was it evidence that, having taken one wrong turn in her youth, the girl never quite found the right path? Or even that her underlying anxieties and problems were never fully dealt with, either when she was young and troubled, or when she was adult and still troubled? How sad that thought was.

Beth dragged her mind back to the Wellesley system. She wondered how that would work in practice. One thing was for sure, it would be labour-intensive.

'That sounds like a massive commitment for the family,' she remarked. Feeding just one child was sometimes, frankly, a pain. Menus developed a certain tyranny, likes and dislikes loomed large, there was always shopping to be fetched and carried. Sometimes Beth wondered if there was a single fish left in all the oceans with its fingers intact, so many orange digits had she and Ben scoffed over the years. She imagined that catering for an endlessly picky and resistant child, hell-bent on starving themselves, must make every mealtime a purgatory. And everything would, necessarily, dance around the one affected child. Fine, in a way, if you just had the one, as she did – though parents might well feel all the more desperate about the war they were waging against an unseen foe, if it threatened their only progeny. But say you had several children. How would the other siblings feel? Or a needy partner? There would have to be strong bonds and resilient egos elsewhere for the group to withstand so much narrowing of focus onto one solitary member. Families in this predicament had her every sympathy.

'It is a huge commitment, you are quite right, Beth.' Maria permitted herself a smile tight as an elastic band. 'But in a way the framework is a great comfort, and we know the results can be fantastic. With other conditions, we can be less sure of our ground, we can encounter other problems.'

'Wait a minute, I'm not sure if you're saying our group of girls is anorexic or whether they've got something else going on?'

'The point is, Beth, that I *cannot* give you any details, as I think I have made very clear. In fact, I have now said more than enough. And,' Maria glanced pointedly at the slim, expensive-looking watch on her wrist, 'I now have another patient I must give my attention to. But you must feel free to come back if you have more questions. The receptionist can always find a time.' With that, she started shuffling papers together on her desk in what was obviously a brush-off.

Beth looked at York and they both got reluctantly to their feet. The interview was over.

Outside the Wellesley, before they got back into the car, Beth put out a hand to York. 'Before you drop me off, I just wondered whether you'd considered…'

York sighed. 'What is it? When your sentences start tailing off like that, I just know there's a whole world of trouble in store.'

'It's just that we've got so few people in the frame, really. Well, there are groups of people who might have drugged Simone, like the people at the drinks party. But neither the bigwigs who were having cocktails or the other waiters and waitresses seem to have had much reason to bump her off. Agreed?'

York, a master of the non-committal answer, merely twitched one shoulder.

'Well, we were talking about her father before, in the café. Say she'd actually found out who he was; say she was blackmailing him...'

'Whoa now! What have I told you about bandying about these accusations? Do you have any reason at all, the smallest bit of evidence, even to lead you to believe that Simone had got in touch with her father?'

'Well no, not yet, but you're better placed to do that sort of work. The important thing is it would be a reason for all this to have happened.'

York took a deep breath and leant against the car, arms crossed, while Beth faced him. Anyone looking on would probably have thought they were arguing about who was going to drive.

'I hear what you're saying,' said York, his tones patient. 'It's frustrating. I get it. There are loads of people who might have administered something to Simone, yet there's no obvious suspect unless you count the girl herself... But what about all that stuff on anorexia? Didn't that make you think that the girl's own peer group might have been involved? And don't forget we've also got a second girl in hospital, now, and that's very unlikely to be anything to do with Simone's father, isn't it? Meanwhile, we've got a bunch of troubled teens, all a bit doolally because they haven't had a bite to eat for days. I really wouldn't rule out those waitresses yet.'

It shouldn't have been reassuring, but somehow the thought raised a smile from Beth. York unlocked the car and she was just about to hop in when he said, 'And by the way, thanks for implying that the police can fabricate evidence to support any old crackpot theory of yours. I appreciate that one!'

'Thought I'd slipped that past you,' admitted Beth with a cocky grin, and ducked inside the car.

York took a moment, then she saw him give a tiny smile.

She knew she infuriated him – but she also made him laugh. And, heaven knew, he probably needed that in his job.

Chapter Thirteen

York thought about Beth's latest wild idea, back at the station, as he flipped through his notebook, trying to work out what he had to go on so far with this case. It wasn't a lot.

His standard-issue, allegedly ergonomic chair creaked as he leant back, and his gaze lit irresistibly on the nasty polystyrene ceiling tiles someone had put up in the 1970s, which dearly wanted to cascade down on all their heads. The walls were smothered thickly in institutional magnolia, and the noticeboards everywhere were deep in curling posters, mugshots, and procedural updates, as though everyone at the station was an earnest scrapbooker trying to create the *découpage* from hell. In truth, no police worker ever threw anything away lightly, they were all so used to scouring around for evidence, not binning it. Any one of these flyers could turn out to be vital, might even crack a case. Well, that was the theory. Maybe he just needed to delegate someone to go round and rip down all the stuff that was more than five years old.

But it was comforting to work in the big, tatty, open-plan space. Some of his colleagues, he knew, found the jumble of desks, the low-level hum of conversation, the phone calls, and the perennial coffee corner gossip a big stumbling block to proper concentration. But he loved the white noise. He was entitled, now, to one of the partitioned-off offices that the high-ups used, but he much preferred to be out in the body of the room with the troops. There was a solidarity in working closely with colleagues. And also, if he was honest, he spent enough time on his own. He was a sociable type but, with no partnership at the station that really meshed for him work-wise yet, it was nice sometimes to have Beth along for the ride. Plus, her insider knowledge helped him cut some corners.

York turned determinedly from any detailed examination of his own motives to the much easier, though flimsier, list of concrete leads in the case.

So. What had he got?

One dead body. That poor waif, Simone Osborne, whose still, pale form would haunt his dreams forever if he couldn't find the bastard – or bastards – who'd fed her drugs.

Or had she just taken them herself? She could have done it in a moment that was maybe out of character for her, but all too typical of teenagers up and down the country. They felt they were immortal, or they succumbed to peer pressure, or they just thought 'what the hell?' and sought quick oblivion for an hour or two. Not for eternity, which was what Simone had got.

Meanwhile, he still had one other girl out for the count in hospital. Lulu Cox. He made a mental note to check up on her status, see what, if anything, could be gleaned about her circumstances. There must be similarities and connections with Simone. They had been friends. How close were they? Were they in the same friendship group, and who else was in it that was still conscious and questionable? Where had they all been recently? Could they have accessed drugs?

If the girls had not got hold of the drugs themselves, then who else could have supplied them, and with what intent?

As far as suspects went, he still had a ridiculous number, most of whom he'd ruled out on grounds of absurdity alone. Why would, for example, a Gallery trustee like the former director of programming at the BBC want to drug a teenage girl? Unless Beth was right, and the first girl's parentage was somehow involved. Could Simone's father have been present that night, and been unhappy about being unmasked? It was melodramatic, straight out of one of the books that, unbeknownst to Beth or his colleagues, he was addicted to. But he was willing to bet his entire collection of Margery Allinghams – including a pristine edition of the *Tiger in the Smoke* – that nothing as ornate lurked behind this killing spree. Plus, it didn't explain the second girl's overdose, unless the murderous father was trying to cover up the motive for the first?

He sighed. Deeply. The easiest way to put that side of the investigation to rest was to ask the mother. Little though he wanted to intrude on her grief, he needed to chase up this loose end and tidy it away. And, unfortunately, it was not the sort of interview that he felt happy about delegating to a subordinate. The woman was facing the most terrible loss a parent can confront. She had to be approached with great sensitivity.

Not for the first time, York wished that Beth actually was a member of his team, instead of just being an intermittent thorn in his side. She would have been great at an interview like this. She could do empathy, all right, but she also had an edge. And no-one found her threatening. He supposed that was a height thing. In a way, it was a perfect disguise. She was more or less the right size to fit in his pocket, but with an attitude that even this room couldn't contain.

He flipped the notebook shut, cross with himself for going off at a tangent again. OK. He needed to focus, and he needed to get this done. No point in putting it off forever. A duty avoided was, in his experience, a duty that just loomed ever larger. He should get it out of the way now.

Just as he was finally collecting up his phone and scooping the loose change off his desk, the landline rang. He pounced on it in relief.

A couple of minutes later, he bounced out of the office with a spring in his step. Yes, it was unorthodox but, shoot him, he was going to take Beth along for the ride. She didn't know it yet, she'd just requested one of her speciality coffee meetings at that God-awful place she always picked. He didn't understand it; there were some decent places in Dulwich. But she chose the same appalling spot.

Well, this time, he was going to whisk her off to see Simone's mum. She'd brought it on herself in a way. She'd been the one to suggest that the father might have played a part in the crime, never dreaming of course that she'd have to be in on confronting the mum. York, despite himself, was going to rather enjoy this. He had no desire to upset Jo Osborne all over again, but it might show Beth that throwing out crazy theories had consequences. You had to test them, and that often involved stepping on people's toes, or in this case, the much more fragile feelings of a recently bereaved mother.

***

'Ok, Ok, I realise that was all a totally pointless exercise, and so painful, too. Next time I have an idea like that, can you please just shoot me?' said Beth, her fringe drooping over her face.

The last twenty minutes spent with Jo Osborne had been agony. The woman's eyes were not just red-rimmed with prolonged crying, but seemed to have sunk back into her head. If it wasn't for her little son, Lewis, York would have seriously worried about her. But keeping going for her one remaining child was giving Jo a reason to put one foot in front of the other.

Paula – the fresh-faced police Family Liaison Officer, or FLO – had left them to it pretty sharpish, legging it outside for some fresh air. It wasn't that Jo's place was stuffy. It was small but carefully kept. But grief hung around her and her surroundings like a pea soup fog. At least here, Paula didn't have to act as the spy in the camp, befriending an ostensibly shattered family only to help build the case against them if it turned out that things were more sinister than they seemed. There was no suspicion that Jo had had the slightest involvement in Simone's overdose.

But in a way, having been trained to play a double game, Paula seemed to have found watching sincere and harrowing grief, unalloyed with guilt, more taxing than trying to catch out a criminal. Her own eyes were red, a fact which York had noted. He'd sort it out when he got back to the station. There'd either be a change of officer or the decision that the family could manage from this point on.

From a budgetary point of view, the latter decision would be miles better, but he wasn't sure that Jo could hack it quite yet. He'd get a nice lad in just for a day or two. Be good for the boy, Lewis, to have some male company, and Jo might get back on her feet with someone else to cook for. It sounded crass, but York had seen this sort of thing up close more times than he would have liked, and tasks that had to be performed – no matter how routine they were – really helped people from disappearing into depression. Things were going to be very tough for Jo for months to come.

One of the worst things she was going to have to face, and that would come quite soon, was the horrible realisation that they wouldn't be able to have a funeral for Simone, possibly for some time. Until someone was brought to book, the girl's body remained the most eloquent weapon at the disposal of the prosecution. And once someone was charged, the defence then had the right to conduct its own forensic tests. It was a last indignity, but one which all families in this position had to face, in the interests, he sincerely hoped, of justice.

When the time was right, he would suggest to Jo that she hold a service of remembrance or thanksgiving for her daughter, which would have to take the place of a funeral for now. He wouldn't be dragging Beth with him to have that little chat, though, and he was sorely regretting his decision to take her with him this afternoon. He glanced over at her sympathetically. She still looked broken up.

'Look, you were right. It was worth going into,' said York reassuringly. 'And now we know. Jo's dad was just an ordinary shit of a lad, who scarpered the way the feckless ones do, all of 14 years ago. Luckily, he didn't get so far away that we can't check his whereabouts. But I'd say that not in a million years is the type of waster Jo described the kind of person who'd be on that St Christopher's Hospice drinkies list, for sure.'

'I'm surprised at Jo. But she didn't know she was going to get pregnant, I suppose. It was just a fling. And she didn't know he'd abandon her either. Poor woman. I bet that's the last bad decision she made – apart from giving Simone the chance to go to the College School.' Beth sighed again and stirred her cappuccino in lacklustre fashion. York was casting about for ways to cheer her up when she took up another thought.

'Do you really think it might have been any of those other grandees that were there?'

'It's hard to believe,' said York. 'But we'll have a delve. I've got the team on it, and in fact they should be through pretty soon. You can imagine, a lot of the invitees have been quite shirty about being questioned. There's nothing like a murder squad detective ringing you at work to piss off your average company director or banker. It's cheered my DCs up no end, that little job. But honestly? I can't see any of that bunch toting a drugs cocktail like the one Simone had rattling around inside her. A bit of coke, in the 1990s, maybe for that lot. But backstreet dirty drugs, fake MDMA, a nasty bit of acid? Nope, it's not the kind of thing you get round the back of those Soho clubs that media types love, even nowadays.'

'So, where does that leave us?' said Beth. Her voice was monotone, her posture defeated. At least York had persuaded her to go to Jane's instead of that dire place Aurora for a restorative coffee afterwards. They would both have felt like shooting themselves if they'd had to suffer the Aurora's dishwater brew on top of the grim interview they'd just had.

'Look, as you know, I'm a realist. There's a lot of crime in London. There's stabbings, robberies, drugs, terrorism, stuff going on every day. By the law of averages, we can't clear everything up. Not with our own numbers going down, and our resources disappearing the same way. If I were to DNA test Simone's dad, I'd have to scrimp somewhere else – not bother checking all the drinks party alibis, maybe. It's a numbers game. Yes, I like catching the bad guys – that's why I joined the force – but it's naïve to think there's always a neat explanation, or that we can always go on and on until we get to the solution.'

As he'd hoped, the familiar spiel about not expecting results riled Beth. Immediately, she was sitting up straighter, and there was the old fire in her eyes as she pushed her heavy fringe out of the way and gave him a piece of her mind.

'You can't tell me this is one of those random crimes! There's no comparison between some gang-stabbing and the planning and cunning, and, oh, just *sheer evil* that was involved in draping Simone over that tomb. We have to stop this person, or they *will* do it again,' she said, leaning forward and seizing York's sleeve.

He looked down at her little pale hand, the nails neat but free of the frippery of varnish, and thought how it summed her up – strong, capable, but also in need of protection. His other hand came down to settle over it, but too late, she'd taken hers away and was now fussing with her coffee spoon, eyes lowered, clearly feeling she'd said, or done, too much.

'A second girl has already been drugged, after all. This isn't an isolated thing. So, we *have* to go on.'

York tried to suppress a smile at the effectiveness of his tactic. Luckily, his phone buzzed as a message came in, and he could legitimately bend over it and press a few buttons. Then he was sitting up straighter, too, and drinking down his coffee as fast as possible.

'Speaking of Lulu Cox, that was the hospital. She's just coming round. Come on, drink up.'

Beth didn't need a second urging. She was on her feet, and swigging the last of her cappuccino. If they were off to the hospital, who knew when she'd next get a decent cup?

***

In some ways, it was a replay of Beth's earlier scene with Simone Osborne. The room was as functional and cheerless, the view of the car park as uninspiring. The figure in the bed was pale and lying under a cheerless NHS standard-issue, blue blanket, which could have been the twin of Simone's. It might even have been the very same coverlet, boiled to aseptic cleanliness in between usages.

There was one important difference, though. The girl in this bed was propped up on pillows and, though her long

211

rusty-red hair was lank and sweaty and her face pinched, there was colour in her cheeks. A stern-looking nurse bustled over and checked her pulse, then said, 'Not too long with her now. Five minutes at most.'

York and Beth approached the bed as the nurse pottered out of the room, setting the folder of medical notes on the window sill and then shutting the door emphatically. The mild kerfuffle seemed to disturb the girl, who moved her legs restlessly. Then her eyelids fluttered, and green eyes squinted at them, confused. The girl struggled to sit up and shade her eyes against the sun from the window, then winced at the stab of the cannula in the back of her hand, feeding into a drip which tethered her to her bed.

'What's going on?' she said, her voice croaky with disuse.

Beth went over to the bedside table and poured some water from the plastic jug, handing it to the girl, who gulped it gratefully. Some ran down her chin, and Beth wiped it away with a corner of the coverlet, having cast around in vain for some tissues.

'Lulu, I'm a police officer,' said York, scooting a chair up to the bedside and leaning earnestly toward the girl. 'Can you remember what happened to you? Anything you tell us will help us to find out who did this. And who gave the drugs to Simone, too.'

'Simone?' said Lulu. 'How is she?'

There was a pause. Beth looked at York, who shook his head silently, but Lulu was watching them carefully. 'Something's happened, hasn't it? Where is she? What's happened to Simone?'

'Shh, shh, don't distress yourself,' said Beth quietly, stroking the arm which was free of tubing, while York glanced quickly over at the door. He didn't need that officious nurse to walk back in and terminate the interview before they'd got anywhere.

'Don't worry about all that now,' said York. 'What matters is that you should tell us exactly what you remember, before you started feeling ill. Where were you? And what

212

were you doing?' He didn't want to make it sound accusatory, but they needed some facts. And soon, if they were going to get anywhere. The trail was cooling with every hour that passed and, while he was philosophical about the prospect of never finding a culprit, he knew Beth would never forgive herself if they couldn't wrap all this up neatly.

'Anything you can tell us would be really helpful,' Beth cooed gently at the girl, smiling reassuringly. She was fitting effortlessly into the good cop role – anything to get some information.

Lulu Cox wrinkled her forehead with the effort of memory, her fingers pleating the covers. 'It's all a bit vague. I had my meeting at… well, my usual meeting… then I don't know.'

'Sorry, Lulu, but what was that meeting? Can you tell us?' Beth leaned towards the girl earnestly.

Lulu averted her eyes and, if York wasn't mistaken, the colour in her cheeks mounted. Whatever it was, either shame or embarrassment – maybe both – was keeping her quiet.

'Lulu, I shouldn't have to remind you that this is an ongoing police investigation. There are very serious crimes that have been committed here, and you may be the only person who can help us at this stage. You have a duty to tell us everything that could help.'

York didn't want to sound too aggressive – the girl had only just woken up from a coma, for God's sake – but on the other hand, if she didn't get on with her story, then there could be another victim, and he didn't want to be breaking bad news to any more families.

Lulu swallowed, her throat clearly painful. Probably had her stomach pumped in an effort to stop the drugs mashing her organs, the way they'd eaten through Simone's. He hated having to bully someone so vulnerable, and a girl who was of an age to need a responsible adult with her during questioning, at that – but needs must. Just when he thought he was going to have another go at her, and go in hard this time, she broke into speech.

'It was at the Wellesley, OK? That's where my meeting

was. I go there every week for a session. They say I'm getting better and *I* think I'm fine without all this stuff, but my parents, well, they push me to keep going with it.'

York saw Beth take a covert glance at the girl. Probably wondering what she was having all these meetings at the Wellesley for. Fair point. He was no judge of the heft of a normal teenager, but Lulu didn't look anorexic to him. OK, she was slight, but surely within normal bounds; not the bags of bones he'd seen some girls reduced to on the pro-ana websites he'd checked out after talking to Maria Luyten. Then he saw Beth's eye go to a swathe of bandages on the girl's other wrist. He'd assumed they had something to do with the drip. But on the other hand…

Lulu saw Beth and York's glance and she hugged her arm in defensively, looking downwards. Looks like they'd found themselves a cutter. York sighed. If he'd been doubtful about the wisdom of talking to the girl on her own before, he was now doubly concerned. She was clearly mentally vulnerable as well as having been through the wringer physically. Just as he was about to call a halt, Beth spoke again, in the soft quiet voice that seemed to be doing so much to get the girl's trust. Good for her, he thought, and relaxed back into his chair again.

'Lulu, I'm a mum, and I know how worried your own parents must have been about you. They're going to be so pleased that you've woken up. Believe me, it's the best news they'll have ever had.' York noticed that her large grey eyes were bright with unshed tears. Must be imagining herself in their situation. Well, any parent would sympathise. It must be agony. 'Can I just ask you, do you remember anything after the Wellesley?'

'Well, not really. I sort of remember going to the café and thinking maybe I'd pop in on Simone while I was around here.'

'Oh. Well, I suppose it is quite close…' Beth said, then fell silent, an arrested expression on her face.

'Well, *duh,*' said Lulu, a ghost of her normal sarcastic teenage self flashing to the surface.

214

'Really? They're quite a way from each other, though, the Wellesley and this hospital, aren't they?' said York.

'The Wellesley's only across the car park from the main building, bit of a schlepp, but it's all exercise,' said Lulu defensively.

Maybe, as well as the cutting, she was interested in burning off calories as well, York thought.

'Yes, that's right,' said Beth, as though she was talking to herself. 'We've parked in different car parks each time we've come, and they're on different roads, but it's all inter-connected. Granted, it's about a ten or fifteen-minute walk.'

She'd lived in Dulwich all her life, and King's was her nearest A & E, as well as the place where James had spent his mercifully brief illness, but she'd never actually been to the Wellesley before their interview with Maria Luyten. She'd just heard tell of it; the place kids got bundled off to. A germ of a thought was beginning to sprout. She remained silent, thinking, while York carried on.

'So, did you visit Simone?' He knew the answer would be in the negative. No-one had been allowed through the door, apart from her mother. But he wanted to keep Lulu talking.

'Well, I was in the café, I got a drink, I was thinking about going over to see Simone, especially as one of the, erm, one of the doctors' kids was hanging around, and I didn't want to talk to him.'

'He's your age, is he?' York said with a smile. They wouldn't be the first youngsters to meet in inauspicious surroundings. But he was way off in his suspicions, if Lulu's look of disgust was anything to go by.

'No, just a boy. About the same age as my brother. I wasn't in the mood to talk to *kids*... can't remember what happened next... I sort of remember the lobby, or the car park, it was warm and I was tired.'

There was a frown on the girl's face and she was looking pale again. Even if the nurse hadn't hurried in and officiously shoved him from the bedside, so that she could take Lulu's temperature again and exclaim how exhausted she looked,

York would have been wrapping up the interview anyway. There was only so much the child could take.

Beth was unusually quiet as she gathered up her bag and gave the girl in the bed an absent pat on the arm and a smile. As they walked down the corridor, York's shoes squeaking on the lino as usual, he turned to her. 'What did you think of all that, then? We didn't get much out of her, did we?'

He was braced for her disappointment. What he wasn't expecting was the maddeningly impish smile that peeped up at him from under Beth's unruly fringe. 'On the contrary. I think we may be close to a breakthrough.'

York came to a halt. 'This isn't going to be the moment when you hare off on your own to do something stupid and incredibly dangerous, is it?'

Beth looked up with every appearance of injured innocence. 'I don't know what you mean. I just need to go away and think about it all for a time. But I do think we've had such great long lists of suspects, all the waiters at the party, all the invitees as well, that we haven't been able to see the wood for the trees. The thing about Dulwich is that it's a small place, and small things matter. We should be thinking *small.*'

York, staring down at the diminutive figure, muttered something indistinct but decidedly aggrieved under his breath, and stalked down the corridor as fast as he could. Knowing that Beth was having to break into a canter to keep up was a small consolation for the sudden worry that, once again, she was going to come up with a solution before he did.

They were almost at his car, with Beth seriously pink in the face and even York a little out of breath, when his mobile shrilled.

'What? *Another* one?' he barked into the phone.

Suddenly, resentment was flung aside and it was all business, rushing back to Dulwich with the siren screaming. Second time around in a speeding police car with the blues and twos going, Beth couldn't help a thrill at the way other cars had to scurry to avoid them like courtiers making way for a monarch on the warpath. Best of all, she felt a lot less like throwing up. As soon as the first white picket fence came into view, though, York screeched over to the side of the road, reached over her to fling the passenger door open and said, 'I'll catch up with you as soon as I can.'

She'd been summarily dismissed. No sooner had she scrambled out than the car was off again at break-neck pace, threading through the traffic and into the distance. Damn. She couldn't make out where he was going, but it was somewhere in the village. And it certainly looked serious. She'd never seen him quite so silent with concentration before. She checked her watch. Still quarter of an hour 'til pick-up time. She shrugged her shoulders, and started to walk. No point, as usual, in going back to Wyatt's. She might as well go early to the Village Primary, get some brownie points with Ben for not keeping him waiting for a change.

Beth wasn't quite the first at the gates. There was already a fair sprinkling of mums waiting for kids from the first years of Primary, where dependency levels ran higher – amongst the mothers. She recognised one whom she'd chatted with before, and went over to say hello. The woman – a pretty, assisted blonde in her mid-thirties – was wearing the bright mismatched florals that gave away the fact that she had daughters, and did all her own clothes shopping, as well as theirs, in bulk online from the same scrummy store. Possibly after one too many glasses of Chardonnay.

'Haven't seen you for ages. How've you been?' Beth asked politely.

'Well, Jocasta's just got a distinction in her Grade One violin, and Veronique only got a merit in ballet, but she started less than two months ago. So, we're all good! And how's… erm?'

Beth was past marvelling at the thought that this woman had once had a job and a *life* of her own, and went straight to racking her brain to think of something Ben had done recently that she could ante up.

'Um, I'm pretty sure he's just moved to a new level in Angry Birds?' she said tentatively, and caught sight of

Belinda MacKenzie standing a couple of metres away, with her usual friends in tow. Belinda was beckoning her over and, for once, Beth was relieved to do her bidding. ''Scuse me,' she said, gesturing in Belinda's direction.

'Oh, *of course,*' said the other mother, all but dropping a curtsey to the Queen Bee.

'So, have you *heard?*' said Belinda, with no preamble at all, the moment Beth reached the group. 'No, you must have done, you know all the insider police info, don't you, Beth? That handsome inspector and you are virtually inseparable, I hear.'

Beth, immediately regretting her hasty decision to come over, tried to keep Belinda on track. 'What's the news, Belinda?' she said crisply.

Instantly, Belinda's face lit up. 'Well, you'll probably have all the details, but I've just heard there's been another, *you know*, at the College School.'

'Another what?' said Beth, feeling as usual that whatever game Belinda was playing, she didn't have time. Or the rules. Or the inclination to participate, even if she'd had the other two prerequisites.

'Another girl... who's killed herself. Or tried to. Isn't it *awful*?' There was no disguising the relish with which Belinda imparted her juicy chunk of gossip. Her tone might be low and serious, but her eyes were shining with excitement.

Beth was aghast. 'No! Are you sure? How do you know?'

'My au pair was sneaking off to meet one of her friends in the park. I wouldn't mind but she scrimped a full hour off the cleaning today, and the packed lunches she made for the kids, well, she didn't even peel the carrots before chopping them into sticks,' Belinda said, gazing round at her coterie, who looked suitably scandalised at this slipshod behaviour. No child of Belinda's should ever have to tangle with carrot skin, although since the carrots were organic presumably no harm would befall them even if they did. But you *never knew*. And it certainly wasn't down to any au pair to play fast and loose with the poor darlings' immune systems.

'So, how did *she* know?' said Beth, trying to get things back on track and away from the carrot skin *débacle*

'She heard all the sirens, of course. It was a few doors down from us. The Jones-Creedy girl. She was carried out on a stretcher. Oxygen mask, paramedics. It was the full *Holby City*, she said. She loves that show. I never watch it, of course,' Belinda tacked on, and the heads around the circle of mothers nodded reflexively. You could admit to watching *One Born Every Minute* under torture, as that was about babies and, by extension, the glory of motherhood. But a medical *soap* was out. Officially, Belinda and her friends watched nothing but challenging Scandinavian dramas on BBC4, and absolutely adored them. What they were glued to in the quiet afternoons was their own business.

'Wait a minute. What time was this?' said Beth.

'Um, I think it was around 2.30, 2.45 – not long ago,' said Belinda. Then she finally asked a question of her own. 'Why?'

'Oh… just testing a theory, that's all,' said Beth, her brows pulled low under her fringe. The news about Sophia Jones-Creedy was dreadful. A third overdose. And this girl, everyone agreed, had been a string-puller, not a victim. This was no doubt what York had rushed away so importantly to deal with. On the face of it, they must be connected, if it was drugs all over again. But it did throw out Beth's new and cherished brainwave completely.

'What do you think's going on, Belinda, you must have an idea?' Beth asked her point-blank.

Belinda raised her eyebrows in surprise – as far as she was able. 'Well, Beth, I thought you were the one who was good at these puzzles? To me, it seems obvious.'

'Really?'

'Yes, it's all part of that awful gothic teen stuff, you know, like that show on cable, *Thirteen Reasons Why*. Of course, we only have the cable for the au pair,' she added quickly, and the circle nodded devoutly.

'*Thirteen Reasons*?'

'Yes, it's some extended suicide note from a teenager, showing how everyone was horrid to her and then she tops herself. You know the kind of thing they love. Very gloomy but a massive hit. Haven't you heard of it?'

'Ben's not at that age, thank goodness.'

'Nor are mine, Beth, but forewarned is forearmed, you know,' said Belinda severely. 'It's our duty to be informed, isn't it?' It was true, everyone knew she spent a huge amount of time scanning child safety websites while the au pair took the kids to the park.

'Oh, but isn't your Allegra a teenager now, Belinda?' said Jen Patterson, one of the bolder mums in the circle.

Beth had always liked Jen's no-nonsense daily uniform of jeans, stripy Breton top, and a nice but weathered Mulberry messenger bag slung crossways across her slim frame. She had a narrow, freckled face, dead straight mid-brown hair, and an easy smile. As a freelance IT consultant, Jen had been called in a few times to untangle the MacKenzie home hub, and Belinda now looked on her as her own personal Internet wizard, which Jen appeared to take with easy grace.

Belinda looked nonplussed for a moment. She was not used to being second-guessed, especially not by those she looked on virtually as staff. But she needed Jen – she had a suspicion that her second son had found a way around her firewalls – so she trilled a laugh.

'Well *technically*, Jen, *technically*, you're right, Leggy is just thirteen. But she's such an innocent. She doesn't give me a moment's trouble, you know.' Belinda smiled blithely round the group.

Beth was pretty sure that Leggy MacKenzie had been in at least one group shot of rowdy teens she'd spotted on Facebook, marauding around the park one afternoon with what looked suspiciously like three-litre bottles of Frosty Jack's cider. She said nothing, but the glances left and right from some of the other mums told a story. It was going to be a very brave woman indeed who broke through Belinda's blissful ignorance.

Beth also shuddered inwardly at the casual nickname 'Leggy', wondering what on earth would have happened if her own parents had bestowed the name Allegra on *her*. It was fine for Leggy Macky, as she was known. She'd inherited her mother's commanding height and both parents' blithe confidence. But for Beth, well, she didn't even want to think about it.

More alarming, though, was the thought that maybe all parents wilfully ignored the signs of burgeoning adulthood in their children. Would she, too, be caught in this trap? There would come a time when Ben was the one sneaking out with friends, drinking in quiet, or not so quiet, corners, and behaving like the teenage idiot he would doubtless become. She hoped that Katie, at least, would be bold enough to tell her what was going on to her face, if she ever needed to. In fact, they needed to make a pact to do the same for each other.

There were certainly things that no parent wanted to know about their child, and vice versa. Puberty, adolescence, interest in the opposite sex – these were not the things they signed up for when they first started to moon over impossibly tiny bootees in the John Lewis baby section and decided reproduction was a great idea.

Beth realised that she and James had thought of babies as human pets, which would probably turn out to be no more burdensome than Magpie or her tabby tomcat predecessor, Sparky, who'd been around in James's day. As long as they had an open cat flap and access to the food that nine out of ten felines preferred, all was pretty much right in their world. Unfortunately, little of that worked with children. Food and shelter were just the start. None of the things that you took for granted in civilised adults – like good manners, consideration, and empathy – seemed to come as standard with a child. You had to input all the circuitry yourself; a process which often seemed unbelievably laborious. *Say please, say thank you, don't push that little boy over*, on and on went the litany. You had no sooner got used to, and found clever ways to deal with, a difficult phase, than it was over

221

with no warning, and something even more challenging had sprung up its place.

Beth had been patting herself on the back for a while now, for negotiating all the early stuff reasonably successfully, much of it on her own. But maybe, just maybe, the coming years were going to prove the real test, after all. Just when she thought she'd got this parenting lark cracked.

'Does Allegra – um, Leggy – know Sophia at school?' said Beth, remembering that, of course, Belinda's daughter was at the College School

'Just slightly. She's in the year below. I shouldn't say this, as the poor girl's in hospital...' The group of mothers leaned in fractionally, like birds expecting breadcrumbs to be scattered before them. Gossip was a currency, and no-one wanted to miss out. '...but Leggy says she's a bit of a ringleader. You know the type. She's somehow got a bit of a clique going, makes all the rules, lays down the law, and everyone just does what she says. Quite ridiculous, the way these teenage girls let themselves be bossed around, in my opinion,' said Belinda definitively.

All around her, heads nodded. Jen Patterson caught Beth's eye for a second and both smiled, then looked away quickly. Belinda, catching the exchange of glances, narrowed her eyes at Beth. The high priestess had sensed a doubter in her ranks. For a second, Beth felt again the chill wind which had kept her so far from Belinda's group for so long.

Then Belinda remembered that if anyone knew the inside story on the other girls at the College, it would be Beth. She half smiled at her, and said, 'Well, you probably know more about what's going on than anyone. What do *you* think is behind it all?'

Beth paused for a beat. It was a question that had been baffling her. Up until a few minutes ago, she'd thought she might be close to cracking it, but now she was back to square one again. But that didn't mean that she had no ideas. And this might be a good forum to float some of them, and see if she could glean any new information.

'I think it's very difficult being a teenage girl now. I'd

hate it, myself.'

'Why on earth do you say that?' said Belinda, with a contemptuous shrug of her shoulders. 'Our girls have so much that we didn't.'

Beth stored this away as interesting. She'd always assumed that Belinda came from a moneyed background, but something in her tone implied that she was consciously ensuring her own children had things that she herself had been deprived of.

She answered slowly. 'In material terms, maybe they do have more than we did. We all have lovely homes and they go to great schools. But think of what they *also* have that *we* didn't. Social media. It's breathing down their necks the whole time. The pressure to be out there all the time, living a perfect life, on Facebook, Instagram, Snapchat, or whatever the latest thing is this week. It's like Big Brother watching them all the time. And worse than just watching, judging and ranking them on how they are performing. They're not wise enough, yet, to know that half the pictures they see, or probably way more than that, are airbrushed, filtered, altered, tinted, and nothing like the originals. And not everyone smiling their heads off with friends is really having a good time. There is so much pressure on them to be having fun, getting 'likes', be out there, and be happy, happy, happy. I'd hate it.'

There was silence after Beth's speech, and she wondered if she'd said way too much. If she were a teenager these days, she would just stay off social media as much as possible and try and live a life under the radar. But that took a certain sort of insouciance and inner confidence. Much though she often felt like an imposter about to be found out, Beth knew she did have hidden reserves of strength that had already got her through some terrible crises and would always stand her in good stead. Not everyone was as forthright, or as doughty, as she was. And teenage girls were notoriously flaky. Small wonder they couldn't all hack it.

'Well, I'm not sure about all that,' said Belinda, slowly smiling around her little group and almost daring anyone to

223

agree with Beth. 'Being popular is just something you're either born with or you're not. You don't have to work at it, do you? By the way, just wondering who's coming over to coffee at my place tomorrow after drop-off? Just the usual gathering, and Juanita's making some pastries. All welcome,' she said with a bright smile of dismissal, and made for the playground, where one of her sons had emerged from the classroom and seemed to be clouting another boy around the head with his book bag.

There was a shuffling of feet and an exchange of glances around the little group, as though the headmistress had left the assembly.

Jen Patterson piped up. 'I think there's a lot in what you say, Beth. My friend's daughter's in the same class as Leggy, Year 8. She's twelve, but already she spends hours on her phone after school. I remember when I was that age, I'd drive my mum mad ringing my best friend, who I'd sat next to all day at school, and chatting for hours. I've no idea what we talked about now, but it seemed important. Ran up the phone bill hugely! But now, with these girls, it's not about chatting to a friend, it's about posing, taking all these selfies, posting stuff to Instagram – it's hard work, not fun at all, as far as I can see.'

There was a little murmur, as the mothers started agreeing and exchanging notes.

'My daughter seems to see herself as a brand, it's as though – I don't want to say it as it sounds so bad – but as though she's marketing herself online. Looking for the best angle,' said one.

'They see celebrities doing it, like the Kardashians, and they think that everyone can make a fortune and be really popular just by having a big smile – and a big bum,' laughed one of the other mums. The giggle took the tension out of the group. Then the trickle of children into the playground became a flood, breaking up the huddle of mothers as they greeted their children and wandered home with them, admiring proffered artworks and shouldering PE bags and instrument cases.

Beth, wincing as Ben slammed his book bag into her leg by way of an affectionate greeting, rumpled his hair and set off for the short walk home, her mind turning over the news about Sophia Jones-Creedy. She waved across at Katie, who was busy shepherding Charlie off to his piano lesson. Should she ring York after Ben's bedtime and try and extract the details from him?

As it turned out, she didn't have to call. At 6pm, the doorbell rang. Just about to dish up platefuls of chicken stir-fry – one of her sporadic attempts to sneak more vegetables into Ben's diet by hiding them amongst his favourite egg noodles – Beth sighed and went to the door. York blocked out most of the light as he stood there on the step.

'I shouldn't really be here, but…'

'Come in, come in,' ushered Beth, surprised but shooting back along the corridor which, all at once, seemed full of large policeman. The food would be getting cold. 'Would you like some?' She gestured at the wok, rummaging in the cutlery drawer for another knife and fork.

York, who knew there was no possible supper to be had in his flat, unless you counted Shredded Wheat with milk so long past its sell-by date that it clanked, tried to hide his delight. 'Well, only if you have enough.'

Beth, who was already throwing another nest of noodles into the covered pot on the hob, smiled and got a plate down from the cupboard, then slid a water glass across. 'Could you call Ben for me?' she said, turning back to the wok for a final steamy stir around.

Five minutes later, with them all settled around the table, Beth smiled. It felt cosy and domestic, and the usual silence which fell when Ben was concentrating on eating seemed harmonious and strangely comforting. York, looking up at that moment, smiled back.

Ben, having carefully separated his noodles from all known and unknown forms of vegetation to his satisfaction, and having polished off the chicken, sat back with a virtuous air. 'We learned about sperm today,' he announced loudly.

Beth, who'd been sipping her water, choked and felt her

eyes fill with tears and her face turn crimson. Oh great, she thought, as Ben leaped from his seat and gave her a hearty thump on the back that made her feel several times worse.

What on earth had been going on in class today? They usually got a note from the school when sex education was on the agenda, so that sensitive parents could take evasive action by pulling a sickie on behalf of their children. And of all the times suddenly to want to chat about school... Normally, Beth couldn't get a word out of the boy about what he'd been up to from 9am through to 3.30pm. *Now* he wanted to talk about what he'd learned?

Beth wiped her eyes on a bit of kitchen towel and tried to look receptive. No point in making a big deal of it. She should be fine talking about sex with her son. Even in front of a comparative stranger.

'Sperm?' she said, in carefully neutral, *let's talk about this calmly* tones.

'Yep. Sperm, blue, killer, humpback...' Ben intoned, bored now with the whole subject. For a beat, Beth was flummoxed. What kind of perversion was this? Then she realised.

'Whales!' she and York chorused together – catching each other's eyes and bursting out laughing. A moment later, though, Beth was serious again. It was lovely sharing a parenting moment – but somehow it just reminded her of all that she was *not* sharing, with James.

Though she told herself it was ridiculous to feel guilty, she couldn't help a twinge of sadness and regret, even while she was feeling happy. James, who had loved them both so deeply, had been cheated of so much.

Still, that was in the past now. Things had moved on, and she had to as well. Besides, there were more pressing matters on hand. Once again, the serene way of life of her little corner of the world was being threatened. When James had been snatched away, she had been powerless. But, with the strange events unfolding now in her midst, was it possible that she could actually shape events, even stop something evil that threatened them all? It was worth a try, wasn't it?

With these musings at the back of her mind, Beth was on autopilot as she read a story, tidied around her boy, and finally packed him off to his bed. York, meanwhile, had made himself comfortable on the sofa with yesterday's paper and his own thoughts.

It wasn't until Ben was finally asleep, an hour and a half later, after various curtain calls for glasses of water, last stories, and playground jokes that simply had to be told to York that very minute, that Beth finally got a chance to talk to the big policeman about the matter that had been burning away at her. But when she walked into the sitting room, he was asleep, head thrown back among the sofa cushions, long legs stretched out so that she had to jump over them like a steeplechaser to get to the kitchen. He must have been exhausted, she thought, as she noticed the way that his habitual frowning expression of laser-sharp concentration was smoothed out by sleep, leaving him looking ten years younger and oddly vulnerable. Not all that much more grown up than Ben, in fact.

Smiling, she flipped the kettle on, then started clattering about extra-loudly with the supper plates so that he'd come back to consciousness in his own time. Eventually, as she wiped the last spoon and rattled it back into the drawer, she heard stirring next door. She bustled in with a tray as York was sitting up, looking for all the world as though he was plumping the sofa cushions, rather than emerging from a deep and apparently much-needed snooze.

'So. Tell me about Sophia Jones-Creedy,' she said, putting a mug of coffee down in front of him and absently stirring her own mint tea. They were side by side now on the sofa, all remnants of PlayStation and homework tidied away, and Magpie the cat for once curled up in her designated bed instead of draping herself across the nearest human. The light was fading outside, and Beth had lit a couple of scented candles on the mantelpiece – partly, she told herself, to rid the kitchen of the last of the cooking smells; partly, because they just looked so pretty.

York, sitting across from her, looked as though he was

admiring the view. Though whether he was thinking of the candles, the garden, or even the woman, Beth had no idea.

'I knew you were dying to ask me about that. The truth is, we're not sure yet what happened. All I can tell you, really, is that it's not quite the same as the other two.'

'Not the same? You mean it's not an overdose?' Beth suddenly leant forward, the tranquil mood shattered. 'Are you sure?'

'Well, no. It's an overdose all right. And all three could have been self-inflicted. It's just that the drugs seem to be different.'

'Wait. So, you're now thinking the other girls could have been suicide attempts? Both Simone and Lulu?'

'I think it's a fair assumption, given all that's happened.'

'But what about the fact that Simone was *posed* in the Gallery? How are you saying that happened, if it was actually an overdose she took herself?'

'Well, if you think about it, the easiest explanation for that is that – she did it herself. That's what I've been coming round to thinking.'

'Really? But what do you mean?'

'I mean, she could have taken the drugs at the drinks party, then waited in the loos until everyone had gone, then laid herself out on the tomb as, I don't know, a really theatrical way to do away with herself.'

'But do you think she was that kind of girl? Does it fit with her character?'

York leaned back a bit, away from the fervour of Beth's questions. 'Well, I'm not sure. I'm beginning to think that no-one really knows what goes on in these girls' heads, least of all their parents.'

'I just don't think Simone was like that. Having met her mum, and heard about how hard she was working – and was she that into grand gestures? That was such a stagey set-up, the crossed hands, the mausoleum... No, I don't buy it. And what about Lulu? We both questioned her. She couldn't explain what happened, but I didn't get any sense that it was a suicide bid. Who'd commit suicide in a hospital canteen, for goodness' sake?'

'Well, what do you think has been happening, then?' York crossed his arms, stretched out his legs again across the rug – and inadvertently kicked Beth's foot. She shifted it quickly as he apologised. Somehow, the mood between them had been broken. Beth withdrew under her fringe and thought hard. Something was awry here. She wasn't sure what.

They just weren't on the same page. Beth had sensed something malign, right from the start of this whole affair. From the moment she'd clapped eyes on Simone, lying there abandoned and still, she'd known that someone had done this to her, that the girl was a victim. She just couldn't believe it was self-inflicted. With Lulu, she wasn't sure; she didn't know the circumstances, and she hadn't seen her when she was found. And Sophia Jones-Creedy? Well, that was something else again.

'You know, this is all wrong,' said Beth suddenly. 'If you'd told me that Sophia Jones-Creedy had been found in the Picture Gallery, laid out over a tomb with her hands crossed over her breast, I'd have thought, yes. She's the type to make that sort of grand gesture. If she'd been feeling suicidal, she'd make sure everyone knew it. You've seen her Instagram, I showed it to you. The girl's a poseur. She's never happier than when she's showing off, and she'll do anything to get a like.'

'Oh, wait a minute, that's harsh,' said York, wrinkling his brow.

'You're just saying that because she's young and pretty. But really, who spends that much time pouting into their phone? She's a schoolgirl at one of the toughest academic schools in the country. She shouldn't have time to be posting fifty pictures of herself a week, wearing next to nothing but tonnes of make-up and a minxy smile. But Simone, on the other hand. She worked really hard for that place, she had a mother who thought the world of her and wanted the best for her. I think her mum would have known if she was unhappy enough to have killed herself. And I don't think she'd have done it in a way that made a total show of her death and

229

dragged her family through all this publicity. She was a shy, hardworking girl, and someone *did* that to her. With Lulu, we haven't pieced together enough yet to work out what might have happened, but I didn't think she seemed depressed enough to want to kill herself. Have you thought about whether Sophia's suicide attempt was out of guilt, though?'

'Guilt? Is that what you think? That Sophia gave Simone the drugs, and maybe Lulu, too, then felt so bad about what's happened that she's tried to top herself as well?'

'Well, actually, no. That's not my theory. But it's better than yours, so far,' said Beth, with a flash of defiance in her grey eyes. The idea that she was brewing was a lot more radical than that. But she wasn't ready to expose it to the light of day. Not until she'd had a chance to test it, anyway.

She and York exchanged a long look. Whatever mood of accord had existed, earlier in the evening, was long gone. They were not seeing eye to eye at all and, wearily, Beth wondered if they ever would be.

'Right. Good to know your views. Well, probably time for me to get going,' said York, rising to his feet. As usual, Beth felt as though she was getting shorter by the second as he stood up. By the time he was upright, she was like Alice in Wonderland after drinking the shrinking potion.

Chapter Fourteen

Beth slept surprisingly well and, by the morning, was resolved on her course of action. Ben was marched off to school in double-quick time, and Beth was soon letting herself into the research institute which she had so woefully neglected in the last few days. To her shame, she saw there was even a thin film of dust on the box file which served as her in-tray. She hastily wiped it off with her sleeve and settled into the chair. Delving in a drawer, she found the internal phone directory which listed numbers not only for Wyatt's, but for its sister establishment as well, the College School.

She ran down the list with her finger then stopped and quickly made a call. 'Yes, it's Beth Haldane here from Wyatt's... Just wondered if you had a moment free this morning to discuss the slavery project... I've been told to keep you informed of everything that's going on, as my opposite number. Would that be possible? Yes, of course I'll hold.' Beth twiddled the phone cord as she waited. 'Hello? Yes, that would be perfect. See you soon, then.'

She replaced the receiver with a decisive click. A slow smile of satisfaction spread across her pale oval face. At last. She was really starting to get somewhere.

Forty minutes later, Beth was trotting through the plain gates of the College School. Though the red-brick, solid Victorian building spoke of well-heeled prestige, the girls' school, like any hard-working blue stocking, had been intended always to stay in the shadow of its glamorous, entitled brother establishment. But, thanks to the efforts of a succession of determined and dedicated headmistresses like Angela Douglas, the College School had crept up and up in the rankings, until today, where it had the audacity to rest a rung or two higher than Wyatt's. Despite this, Wyatt's was still the best-known and best-beloved of the two schools, and College girls were try-hard also-rans compared to the swaggering young gents turned out by the annoyingly cool Wyatt's machine.

Although Beth had been briefly introduced to her College School counterpart at the launch of the research institute, this would be their first proper one-on-one meeting. And, as ever, Beth had an ulterior motive. Would her job ever come first for her, she was beginning to wonder? Or would she always be using it as a pretext to get at some other, more pressing matter? Well, as long as her opposite number didn't guess her first concern wasn't the archives, then it didn't really matter, did it?

By the time Beth had found her way to the door of the office she needed, her heart was hammering and her fringe was sticking to her forehead. She was taking quite a big chance with this meeting. Was she walking right into trouble yet again?

She was just taking a moment to steady herself with a deep breath, when the door opened and a large figure bombed out, nearly knocking her over.

'Oh, you'll be the archives girl,' said Miss Troughton gruffly, steadying Beth with a large hand.

Beth, whose bag had inevitably gone flying, thanked her stars that for once its entire contents hadn't tipped out all over the corridor. She scooped it up hurriedly and stuck out a hand, hoping it wasn't clammy with nerves. She needn't have worried. Once it was engulfed in Miss Troughton's large, hammily pink fist, and squeezed tight, she could no longer really feel her nerve endings anyway.

'Come in, come in,' said Miss Troughton, guiding Beth with what she thought was a gentle hand but what felt to Beth like a hearty shove into a small room. It was almost like the before version of her own archives lair – unloved, full of large cardboard cartons, and smelling suspiciously dusty. It looked like her opposite number gave her job almost as much time as Beth herself did, she thought guiltily.

'Hum. Got a bit behind,' said Miss Troughton, giving the shelves a quick glance up and down. She was clearly taken aback at the state of the place. 'Getting the girls ready for French GCSE. Head of French, you see. Not always as much time for this rub— er, archive stuff, as I might like. Academics have to take precedence,' she said, her already hectic cheeks turning brick red.

Thank goodness, thought Beth. Miss Troughton was already on her mettle. Now, if she just played this carefully...

'Really? I'd heard smaller and smaller numbers of pupils were taking modern languages these days,' said Beth, head on one side, grey eyes shrewd.

Miss Troughton snorted. 'That's true. Bunch of... well... But makes it even more important, see, that the ones who do take French achieve a decent grade. If they play it cleverly, they can go an awfully long way now with a good French A level. Not a lot of competition, you see.' It was a point which played well at parents' evenings with ambitious parents.

For Beth, who had no axe to grind and no child – yet – to shoehorn into a good university, the whole subject was just a useful *entrée* to talking about Miss Troughton's pupils.

'You teach GCSE as well, don't you? And the run-up? Year 9?'

'Year 9. Yes,' Miss Troughton said it heavily. It sounded as though that particular year group gave her no great joy.

'Shall we sit down?' Beth urged. This archives office did boast a largish table and two chairs – a cut above Beth's own rickety quarters when she'd started in the job, before the transformation to institute status had considerably upgraded her furniture stock. Nowadays, she had a small round table in the corner of her office, where she could hold ticklish discussions about slavery – something she really must get round to doing as soon as she'd straightened this whole mystery out.

'How do you find teaching the Year 9 cohort?' she asked Miss Troughton lightly.

The woman peered at her keenly, but it seemed to suit

her a lot better to discuss her French classes than to talk about a slavery project which she quite obviously hadn't broached at all.

'Year 9 is a nightmare, even at the best of times,' she said with a sigh. 'I can't pretend to have much insight into how girls work these days, but Year 9 is always one of the most difficult years. It can be pretty toxic.'

'Toxic? Interesting choice of word,' said Beth, pouncing.

Miss Troughton looked taken aback. From having a general discussion about classes, they now seemed poised to dive into horribly murky waters.

'Well, I wouldn't know the first thing about *that*,' she said, with a bluff attempt at airy dismissal.

'About *what*, though? About something toxic in Year 9?'

Miss Troughton looked puzzled. 'Well, surely you've heard there've been… troubles?'

Beth put her most sympathetic face on. 'Teenage girls can be so difficult…'

'You've got that right,' said Miss Troughton gruffly. 'Beggared if I know what goes on in their heads. Different breed.'

'Really?' said Beth with gentle encouragement.

'In my day, we just got on with it. No time for all this socialising. Keep your head down, do your work, and get out. Otherwise, fail your exams and end up a *shop girl*,' said Miss Troughton with a shudder. It wasn't hard to see the driven grammar school pupil she'd been, eyes on the prize of university and a career. She could never have been a simpering assistant behind a counter. Unless it was at a butcher's, parcelling up the joints with those huge capable hands, thought Beth.

'You must have seen so many girls over the years. Is this year's cohort particularly bad, do you think?'

'*Bad* isn't the word. The trouble starts when you get a bright child who doesn't need or want to work. There can be a lot of game-playing in girls' schools, you know,' said Miss Troughton, darting a frank gaze at Beth.

Beth wondered whether Miss Troughton, back in the day,

had been on the receiving end of any of the casual cruelties that can make girls' lives agony at school – the deliberate exclusion, the sniggered jokes, the messages passed behind a sadly bowed back. But this wasn't the moment to excavate that corner of history. Beth needed to find out what was going on right now, and what part it might have played in the deadly events still unfolding.

'Is there one girl that you'd say was the ring leader?' Beth cut through any idea that bullying and manipulation wasn't going on in Year 9. Miss Troughton might have been oblique, but the message was clear: there was stuff afoot here that she didn't care for.

'There is. A*lways* one, you know?'

'Would you say she's worse than others you've come across?'

Miss Troughton sighed. 'She's very bright, not very happy, and that's not unusual. I've seen it before. But this time, there's more. It's – a motiveless malignancy.'

Coleridge's phrase fell heavily in the small, cluttered room. There was a pause. Beth marshalled her thoughts, trying to find a way to concoct her next question that wouldn't make her sound a bit loopy. But she needn't have worried.

'Do you think she's... evil?'

Miss Troughton's expression of relief and gratitude said it all. 'Yes, yes, I do. She's evil. There, I've said it now. I've thought it, many times, but I've tried not to believe it could be true.'

Beth absorbed all that Miss Troughton had said. 'So, do you think that this one particular girl is behind everything that's happened?'

Miss Troughton, her doughy features suffused with high colour, closed her eyes for a moment, then opened them to gaze beseechingly at Beth. 'I hope so,' she said finally. 'You know, I really do hope it's her.'

Beth paused. Now they were getting to the sticky bit. 'But... say this girl is, well, out of commission for some reason.'

Miss Troughton's small, worried eyes locked on to her own limpid grey ones. Beth knew she wouldn't get a name from the woman, years of teachers' confidentiality had drilled discretion into her, not to mention the loyalty to the College School which leaked from every pore. But it was evident that Miss Troughton badly wanted this dismal episode in the school's history to be over. How far would she go to help her?

'If the child were indisposed herself, you mean?'

'Yes, in a way similar to the others… Would you think that was just a bit of a smokescreen?'

'Yes. Yes, I definitely would,' said Miss Troughton, nodding with such emphatic relief that her chins juddered.

***

Beth mused on the interview the next day, as she ambled along the road with Ben. It was Saturday morning, and they were off to pay an impromptu call on Charlie and Katie. Normally, Beth would have rung first but, despite the fact that weekends were so closely guarded by Dulwich folk, who frankly needed the recovery time from their hectic schedules, she just had seized the impulse when it struck her.

The night before had been one of those evenings when she'd yearned for a grown-up to discuss things with. She'd tried Katie, but she'd been out at the theatre again and not able to talk. She'd even dialled York, but it had gone to voicemail – and she'd been glad. Her thoughts weren't yet well formulated enough to present him with. Because she was on the defensive so much with him, being the amateur to his professional, she felt her theory had to have achieved a certain degree of polish before she could lay it before him. And this theory was hardly shining – yet.

So, Beth and Ben bounced up to Katie's front door – now freshly repainted a delectable shade of radicchio pink, as part of the ongoing spruce-up – and rang the bell. It took a minute or two for Michael to fling open the door. A lovely man, he always appeared slightly tired and a bit rumpled. Today was no exception, as he stood in a creased blue linen shirt, looking vaguely perplexed before stepping forward into the regulation Dulwich double kiss.

'Ah, Beth. Quite a houseful,' he said, wandering towards the kitchen with them, then peeling off before they got there to take shelter in the swanky and hardly-used drawing room.

Beth just had time to register this as odd, when she saw why. Katie was sitting at the shiny marble breakfast bar with Maria Luyten, who had a tissue to her eyes and a steaming cup of tea at her elbow.

'Oh, I had no idea you'd be busy. I'm so sorry,' said Beth. She felt an immediate nasty pointed arrow of jealousy, at seeing Katie so wrapped up with someone else. It was ridiculous. Katie was allowed to have as many friends as she liked, and her sunny nature drew people irresistibly to her. And there was something else in the mix – a little prickle of alarm.

Before she had time to think it through, she realised Katie was semaphoring something to her with her wide eyes. 'No, no, that's great, have some tea,' she was saying emphatically, flipping the kettle on again and getting Beth's favourite large mug out of the cupboard. 'We were just talking about schools, and grades, and entrance exams and… stuff,' she added rather lamely. It sounded quite intense for a Saturday morning.

Meanwhile Ben, oblivious to the adult undercurrents, had run straight out into the garden, where Beth could see Charlie and little Matteo up to something in the summerhouse. He clearly had no qualms about becoming the third wheel. She went immediately to the sweep of windows, but the boys just seemed to be talking.

Beth wasn't sure whether to address the elephant in the room – Maria's tears – but decided that, as the woman was a psychiatrist, it would be ridiculous not to. 'Hope everything's all right, Maria?' she asked.

Maria looked up from her tissue and smiled gratefully. 'So sorry. You must find me so emotional. It's just that Katie's been such a support throughout all this.' Maria raised

237

swimming eyes to Katie and smiled tremulously.

'I hope nothing's happened?' said Beth. She was being nosey, she supposed, but given Maria's borderline unhelpfulness last time they'd met at the Wellesley, and especially that well-aimed barb about teenage girls and puberty, she really didn't care.

'No, no, not at all. It's more that everything seems to be settling down now at last, and that's made me realise how stressed I have been, all this time. It's such a relief,' Maria said, dabbing her eyes with the now rather sodden tissue.

Katie and Beth's eyes met briefly over the shiny brown hair and, if Beth wasn't mistaken, Katie – the most compassionate and caring woman in SE21 – did the tiniest eye-roll. Sobbing about the good times wasn't very Dulwich.

'Well, that's great,' said Beth in hearty tones which, to her own ears, sounded distinctly fake. 'I'll drink to that.' She raised her scalding tea to her lips and took a tiny, but appreciative, sip. Katie always made an excellent cuppa.

'Oh look,' said Katie, pointing to the huge windows at the end of the kitchen, which were closed today as it was cloudy and hadn't warmed up outside yet. 'The boys are toasting each other, too.'

Outside, they could see the three lads, each raising plastic beakers to each other. It was too far to see anything clearly – Katie's garden was genuinely enormous – but Beth could have sworn there was a twig poking out of Ben's beaker. She put her mug down with a thwack, and tea spilled everywhere.

'Should they be drinking that? What on earth is it?' wondered Katie.

The effect on Maria was astonishing. One moment, she was slumping over the marble countertop, twisting her tissue like a lacklustre romantic heroine. The next, she'd sat bolt upright, and all her attention was focused on the boys. 'Oh no! That's Matteo's game at the moment. He likes making these witches' brews. He calls them medicine. He wants to be a doctor.'

Beth and Katie looked at each other, Beth's eyes wide with horror, Katie's startled, not seeing the urgency or the problem. 'But that's rather sweet, isn't it?' said Katie, reasonable as ever. 'He wants to follow in your footsteps.'

'Oh look,' she added. 'I think they're doing a wassail – they're studying the Vikings in class, aren't they?' Outside, the boys raised their arms to shoulder height and clinked their cups in the morning light.

'Oh, *Dio mio*! I have to get out there,' screeched Maria, bolting for the doors.

She sprinted to the end of the room, fumbling with the unfamiliar catch on the large glass French windows, and Beth followed, scrabbling with the panes of glass and finally flinging the central door open. The two women rushed out into the garden just at the moment when the laughing boys raised their beakers to their lips and took hearty swigs.

***

The next hour had been out of a horror film. Beth would never forget seeing Charlie slump to the ground, moments before she and Maria thundered down the garden, the woman's normally sleek dark hair flying around her head like Methuselah's snakes.

For a moment, Katie was left sitting there in the kitchen, transparently wondering if this was this some new game she didn't know about yet. Pretending to collapse in a faint? Was Charlie about to spring back up again with his usual infectious laugh? But he just lay there, prone, while the two other small boys and Beth looked on helplessly, and Maria bent over him with unmistakably business-like intent, rolling him onto his back and feeling for a pulse.

On the one hand, thank goodness she was a fully trained doctor. Even if her specialism was psychiatry, she still knew all the moves to counteract a hefty dose of poison. On the other hand, if she hadn't been a medic, would her son ever have picked up whatever twisted idea had got into his head? All this flashed through Beth's mind as she watched her friend finally streak up the garden towards her unconscious son.

239

With a trembling hand, Beth walked a few paces away, dialled three nines on her phone, and then rang Harry York for good measure. Voicemail, of course. He was never on the end of a phone when she needed him, she thought in panic. She was just about to rejoin the stricken cluster waiting on the sidelines when Maria shouted for her to bring mustard, salt, and hot water.

Though she badly wanted to stay with Ben – to protect her son from seeing whatever awful fate was befalling his best friend right in front of his eyes – she obediently ran back to the kitchen and started searching the cupboards. The trouble was, Katie had so many of them. And, behind the pristine facades of her kitchen units, there wasn't much of a system, Beth realised with a sinking heart. While she could have laid hands on her own pot of mustard in the middle of the night, wearing a blindfold, Katie's idea of organisation was to stuff everything wherever there was a space, then shut a sleek and beautifully designed door on it and move on with her day. A perfectly valid way of being, but not one which helped much in the current life-or-death contretemps.

After some increasingly panicky ransacking, Beth found a cache of condiments behind some breakfast cereal cartons, and immediately was confronted with a whole new worry. Was Katie just too posh to have the right kind of mustard? Yes, she had several jars of Dijon. She even had an ironic American mild hotdog mustard in a squeezy bottle, and she had wholegrain mustard cunningly flavoured with tarragon, all done up in an ornate jar with a frilly cover, the kind of thing that Dulwich residents gave each other for Christmas. But was there any *real* mustard, of the type that would get your tear ducts running, whether you liked it or not?

Beth was on the point of giving up when she finally found a pull-out, multi-tiered larder affair behind one of the doors. Amongst a vast cornucopia of canned goods that made her wonder if her friend was a secret prepper, she discovered a dusty and unopened jar of good old strong English mustard, the vicious colour alone guaranteed to get anyone retching.

She'd already boiled the kettle, so she loaded up a mug

with a ferocious brew of pink Himalayan salt and huge dollops of yellow mustard, ran out into the garden with it, and knelt on the grass. Though some of the liquid had spilled over her top and jeans, there was plenty left for Maria to trickle into Charlie's slack mouth.

His face was as pale as the sheets on the rotary washing line she could see several gardens along. *And who on earth lived there?* Beth wondered, with one corner of her mind. It really wasn't done to air one's laundry in public here, even if it was freshly washed.

Beth looked up to see Ben's anxious grey eyes trained on hers. Immediately, she tried a reassuring smile, but realised the best thing was just to hold her arms out for a hug. Ben, who normally was now much too grown up to consent to being babied in public, ran to her, fell to his knees on the grass and, to her horror, started to sob into her T-shirt. It had been a long time since he'd cried so hard.

She ruffled his dark hair absently, and her worried eyes met Katie's blue ones, brighter than she'd ever seen them before with unshed tears. They ended up in a little huddle together, the slight damp from the grass beginning to seep into their clothes, as they stayed by the still form and by Maria, who now eased her fingers into Charlie's mouth and turned him to the side. Immediately, he convulsed and started to vomit up the bright yellow, and much else besides.

Maria, holding his head, gave Katie a tremulous smile. 'The worst is over now,' she said. Katie met her gaze and turned her head away.

Beth looked up and wondered where Matteo had got to while all this was going on. He seemed to have the knack for effacing himself when he felt the need.

She finally saw him, a couple of yards away, on the swing which dangled from the big copper beech at the side of the garden. Their eyes locked for a second, then he turned those limpid brown eyes away and concentrated on his swinging. Soon all they could hear was the to and fro swish of the ropes, Ben's slight sniffing and, in the distance, the beginnings of the wail of sirens.

Chapter Fifteen

'It's a funny thing,' said Beth, as she peered into the depths of a particularly fluffy cappuccino at a table at Wyatt's Picture Gallery's outdoor cafe. She and Katie had just been round the gallery for the first time since the tragedy. For Beth, it had been like greeting old friends. The canvases might have their secrets, but they were far less deadly than those locked in people's hearts.

'What's that?' said Katie.

'Last time, I got quite a sense of satisfaction when the whole mystery was wrapped up. This time, it all seems like fragments.'

'Maybe it's more like real life,' said Katie.

Outwardly, she was still the smiling, happy woman Beth had always known. But Katie was a little guarded now, and a little more cautious. Before, she'd chided Beth for her over-protective ways. Now, she was the one who insisted on knee pads *and* a helmet when Charlie and Ben went skateboarding in the park. And Charlie, who before would have protested all the way there and back, now meekly wore the padding and just got on with it. One thing was for sure. He'd never be slathering mustard on a hotdog again, even the ironic American mild kind.

Beth knew Katie's hyper-vigilance wouldn't last forever. People recovered from the worst that life could throw at you. Jo Osborne, for example, was back at work now and, while she'd bear the scars of sorrow forever, she was getting up every morning for Lewis, which was all that anyone could ask of someone who'd lost a daughter so horribly. Beth, when she'd last had coffee with her, had thought her the bravest woman she'd ever known, and one of the nicest.

Lulu Cox had been discharged from hospital with a clean bill of health, and a resolve never to drink *anything ever* in a public place again, after Matteo had laced her drink with drugs in the hospital canteen.

Sophia Jones-Creedy, whose bright idea it had been to pose Simone on the tomb in Wyatt's Picture Gallery, declared to anyone who'd listen that she was beyond sorry. The story she told was that she'd lent Simone her outfit in the loos when they'd finished waitressing, as the girl was desperate to try on such a pricey dress, then been furious to find the girl slumped unconscious in it minutes later. She'd manhandled the girl onto the tomb 'for a laugh,' and to pay her back for passing out. Taking a jokey picture of her, and circulating it to her class had all been entirely in fun too, she assured anyone who'd listen.

And as for the crossing of the girl's hands over her chest, the gothic element of the whole business which had given Beth so many sleepless nights? Well, Sophia had said casually, her arms were just dangling, weren't they? She'd shoved them there, into that symbolic and time-hallowed position, just because she thought they'd look good in the photo.

How could she have known that the girl had been given drugs by her friend's little brother? she'd railed, when questioned by Harry York. It was nothing to do with her. She and all her friends had been drinking, and the rest of them were fine. She'd just thought Simone was 'tired' and 'lazy'. And yes, she'd taken her clothes and phone away with her, dumped them in a bin on the street, and left her there all alone without a backward glance. But she'd had no idea that the girl was *ill*.

And, *of course,* she had had nothing to do with the drugs, despite her connection to a notorious petty thief and dealer. This low-life, who she now insisted was a mere acquaintance, and not the boyfriend she'd boasted to friends about, had taken off, leaving his squalid flat empty. Rumour had it he was now to be found hanging around a rather good girls' school in north London.

243

It was Sophia's guilt and sorrow that had led her to 'overdose' – though it turned out that she'd taken fifty cod liver oil tablets, which should enable her to do the splits with the greatest of ease, but not to meet her maker any time soon.

For a while, it looked as though there'd be no official action taken against the girl. There was no direct criminal evidence against her, said the CPS, and Jo Osborne certainly didn't have the funds for a private prosecution, even if Sophia's lawyer mother hadn't been so vociferous in her daughter's defence. Her surgeon father, meanwhile, made all sorts of promises about future good behaviour.

But in the end, to Beth's relief, Angela Douglas had simply announced that the girl's place at the College School had disappeared. So, Sophia Jones-Creedy was last heard of at a maximum-security boarding school in Scotland, craning out of an upstairs window, desperately trying to get a solitary bar of signal on her mobile phone. It was, thought Beth, a fitting punishment for a social media junkie. If she'd had her way, the girl would have been signed up for compulsory art history classes, too, so that her histrionic flare for drama was at least allied to some depth of knowledge in future.

It was Maria Luyten for whom Beth felt a sneaking pity. The woman had been trying to combine a career and a family, and had come a deadly cropper – especially as far as all the right-wing newspapers that had followed the unfolding story had been concerned. Because she'd been out, easing the problems of other troubled children, her own son had been allowed to become a monster, so the narrative went. Certainly, there was something horrifying about the little boy, who'd decided to dose up the girls who came to his sister's house before the Picture Gallery event with a tiny bit of everything in his mother's doctor's bag.

There was no method in his madness, no dosage control; he'd just put a tablet of this, a vial of that, and a pinch of the other into one of the girls' drinks when they weren't looking. It had been Russian roulette. There was no malice against Simone personally, which was something that Jo Osborne said had eased her mind a little. Simone had been fine for the few minutes until she got to the drinks party, when her increasing clumsiness had caused her to become the brunt of Sophia Jones-Creedy's little digs and the group's teasing. She had then collapsed in the anteroom to the mausoleum – unseen by anyone except Sophia Jones-Creedy – once the hefty amount of diamorphine had kicked in.

The cocktail of strong antidepressants, huge quantities of paracetamol and temazepam, plus pinches of a random collection of street drugs that Maria had confiscated from her other patients, had then worked to destroy Simone's liver and put her in a coma.

Lulu Cox had been luckier; there hadn't been so much of the stuff left by the time Matteo poured his concoction into her drink at the hospital, and Charlie, getting the dregs of the batch, was the least badly affected of all.

Beth didn't know whether doctors usually locked up their pill supplies when at home, or whether Maria Luyten was unusually lax because she was stressed at work and having a hard time adapting to a new country, or because her children had various problems fitting in. All anyone really knew was that her eye was off the ball, and Simone Osborne had paid the price.

Matteo, at nine, was under the age of criminal responsibility, so he'd been made the subject of a Child Safety Order and was being supervised by a youth offending team from the council – at least, until the family moved. Because, call it coincidence, but the bank who employed Theo Luyten suddenly had urgent need of his expertise at head office. What Maria and Chiara would make of life back in the Middle East again was anyone's guess, but at least it would save Maria from the ignominy of being sent on a parenting course by the British courts.

Beth sighed, and stirred her cappuccino again.

Katie looked at her. 'What did your inspector say to you, you know, after we went to the hospital that, *that* day?'

'He's not *my* inspector,' Beth corrected automatically, then turned her memory back. They'd all been a bit out of their minds, with the worry over Charlie, and the creeping

245

realisation of Matteo's guilt, and the horror-struck collapse of Maria. Tempers had been running high. She wasn't sure, though, that that excused York's latest tirade.

'Why do you have to be involved? Why are you even here?' he'd shouted on the doorstep of Katie's house, as the ambulance carted Charlie, Katie, and an ashen Michael away.

'Look, if I wasn't here, then it would still be going on. I've told you what happened, and I've worked out how the Picture Gallery fits in. You could at least be a bit grateful that I've solved the whole thing for you,' she protested, her face red, her fringe pushed up her forehead, her top splattered with the yellow mustard, and her jeans grassy and damp.

'I'll tell you what I'd be grateful for, I'd be grateful if you *stayed out of police business*,' he'd yelled, his face puce now.

Ben, who'd been gathering his things in a shell-shocked kind of way, ran over to Beth and flung a protective arm around her waist. Over his dark head, she glared at York. 'Now you've upset my son,' she'd snapped, and turned on her heel.

It had been the last she'd seen of him. Oh well, she thought. It was for the best. They seemed to wind each other up the wrong way all the time. She yearned, as usual, for the easy relationship she'd had with James. He'd never shouted. Had he? She realised, with a stab of sadness, that she could hardly remember. She shook her head.

'He was pretty cross, let's put it that way,' she said to Katie.

'Just worried about you. You've developed a sudden habit of getting yourself into danger,' Katie said, looking ruefully at her friend.

'Well, one thing's for sure – never again,' said Beth. 'I'm going to be much too busy. I've got that whole slavery exhibition outline to finish off and present to the board – I'm so behind – and I'm getting going on redecorating my hall as well. All that's going to keep me out of trouble.'

She lifted her coffee cup with both hands, and tried to blow her fringe out of her eyes. It flopped back. Beth gave up, shrugged and smiled, head on one side. 'And anyway, seriously, what else could possibly happen in Dulwich?'

THE END

Fantastic Books
Great Authors

CROOKED
CAT

Meet our authors and discover
our exciting range:

- Gripping Thrillers
- Cosy Mysteries
- Romantic Chick-Lit
- Fascinating Historicals
- Exciting Fantasy
- Young Adult and Children's
  Adventures
- Non-Fiction

Visit us at:
www.crookedcatbooks.com

Join us on facebook:
www.facebook.com/realcrookedcat

21649040R00150

Printed in Poland
by Amazon Fulfillment
Poland Sp. z o.o., Wrocław